GW01279520

Lindsey resides in Ocala, Florida, where she lives with her two small sons. She holds a BA in anthropology from the University of Florida but realized years later, her true calling was making up stories with a common central theme of equality.

Lindsey Ormond

A Flaming Fairy Tale

Austin Macauley Publishers™
LONDON · CAMBRIDGE · NEW YORK · SHARJAH

Copyright © Lindsey Ormond (2020)

All rights reserved. No part of this publication may be reproduced, distributed, or transmitted in any form or by any means, including photocopying, recording, or other electronic or mechanical methods, without the prior written permission of the publisher, except in the case of brief quotations embodied in critical reviews and certain other non-commercial uses permitted by copyright law. For permission requests, write to the publisher.

Any person who commits any unauthorized act in relation to this publication may be liable to criminal prosecution and civil claims for damages.

This is a work of fiction. Names, characters, businesses, places, events, locales, and incidents are either the products of the author's imagination or used in a fictitious manner. Any resemblance to actual persons, living or dead, or actual events is purely coincidental.

Ordering Information:
Quantity sales: special discounts are available on quantity purchases by corporations, associations, and others. For details, contact the publisher at the address below.

Publisher's Cataloging-in-Publication data
Ormond, Lindsey
A Flaming Fairy Tale

ISBN 9781643788357 (Paperback)
ISBN 9781643788364 (Hardback)
ISBN 9781645365334 (ePub e-book)

Library of Congress Control Number: 2020900723

www.austinmacauley.com/us

First Published (2020)
Austin Macauley Publishers LLC
40 Wall Street, 28th Floor
New York, NY 10005
USA

mail-usa@austinmacauley.com
+1 (646) 5125767

I would like to thank the many patient people in my life who have listened to my countless stories, encouraging me along the way to never give up on my dreams.

Preface

"Far greater than all the material possessions in the world is my freedom to choose, my freedom to live and my freedom to be happy."

The transformation of a caterpillar into a butterfly is in fact a gruesome act of the caterpillar first digesting itself and releasing enzymes to then dissolve all of its tissues. Most people only have the memory of a storybook that shows a very hungry caterpillar's weekly food intake; then inevitably it turns into a beautiful butterfly at the end. But in truth, not all caterpillars turn into the iconic and gorgeous butterfly that colors our childhood dreams. Maybe we should ask ourselves, "Is that caterpillar still the same being? Does that now-striking butterfly know it was a vile sack of goo before it was born?" Transformations are unstoppable. Nothing remains the same for a lifetime.

Fiona: December 2015
Caged

I wake up and realize this nightmare is in fact my reality. I look around at all four beige walls and feel like a caged animal, once again: just like I felt as a child. There's nothing on the walls but stale paint. My metal bed is cold and hard beneath my bare bottom. My drab, grayish hospital gown is a clear sign that it is laundry day at Living Waters, the institution that now feels like it may be my permanent home. I can hear someone in the room next to me having a complete meltdown, screaming like a child having a tantrum. I hear the doctor coming, so I lay down quickly and pretend, I am still asleep. I want to wait as long as possible to have to take my daily, mind-numbing dose of medication.

"Fiona?" Dr. Clark asks standing next to my motionless body. She seems to know I am faking being asleep.

"Fiona, please get up. You need to take your medication, sweetheart," she insists, shaking me a bit to wake me.

Reluctantly, I open my eyes. I have known Dr. Clark since I was eleven years old, and in almost twenty years she hasn't changed all that much. Though, she is middle-aged now, she keeps herself attractive and fit, with her blonde hair neatly tied back and her square-rim eyeglasses framing her sharp brown eyes. I sit up, frustrated, and sling back all five or so pills, all at once, from the small paper cup, she has brought them to me in. I gulp a sip of water afterwards and open my mouth with my tongue hanging out to prove to her that I have in fact swallowed all of the pills. Though, I've been in here a month, the doctors still don't believe, I will be compliant every time.

"When will my laundry be done?" I ask Dr. Clark as she begins to walk back out into the desolate hallway.

I don't want to look like a mental patient in my standard gown: the kind that all patients with no family to bring them clothes wear.

I want my own robes.

"In about an hour, the nurse will bring it to you, Fiona."

I pull out my cardboard box from under my bed after she leaves and begin reading the letters over and over again to myself out loud.

My Dearest Chloe,

Another day has passed that I haven't heard your voice at all. I am here, in New York City. How are you? Where have you been? How are Kaden and Max? I miss the little dudes, almost as much as I miss you. I'm sorry. I am so sorry for keeping you in the dark for so long. For not telling you sooner what you were getting yourself into. Falling in love with me. I should have warned you. I should have told you I was a disaster. To not fall in love with me. But I was selfish. I wanted you to myself. Because I loved you – because I love you. Have you talked to Trent? I'm not mad at you. I hope you are not mad at me either. I just need to know that you are alright. I just need to hear your voice so I can sleep again. I am not sick like they have told you. I am lying. I am faking it. I want you to know I am alright and I love you. I am doing this for you. To protect you from…me.

Fiona

I tuck the letters away and don't put them into an envelope. I simply slide the box back under my small metal bed.

"I can't send them," I say out loud. "It would be completely selfish of me."

I sit there, thinking of Chloe: of her delicate face and her golden blond hair, and the way she moves when she walks, and the curl of her smile when I say something funny.

I have to stop thinking.

I decide to wander out into the halls to see if anyone else is awake yet besides my screaming neighbor next door.

The halls are empty. I walk towards the common area and fill a Styrofoam cup with black coffee that tastes like they reheated it from the day before. I sit down at the piano and start messing around with the keys. I bang them loudly. It echoes throughout the whole room. I glance over at the game corner where Marjorie and I usually sit. The large red rug is bare, with no board games scattered about yet.

"Miss Lennox!" A nurse comes in, screaming at me. "Please, Miss Lennox. Everyone is still asleep, sweetie. Now is not a good time to play."

I smirk up at her and make a possessed-looking face for fun, and she backs slowly away from me as if I might cast a spell on her if she stays.

"Just play quietly," she insists while walking backwards to her station.

I play, from memory, a song I remember my father used to play for me as a little girl. I hum the tune loudly, not caring if I wake up the entire center. One by one, they start to wander out of their rooms like zombies in an apocalypse. Still half asleep, all in their hospital gowns like me.

We all look the same.

Dressed in the same dull colors, some with their bottoms out, having not even bothered to pretend to wear panties.

"Fiona!" Marjorie exclaims loudly. "That is so beautiful, sugar! Keep playing please," she says while twirling in an awkward circle next to me, dancing. She is in her thirties and heavy-set. Her sweet, plump face wears the innocent expression of a girl and her auburn hair is wrapped into an untidy, frizzy bun on top of her head. She spins around and around humming the tune, but not on key. She smiles and giggles and just keeps dancing. So I keep playing the same part over and over again loudly. I look around and notice everyone seems very entertained by my simple piano playing. I eventually quit and a persistent "Awwww..." resounds throughout the room.

"I will play some more later," I assure them before standing up from the old wooden piano bench.

"Fiona, wait!" Marjorie runs up to me as I start to walk back to my desolate room. "Want to play monopoly with me?" She asks me, hopeful.

"Why not," I agree, and we proceed to the game corner and set up monopoly.

Marjorie asks me to play monopoly almost every day, at least five times a day. I usually agree to play at least once with her. I love to see, how excited she looks, when she wins money or owns a bunch of properties. I can tell, she is imagining it is real life and she is fantasizing about this alternate universe where she exists as a top hat and owns a whole board of property. She looks so happy for just a little while. I love to see her this way. I love to see any of them happy and smiling. So I play piano, play board games with them, and try to take all of our minds off of the fact that we are imprisoned in a cage like wild animals: a threat to the general public for one reason or another.

My reason being, I am a threat to myself.

Marjorie's being she is incapable of caring for herself and has no living family members that can or will take care of her. So she is here alone, cared for, solely by the staff. And me, of course. She relies on me for entertainment and company most days. I don't mind really. It gives me a purpose. I pretend that one day we will both be set free, back into the wild, and drink coffee together at Mugged, the coffee shop my father owns, and play monopoly there. We will be back together in Florida. Chloe might be there working; her boys will come eat lunch with us and all will feel normal again in the world.

But for now, I am here. Doped up on antidepressants, lithium and Ativan and fed food more suitable for the birds.

I let Marjorie win the game.

"I won! I have the most monies and the most places!" she shouts excitedly. "I won!"

"Yes, you did," I confirm with a grin.

"I am going to go write another tally in my journal, that I won, Fiona. Be right back," she informs me before running off to her room to tally her win.

I think about the caterpillars Chloe collected as a child, and imagine this is how they felt. This is how she felt.

Caged.

Acting

It isn't hard for me to pretend, I am psychotic. I mean, I am a little mental in all reality. I have tried to kill myself multiple times in the past, for real. But not this last time. The time I took all of my father's old medication after he passed away. I simply wanted to numb the pain, honest. Why would I want to be away from Chloe? Why would I choose this? Well, now I have decided to stay here.

Maybe even permanently.

I need to force myself, and her, to be away from me. She deserves better. If she knew everything about my family and my past, she might even choose to be away from me herself. So I fake it. Every day. It's actually entertaining to me now, to pretend so convincingly that I am insane. To see the faces of the nurses and doctors as I act like someone with many screws loose in the head. My mother keeps calling. Keeps trying to get me transferred to a nicer, private facility that isn't state funded, of course. It is killing her to know that I am still in the state center Living Waters here in the City, rotting away like a corpse. I haven't taken her calls and have refused her visits, and Chloe's, for about a month now. I am afraid they may see through my acting. They know me better. Some days, I even wonder if Dr. Clark is starting to question my insanity, but I think she enjoys keeping me here, as though she felt liberated by caging me up and keeping me 'safe' from myself.

I look through my basket of 'clean' clothes. They do not smell clean in the least. Besides, they are crisp and rough to the touch: definitely not washed with fabric softener. I decide to put on a terrycloth robe that is solid white: it is the first robe I wore here. The last day I saw Chloe and my mother. It wasn't until I saw what I – what all of this – had done to them that I decided to fake being mentally ill in order for them to be at peace. I guess, at this point, I feel sacrificing my happiness in order for them to live in peace is the only logical solution. I know that my dad was planning on transferring my trust fund to Dr. Clark anyway. That is a whole other problem in itself, if I were to get out of here. I am not even sure I could if I tried. He – my father – was a very manipulative man. But I was on to him. I had been for some time. He didn't think, I deserved any of his money so he planned on keeping it out of my hands at all costs. I didn't want the money anyway. I don't want a dime of his money. It was never about the money. It was about the sad truth that, even at the end, he was still not accepting of who I am.

There is a knock on my already cracked door. It's Marjorie, I assume.

"Come in," I say, slipping my journal under my thin, plastic mattress.

An older man opens the door and takes a step inside. It is Mr. Hammond, the director of the center. His short beard is still salt-and-pepper, though the hair on his head has gone white. He wears a white button-down shirt and blue pants. Their waistline is a little tight under his solid little potbelly and there is a reddish stain between the second and third buttons of his shirt. I guess, he had the Pasta Marinara for lunch today.

"Fiona," he says, smiling kindly. "I just got off of the phone with your mother. She is very adamant about moving you this coming weekend to a new facility. The private clinic, The Meadows. Have you heard of it?"

I have heard of it. That's because I have stayed there. It was one of the clinics, my father sent me to as a teenager.

"No," I say, trying to pretend my memory is as messed up as the rest of me.

"Your mom thought it was the one your father sent you to as a teenager," he informs me. "Maybe she is mistaken. I will find out."

My mother is not mistaken. I am lying.

"Well, I wanted you to know that on Saturday your mother is going to go with you to get you all set up there. It is beautiful. You will have a much bigger room, with people more…your caliber," he suggests, hopeful.

More my caliber? As if I am some spoiled, stuck-up rich kid, stuck in this center against my will. He doesn't know me at all.

"Yeah, okay," I say, as if not affected by this. Inside, I am feeling anxious. Knowing that I am going to have to face my mother for the first time in a month. I'd better step up my acting. I'd better be utterly convincing, to keep my plan in motion.

"Well. You might want to begin to pack some of your things. Or I can send Dr. Clark in to help you…"

"No!" I interrupt loudly. "I mean…I can pack them myself," I say, in a hushed voice now.

I don't want to risk Dr. Clark, seeing any of my journal pages or letters to Chloe. If she reads them my cover would be blown.

"Alright, suit yourself," says Mr. Hammond. "We are going to miss you here, Fiona, but we know you will be in good hands at The Meadows. I wish you all the very best with your recovery."

He takes my cold hand in his. He looks sincere. I've always liked him. He seems very passionate about his position here, as though he really does want me to get better; wants everyone here to get better.

After he leaves my room, I decide to go get a glass of water from the cafeteria. I see Marjorie by the old cloth couch, relentlessly talking to another patient who looks asleep, clearly not listening to her at all. I walk over to her, deciding I need to explain that I will be leaving in a couple of days. After all, she has been my best friend while I've been here.

"Marjorie. I need to talk to you about something," I say, interrupting the monologue she is reciting to her sleeping friend.

"Fiona! Do you want to play Monopoly?" she asks me, excited, as though she hasn't heard me at all.

"Not right now, Marjorie. Maybe later, okay? I need to talk to you, Marjorie. I am going to be leaving Living Waters this weekend. On Saturday..." I try to make eye contact as I am speaking, something which is difficult to do with her.

"Where are you going Fiona? Home?" she asks me, concerned.

"No, I am going to a different facility. The Meadows. My mother is making me. I don't want to leave," I add quickly.

"That's okay. Just take me with you, Fiona," she says, assuming this is a logical idea.

"I wish I could, but you know that I can't do that, Marjorie. Listen, when we both get out of here, we will go get coffee at Mugged together and we can play board games. Monopoly, okay?"

She looks down at her lap and sits in silence for a few minutes. I don't know what to say, so I just wait for her to respond.

"I'm never getting out of here, Fiona," she says with tears in her eyes. It is the first real thing I feel she has ever said to me. The first thing that seems completely logical and sane. Something she actually believes and knows is the truth. She has no family, no money and no ability to get a job. She can't take care of herself. She will probably be here...forever. That coffee date will most likely never happen.

"I will get you out of here, I promise," I say, and immediately realize what I have done. I have made a false promise to a girl who is now thinking there is a glimmer of hope for her one day.

I am not so sure that was a good idea, after all. I am a bad person. I am choosing to stay in a place where she is legitimately trapped. I begin to feel like utter crap and have to swallow hard to keep from vomiting.

"No! You can't leave me here, Fiona!" she screams all of a sudden. She slaps me in the face. Hard. It hurts really bad, actually. I fall over onto the hard, tile floor. Who knew Marjorie was so tough!

"You aren't my friend anymore, Fiona! Friends don't leave each other behind!" she screams as the nurse rushes over to restrain her.

"I'm fine!" I shout. "Don't restrain her! It was my fault!" I yell, trying to save Marjorie from being strapped to her uncomfortable bed, for the rest of the afternoon. "Please. I provoked her!"

"Miss Marjorie Evans. You need to come with me to your room. Now," the nurse says, leading her away.

I feel so helpless that I suddenly begin to cry. My only friend for the past month is going to remain here, without me to take care of her. I run to my room, still in tears. I rip my journal out from under my bed and write…

Get Marjorie Evans better. Get Marjorie out of here. I promised.

Chloe: July 2015
Equality

I drive downtown to, probably, what is the only tattoo shop, I have ever seen in this small town. It has a lime-green neon "OPEN" sign outside, blinking out of synch as if it's about to cash out at any moment.

"Can I help you?" This burly tatted-up guy says as I walk in. He gives me one of those head-to-toe assessments and I think he realizes that unless I'm a complete closet freak, I have no tattoos anywhere. I immediately feel completely out of place, hearing nothing but tattoo guns buzzing in the background. What must a twenty-something, minivan mom with long, sun-bleached, blonde hair and a Florida tan seem like to them? Ridiculous? A total amateur? Totally vanilla and totally bored with her life?

"Um…I'd like to get a tattoo," I say.

He looks at me like, No shit. So I immediately follow with, "I know what I want. I don't need to look through those binders over there or anything," I say confidently, pointing to the large stack of tattoo binders in the corner of the shop.

"Do you have any preference on the artist?" he asks.

"No. As long as they know what they're doing." Oh God, now I've insulted them.

"Fiona!" he calls loudly towards the back of the shop.

"Yeah?" answers a somewhat rough but female voice from a back room.

"You free to do this girl here's tattoo?"

"Yeah, be right there," she answers loudly.

"Miss, I'm going to have you sit over here at Fiona's chair, alright?"

"Thanks," I say as I sit down in a cracked pleather chair.

And I wait.

About five minutes later, this very edgy yet beautiful creature emerges from the back room and I assume, she must be Fiona. My personal tattoo artist. She looks questionably female, but I know from the name she most definitely is. She has a rock star-like, James Dean hairstyle and is covered in tattoos. Like probably the most tattoos, I have ever seen on someone in person, especially in this small Florida town. Her eyes are strikingly jet-blue and she looks right at me and smiles.

"Hey! So, what can I do for you today, love? I'm Fiona, by the way."

Her personality seems much more delicate than her looks, so I feel a slight sense of relief.

"I would like to get my first tattoo," I admit.

"Oh, shit! A virgin," she says excitedly. "So much prime real estate just waiting to be inked!"

I get goosebumps all of a sudden, watching her eye my skin like that. "Hah. Yes," I say. "I would like a caterpillar," I explain, "On my foot."

"Ehhh..." she says, and gives me a kind of disappointed look.

"What?"

"Oh, nothing. If that's where you want it then that's where you shall have it, my dear."

"No, wait. Is that tacky or something?"

"No, not really tacky, just didn't pin you for one of those girls."

She didn't? I was almost sure, I would be pinned for being one of 'those girls' by my looks, whatever those girls may be.

"You didn't?" I ask.

"Nah. If I were you, I would get it somewhere on my arm. Visible and bold where everyone could see it. But that's just me."

"Okay," I say confidently. "I'll get it on my arm. Right here on the inside of my wrist."

"You sure?" she asks, looking right at me with her striking blue eyes.

"Yes. I'm sure."

"Alright. Do you have a drawing of it?" she asks.

Oh, shit. I told the guy I didn't need to look through the binders because I knew what I wanted, but I didn't even think to bring a picture of what I want this creature to look like.

"No, I guess I'm new at this. I can just come back tomorrow and bring a magazine picture back or something," I say as I stand up to leave.

"Psh," she says, and shakes her head. "No, you won't. Do you trust me?" she asks.

"Hypothetically speaking, I guess I have to, so...yes?" I say unconvincingly.

"I'll do the caterpillar free hand, then. That cool?"

"Yeah, okay," I agree, and she starts up the tattoo gun.

It doesn't hurt as bad as I had imagined. It feels like a dull, but constant pain. More annoying than anything else.

"I have to ask," she says, distracting me, "Why the caterpillar and not the infamous butterfly for a first tattoo, huh?"

"It's symbolic to me, I guess. I'm not quite the butterfly yet."

"Hm. Interesting."

It doesn't take very long, but it is perfect. It looks exactly like a caterpillar and just like the one I imagined and remembered as a child. "I love it," I say as I admire my new wrist, with a lifelike-looking caterpillar now on it.

"Now, you know…I probably should have mentioned tattoos are very addicting, so don't be surprised if you find yourself back here, wanting more in a few weeks or so."

Clearly, they are addicting to her: she has them everywhere.

"Thanks for the warning," I say, standing up slowly to make sure I'm not woozy.

"You take care, sweetheart," she says and hands me her card.

Fiona Lennox, it reads. And the name and number of the tattoo shop underneath.

I watch as she confidently walks away towards the back room again.

On the drive home, I can't get her blue eyes and slicked-back hair out of my mind. I can't decide whether I want to be with her or just be her. As a married woman, this is very confusing.

"Hey, I'm home!" I say as I finally walk in the door.

"Hey. What did you end up doing, babe?" asks my husband Trent. He's wearing his favorite Wrangler jeans and the ever-present baseball cap.

"Oh. Well I, uh…I got a tattoo."

"What?"

"A tattoo."

"Yes, I heard you Chloe," he pipes up. "Is this like some quarter-life crisis, you're going through?" He pulls me aside so our children Kaden and Max can't hear us.

"No. I've always wanted a tattoo, you've known that."

"Yes, but it's not really like you to just go off and get one without even telling anyone. Whatever. I'm glad you're happy," he says, adjusting his baseball cap tensely.

He didn't even ask me what it was, I think to myself.

Fiona: December 2015
Contact

By the time Saturday rolls around, I have everything I came here with, packed up and ready to go. I didn't sleep well last night, even after taking my Ambien. Awaiting my mom's inevitable arrival is enough to send me into actual insanity.

Dr. Clark arrives first.

"Fiona. Are you all packed and ready to leave?" she asks me, holding a stack full of papers in her hands.

"Yes," I unenthusiastically respond.

Crazy people either show no emotion or too much. I know this from experience. It's the manic tendencies we are all prone to, I guess.

"Alright, then. Your mother should be here any minute," she explains, and I see my mom walking up to the door.

She puts her hands over her mouth and gasps. "Fiona! Oh, Fiona! It is so good to see you honey."

She pulls me close and squeezes the life out of me. I don't respond. Looking detached is essential to appearing insane.

"Well, let's get moving ladies," she says, taking my big suitcase for me.

As we start to walk down the hall towards the check-out counter, I remember I haven't had the chance to say goodbye to Marjorie.

"Wait!" I suddenly shout. "I need to say goodbye to Marjorie." I look hopefully at Dr. Clark.

"Who? Who is…Marjorie?" my mother asks with distaste.

"Marjorie is a…a friend Fiona has made here over the past month," Dr. Clark explains to her.

"Oh, sweetie…Why don't you just visit her another time, dear?" my mother suggests, hurrying me along down the hallway.

"No!" I say, and run back towards her room.

"Marjorie," I say, out of breath as I finally reach her room at the end of the hall.

She is asleep in her bed, still strapped down tightly. It is very dark and quiet in her room and it suddenly starts to remind me of my father, lying helplessly in bed those few days, before his death. How sad a sight it was and how sad a sight it is now, to witness Marjorie this way. I don't know whether I should risk waking her from what might be the perfect dream of a happier place, or to let her stay just a while longer in her alternate reality.

I decide to just walk out of her room, but she wakes to my footsteps on the hard tile floor.

"Fiona!" she yells.

"Marjorie. I didn't want to wake you, but I wanted to say goodbye. I am so sorry, I have to leave you here. I will come back for you, okay? And I will visit when I can," I assure her.

"Fiona. You are my best friend," she says. "I'm sorry for slapping you."

"It's okay. You are really strong. You hit like a body builder."

She giggles innocently and says, "Yeah. I know…I am really strong."

"Try to get some more rest," I tell her, and I walk out the door and don't look back.

When I walk back up to Dr. Clark and my mom, they are filling out my discharge papers at the front desk.

"Okay, you're all set, Fiona," Dr. Clark says. "All we need is your signature right here." She points to a black line on the final page that reads: Patient's consent to be discharged.

What if I don't sign? I think to myself. Can I stay?

I quickly decide to sign the line with a shaky hand to appear weak. Or maybe, I am just weak from all of the medication numbing my brain.

We all three rode over to The Meadows together in my mother's fancy car. A car that probably cost more than some people's houses.

As we pull up, it is complete culture shock for me. Here I was, living in the slums – for lack of a better word – during the past month, and now I am going to live in some huge palace with a bunch of rich kids who probably got hooked on drugs using their parents' money. But who am I to judge? I have been there, I guess. I start to remember this place. I have a long history of being able to block things out of my memory, permanently. Or at least I thought I did. But seeing the front of The Meadows is like reliving it all.

I remember my dad driving me here when I was fifteen, convincing me, it was for my own good and telling me, it would be like Spring Break. Actually, it was the Spring Break of my freshman year of high school, now that I think about it. I spent a week and a half here with a few other spoiled kids who had stolen things or done a cocaine buffet and got caught. I didn't relate to them at all, though. They were meaner than the kids who bullied me in high school. Called me Fiona, the Flamer. It was a week and half of pure hell.

"Fiona?" Dr. Clark is still waiting for me step out of the car.

"Sorry," I say, and gather my things. I walk slowly up to the huge double doors of The Meadows. My mother takes my hand.

"You're going to love it here, sweetie. I have a lot of faith that they are going to get you the help you need and you will be out of here in no time."

But I don't want to be out of anywhere. I want to be sick: to stay here locked away from Chloe so I don't hurt her any more than I already have.

We walk in. It is even more glamorous than I remembered. There is an actual Barista to my right serving fresh, hot, brewed coffee and it smells delightful. I try to hide my excitement at the fact that I don't have to drink the stale coffee from Living Waters any longer.

There is an enormous chandelier, hanging in the common area. From underneath it, several girls eye me as I walk in. All are wearing Michael Kors jump suits, each in a different color. They give me an evil glare and whisper among themselves while they settle onto an expensive leather couch in the middle of the room.

I turn away, pretending not to notice. Because I am so mentally ill, that is.

My mother and Dr. Clark help me get the paperwork filled out and we take an elevator up to my room.

I apparently have a roommate for now, which is the only downside to being here. They are extremely booked up and my mom pitches a huge fit about this to the Director, Dr. Hall, who I can't seem to find anything wrong with yet. He seems nice enough: polite, clean-cut, and handsome in a boring, Ken Doll way.

"I was under the impression that Fiona had a room all to herself," says my mother in a flippant tone.

"We apologize. As soon as one opens up, we will move her," the Director assures her.

"Well, alright." She still looks rather irritated.

My roommate walks in. It is one of the girls who glared at me downstairs. Of course, it is the one in the bright pink, Michael Kors.

"Excuse me," she says, and waits for me to move out of her way as she stands there in front of me, still wearing an evil look on her face.

I stand motionless.

If this is like prison, I need to make a good badass first impression and not back down.

"I said, excuse me," she repeats, louder now.

"Trisha," says the Director, "You need to introduce yourself to Fiona. She is your new roommate, for now."

"Yeah. I'm Trisha. Can you move?" she says, giving me a little shove to the shoulders.

"Trisha! That is enough!" says the Director. No restraints, I assume, are used here at the rich-kid center.

I decide to move slowly while staring viciously into Trisha's eyes.

She makes a scared face at me. "Freak!"

"Oh, this is just wonderful," my mother says. "Maybe we should have just kept you at the state facility."

"I will take care of it," the Director reassures my mom. "Trisha, please come with me, sweetie," he tells her, walking her out of the room.

I begin to place my things in drawers and in a closet, I have all to myself. I come across my box of journals and letters and decide it's best to leave them in my suitcase until my mom and Dr. Clark leave the room.

"Are you hungry? Should we go have lunch and a coffee?" my mom asks.

"No," I respond shortly. I just want her to leave, at this point. Although, I miss her tremendously, it is too hard to put on this act around her: the detached-mental-patient act.

The director walks back in a few minutes later and informs me we have 'group' in twenty minutes in the conference room down the hall, so my mother decides to go ahead and leave. She gives me a huge hug before walking out with tears in her eyes.

I immediately run downstairs and order a piping-hot, large coffee from the Barista. I haven't had good coffee in over a month. I sit by myself at a small table and sip it, savoring it.

Suddenly a girl walks up and sits down at the table next to me. "Hey," she says casually, as if we knew each other.

"Um…Hi," I say, wishing she would go away and leave me alone with my coffee.

"I'm Jade," she says.

"Fiona," I answer, still looking down at my coffee.

"Don't let the mean girls get to you," she tells me. "It's like high school all over again, right?" And she laughs a little to herself.

Jade wears trendy-looking glasses and has a cute, straight-bob haircut. Her hair is almost black, but her eyes are really blue – maybe bluer than mine. She is really beautiful in a nerdy way.

I try to act unaffected by her, because I have to appear crazy and detached still.

"Well…Want to walk over to group together?" she asks me, looking up at the huge clock in the coffee shop.

A loudspeaker suddenly announces, we are to head over to 'small group' in the conference room. I decide to walk with Jade. She talks to me the whole way, even though, I don't respond.

"Your tattoos are really awesome. I have a lot, too." She pulls up her sleeves, revealing all the ink on her pale skin. I am surprised she has as many tattoos as she does. She looks really nerdy, but I am starting to realize she is just a true artist. Like me.

"This one was my first." She points to a Hawaiian-looking flower on her wrist and I think of Chloe, and of how that is where she got her first tattoo, by me, that day at the shop.

I think of Viv and Winter and all of my other friends back home, and I have to open my eyes wider for a second to keep from crying.

"I'm not actually Hawaiian or anything," says Jade. "I was like sixteen and convinced that this was something I would want my whole life."

She just keeps talking and talking the whole way to the conference room.

We finally get there and sit down in a circle with what appears to be the whole facility. Trisha sits on the opposite side of the circle from me and makes a bitchy face as she crosses her legs.

"Welcome everyone," the director Dr. Hall says. "We have someone new with us today. Fiona, would you please stand up and introduce yourself?" he asks.

I hate this, I think. I don't want to stand up. But I do.

"Hi. I am Fiona," I say, frowning, and immediately sit back down.

"Wait. Tell us about yourself," he insists.

I stand back up, slowly realizing this is not going to be like the state center, where I could go unnoticed and be crazy under the radar. They are very intuitive here. Way more observant. Shit.

"I am Fiona. I was an artist before…before I tried to kill myself."

"An artist?" Trisha asks in a mocking tone. "What a nerd."

"I was a tattoo artist," I say, looking right at her.

She gives me a more accepting look now, as though I have suddenly become a badass for being someone who draws on skin instead of paper.

That was what I'd hoped for, actually. Be scared, bitch.

Chloe: July 2015
Friendship

Fiona and I sit inside The Bean Hut in the tiny downtown of Middleton, Florida, studying each other carefully as we sip our hot coffees together.

"Which tattoo was your first?" I ask Fiona curiously, wondering what unique drawing it will be.

"Oh God," Fiona mumbles, "This gem right here."

She stands up, turns around, and lifts her shirt just enough so that I can see the 'iconic butterfly' she referred to in the shop stamped on her lower back.

"A butterfly tramp stamp. I wouldn't pin you to be one of those girls," I say mockingly.

"Touché, love, touché." She smiles.

We talk about several more of her tattoos. She has quite a few really interesting ones: a gravestone for her first dog on her arm, Cheetara from the Thundercats on her back, and the word, "fluidity" on her collarbone. I want to ask her more. I want to know about each and every inch of her decorated skin, but will I sound too meddlesome? Or like some kind of stalker? So I stop inquiring about her ink and let her know that it's nearing the time I have to leave. I have to get home to my boys and my husband. We agree to meet up again, here, a few days from now. I guess, this was going to become a regular thing, getting coffee together.

Fiona: December 2015
Permanent Ink

Circle time comes to a close after I get to hear several of the other patients' back stories, including Trisha's and Jade's. Trisha's is about as predictable as can be. She comes from a very wealthy and prestigious family, got addicted to cocaine – go figure. Ended up here and is only supposed to be here another month or so. Thank God. Jade's story was captivating to me. She was an artist, working for an architect here in the city doing the geometrics for his company. She had a bad accident and ended up addicted to the pain meds they gave her. She had a hard time withdrawing so she decided to come here until she gets off of them completely. She doesn't have much of a stay left either, it sounds like. Apparently, the fall she had was really serious. She broke her back and they thought she might actually be paralyzed, so she is lucky to be able to even walk. She has come a long way. Her story touched me because she sounds like such a positive person despite all the things she has had to overcome the past year.

I wish I was more like her.

I start to head back to my room, but Jade runs up to me before I make it out of the conference center.

"Hey. That's pretty rad, you are a tattoo artist," she says.

"Yeah, I was. Who knows if I will have a job anymore after this stent," I say, realizing how lucid I sound. I am not doing a good job so far sounding crazy, here at The Meadows.

"Oh, I'm sure it will make for a great comeback story," she says brightly, and I kind of want to just smack her in the face like Marjorie did to me back at Living Waters.

Her upbeat personality is giving me a headache so I decide to walk faster. I feel like I am losing a race when she catches up to me again down the hall.

"So, do you want to go play a game in the game room?" she asks. What is with these people and their games? I have played about as many games as anyone should play in a lifetime over the past month.

"I'm just going to go lie down for a bit," I tell her as I practically run to my room.

Trisha is already there, reading some lousy fashion magazine on her bed. She doesn't say anything rude to me when I walk in. She actually smiles this time.

"So, you're a tattoo artist, huh?" she asks me again. For some reason, this is always a fascinating job to people. A good conversation-starter, I guess.

"Yes," I say shortly. She needs a taste of her own medicine.

"What do you think about this tattoo, I got a while ago?" She lifts her shirt up to her bra-line, showing me the side of her waist where she has a beautiful tree drawn on her. It is really big, but nicely done. The artist seems really talented. I actually love it.

"It's pretty sick," I say, admiring the artwork sincerely.

"Really? You really think so?" She seems so insecure all of a sudden.

"Yes. It's a great drawing," I reassure her. "Why?"

"It's just a lot bigger than I had wanted, and I've been kind of ashamed of it ever since."

"Nah. You should never be ashamed of a tattoo. You wanted it at that moment, which means it meant something to you once. It's beautiful," I say to her, and mean it.

"Thanks," she says, and looks more comfortable in her skin. I am glad, I can make someone feel more comfortable again.

"Check this out," I say, and lift my shirt to show her the butterfly tramp stamp on my lower back. "This was my very first tattoo. Most people would be really ashamed of it, but I kind of love it. It is this totally unoriginal marking that shows I fit in with the masses once."

She laughs loudly. "Yeah, I guess you're right…It did mean something to me once," she reveals to me. "My tattoo…There was this tree my boyfriend and I used to picnic under all of the time. I would pack like peanut butter and jelly sandwiches, you know, with the crust cut off, like I was his little mommy."

I look at her and feel kind of disgusted by the typical gender roles her and her boyfriend must have abided by, but I smile agreeably and say, "Yeah."

"Well, I tried to draw a picture of the tree for the tattoo artist to do, and this is really beautiful like you said, but it doesn't look like the tree. And it is just so big. I don't know…It just isn't what I had in mind. I really wanted it to look just like that tree. But it isn't the artist's fault, you know…"

"So you and your boyfriend, aren't together anymore?" I ask her, trying to make conversation.

"Nope. He broke up with me after he decided I was a coke head." She laughs awkwardly.

"Well, then he wasn't a keeper. If he wasn't going to stick around for the long haul, you know?"

"Yeah. You're probably right…What about you?" Trisha asks me. "Do you have a boyfriend on the outside?" She smirks.

Man, I haven't been asked if I have a boyfriend in years. She can't possibly think I am straight, I think.

"No, no boyfriend," I say.

"Well, you're probably better off…And you really tried to…Never mind." She stops.

"Yes," I respond, knowing what she is referring to. "I was in a low place."

There is a tap on the door. I look up and see Jade. Trisha must still not have broken the ice with her because she rolls her eyes and walks out of the room, turned back into her mean-girl self all of a sudden.

"Sorry to interrupt," Jade says while walking in confidently.

"Nah, it's okay," I say, feeling bad, I blew her off about the game thing a few minutes ago.

"I feel like you're purposely avoiding me," says Jade.

She is so upfront and bold about things it is a little off-putting to me.

"I am just…trying to acclimate today," I say, hoping not to upset her any more than I already have.

"I guess, I just saw all of your tattoos and assumed we might have something to talk about, or something in common. There aren't that many people I connect with in here…"

"No, you're right. I'm sorry. It's just been a long day with a lot of adjusting," I say.

"Right. I get it." She starts to walk out of the room.

"Wait. Jade, how about that game?" I ask before she turns the corner.

She smiles and nods her head. We walk to the game room and of course, she chooses monopoly to play. I think about Marjorie and hope she is surviving at Living Waters without me. I win monopoly for the first time in a long time. After we are done with the game, I walk to my room and remember we are allowed to make a phone call before dinner. I walk to the front desk and decide to use my call. Chloe answers on the first ring.

"Hello?" she says.

I want to speak. I want to tell her I am okay. But I panic and regret calling her.

"Who's there?" she asks.

A few more seconds pass.

"Fiona? Is this you…? Are you there?"

I hang up the phone.

I tell myself; I am starved for affection. I am selfish. It would be completely selfish. After letting her come this far without talking to me, she has probably moved on. I look down at the engagement ring I am still wearing. I decide, I need to be more approachable to the women here. I need to develop friendships with them so I don't crave Chloe so much; so I can let her go. I find Trisha in our room when I return and ask her if she wants to go smoke a cigarette with me. I figure she smokes, and she does.

"Yeah," she says. "I'm in."

She catches me looking down at my ring while we smoke our cigarettes on the glamorous upstairs balcony overlooking the water.

"Who got you the ring?" she asks me. "I thought you didn't have a boyfriend."

"Yeah. Well, I don't. I have a fiancée, technically," I say in a smart-ass tone.

"Well, who is he?"

"He is a she."

"Oh, I see. I guess I should have guessed by the short, dikey haircut."

"Oh, dikey, huh? Now I am dikey."

"You know what I mean."

I feel like it is getting harder for me to pretend I am insane anymore. I am clicking with the people here. They aren't crazy like the patients at the state center: they are just like me. Mr. Hammond was right. Maybe they are more my caliber, and I truly need friendship right now in my life.

I lie in bed in the dark while Trisha snores loudly in her own bed. I begin to journal to Chloe.

Chloe,

I heard your voice today. It was me on the other end of the line. I hung up before I could tell you I love you…I love you, Chloe. I love you so much, baby. I miss you. Kiss the boys goodnight from me, okay? I want to take them to the park. I want to push Max on the swing. Does he still like to swing? Tell them, I will take them soon, okay? I miss you. Goodnight.

Fiona.

I begin to actually feel like I have a twisted mind as I scoot the box of unread, unsent letters to Chloe back under my bed. Maybe I am actually psychotic after all.

Chloe: July 2015
Choices

I think back to yesterday at the coffee shop with Fiona. Did people think we were a couple? Did I want them to? Was my skin as transparent as I thought it was all the way through to my heart?

I decide I will talk to her, about everything I am feeling, before it eats me alive. We are supposed to meet at the coffee shop on Thursday. It's Tuesday. I can't wait that long, so I impulsively call her at the tattoo shop again.

"Fiona isn't in today, ma'am," says a man who I'm pretty sure is the big, burly guy, I was confronted with when I walked in that first day.

Where is she? I wonder.

"Oh, okay, well, do you happen to have her cell number?" Okay, that was definitely crossing some kind of line, I'm pretty sure.

"Uh, sure, yes. I'm not really supposed to give it out to just anyone," he informs me.

"It's about my tattoo," I lie.

"Yeah, I kind of figured, so here you go, miss."

Ma'am? Miss? Really? Is my voice aging?

"Okay, thanks so much." I hang up the phone.

I now have in my possession, her personal phone number. So I sit and stare at it for about an hour before I actually dial.

"Hello?" she answers, after the second ring.

"Hey, Fiona, it's Chloe."

"Well, hello."

"I got your cell phone number from the guy at the shop," I try to explain.

"That's probably Joe," she says. "He's actually the owner."

"Well, I know we are supposed to meet Thursday at The Bean Hut but I wanted to talk to you about something so I was just wondering if we could meet up today, or tonight."

"Sure," says Fiona. "How about you come over for dinner tonight? I want to try out a new recipe anyway."

"Like to your house?" I ask, surprised.

"Yeah. Let me give you my address and you can map it out and I'll just run to the store later and pick up something to cook up. Anything I should steer clear of? Any weird food allergies or aversions?"

"No...I mean, yes to dinner, but no to the allergies. I'll pretty much eat anything," I say.

"Well, alright, then I'll see you at seven? That work?"

"I'll see you at seven."

I can't help but look at the clock almost every hour of the day. I spend nearly two hours getting ready while the boys nap.

It's almost five. Trent should be home soon. I pace around for the next few minutes, going back and forth between feelings of excitement and guilt.

"Hey, guys! Daddy is finally home," he says as he walks in the door. His Wrangler jeans look even tighter than usual. Maybe he is stress eating.

"Okay, so I'm going to head over to the girls', honey," I say after he kisses the boys and places his keys on the counter. "Want me to call when I am headed home tonight?" I ask as I gather my things anxiously.

"Nah, I'm sure, I'll be asleep already. Long day. I'm just glad you have been more social lately, Chloe. It's healthy for you to do stuff even if it's without me sometimes, you know?"

Way to make me feel like total shit, I think. He's trying to make me feel good, I know, but I can't help but feel awful instead. Like I am lying about my whole life to him.

I pull up to this really cute house in the Historic district of downtown Middleton. It's exactly the house, I would picture her renting. It has an adorable front porch with two wicker rocking chairs and shutters on all of the front windows. I take a big breath in, as if I am about to swim a long distance under water, then blow out the air as I shut the car door. As I walk up to the front door, she swings it open wildly and greets me excitedly.

"Hey, girl, perfect timing! I've got some shrimp going on the stove and some roasted veggies in the oven. Hope you're hungry."

"Absolutely," I say. "Sounds great!"

Her house is filled with little knickknacks. She has tons of shelves of books and tattoo magazines, and a poster of a dog and a cat snuggling, that doesn't seem to fit in with the rest of the decoration. It hangs on the living room wall.

We don't talk much during dinner, probably because the food is fantastic. Is there anything she isn't good at?

"So, you said you wanted to talk to me about something?" she asks while drying a dish at the sink after dinner.

"I did...I mean, I do."

"Well, shoot then."

I realize in this moment that I've had all day to plan what I am going to say, but I haven't.

"I really like you, Fiona," I blurt out. I really like you? God, sometimes I can be such a tool.

"I really like you, Chloe," she says. I can see her smile as she says it, in the reflection of the window in front of her.

"I have dated a few girls before. I don't think you know that about me," I say proudly.

"No, I didn't know that about you. Well, aren't you just full of surprises?" Fiona says.

"Look, I know I am married, and I have two kids, and I don't really know what this is, what we are doing, but I just feel compelled to be around you. Ever since I met you, really. Ever since the tattoo shop."

"You are married, Chloe. You are right about that. I can't be some girl that saves you from some mid-life crisis you may or may not be having," she says.

That wasn't exactly the response, I had hoped for. Mid-life crisis? I wasn't mid-life yet. How old did she think I was? Had I even told her my age? I couldn't remember.

"Well, I just didn't want you to think, I was some 'virgin' at being with a woman, like you said about me getting a tattoo."

"Aw. Did that upset you, sweetie?" she says condescendingly, and gives me the cutest pouty lip I have ever seen.

"Ha-ha, very funny. Well, thanks for dinner, it was delicious. I guess I should…you know…head home now."

"Listen," she blurts out as I'm leaving, "The last girl I dated was straight. She used me for what felt like some experiment, to see if she was capable of being gay. So if I seem pretty guarded, that's why. I can't be someone's experiment again. I'm a lesbian. Always have been, always will be. Now, that's cool that you are bisexual and all, but I don't do well with you inbetweeners. I kind of feel like you are just stuck in a purgatory trying to make up your mind. I'd be lying if I said I wasn't incredibly attracted to you, Chloe. And I'll be here to do coffee dates or dinner dates or whatever you need in your life right now. But don't fall in love with me unless you are sure about what you want. I wear my heart on my sleeve and it would be too hard for me to say no to you. Take that how you will," she says.

She grabs my wrist to check on my tattoo. We lock eyes and I stare at her for what feels like a lifetime.

"Thanks again for dinner," I say, and I bolt to my car. I can't even remember if I closed the front door behind me.

I get home before the kids are asleep, kiss them goodnight and try to hide my emotions while lying next to Trent in bed. He falls asleep quickly and starts to snore loudly, as usual. He barely touches me anymore, probably in fear that he will get shot down like so many nights the past year or so.

I wake up in a panic the next morning and start to remember what a weird and horrifying dream I had had. I dreamt that Fiona and I were a couple and we were trying to explain to Kaden what to call "us".

"Do I call you both mommy?" he asks in my dream.

"You can call us Mom 1 and Mom 2," Fiona responds in this weird monotone voice. We are both dressed in those creepy Thing 1 and Thing 2 outfits, all the way down to the wild, mop hair.

"Man, that was horrifyingly weird," I say out loud. I must be reading too much Cat in the Hat to the boys lately, I decide.

I go over and over my conversation with Fiona last night. Was this her way of telling me to back off, in a very sweet and non-confrontational way? Or was this her way of telling me to make up my mind? As in, choose between her or my husband. How could I choose? I have a family: two miniature human beings who depend on me for basically everything right now in their lives. And I start to realize, how needed I am by this family that I have played such a huge role in creating. I picture what each and every person in my life would say and think if I told them, I was "Breaking apart" my family to be with a woman, I had fallen madly in love with, whom I believed was my true soulmate. There is still so much I don't know about Fiona. I don't even know how old she is.

I get a pen and paper and write down questions I have for her so that I don't forget to ask them the next time I see her, which is supposed to be tomorrow, as long as our "Coffee date" is still on.

"Oh, what the hell, I'll just call her," I say out loud.

"Hello?" she answers.

"Hey, it's me." Was I a 'me' already?

"Good morning," she says.

"I have some questions to ask you."

"Questions? Nooo, not you!" says Fiona in a sarcastic tone.

"Very funny. How old are you?" I ask her.

"I'm twenty-eight."

"Why did you move here from New York City?"

"My girlfriend and I broke up and my mom pissed me off. Also, it was really far away and seemed to have beautiful landscapes."

"Do you want a family one day?"

"Really, Chloe, this is starting to sound like an interview on The View."

"Just answer the question. Please."

"Oh, I don't know. I guess if the person I was with did, or had one already, then yes. I love children and animals."

"You do know those are two very different things. Children and animals."

"Chloe, God, get to the point."

"Do you want me to choose? Between you and my husband?" That was most definitely not on the list.

"How could I ask you to do something like that? First, you wouldn't be choosing between me and your husband. You would be breaking apart your family"

"Oh Jesus, is that what you really think? That I would be breaking apart my family?" I ask, somewhat annoyed.

"No. No. It just...came out wrong. Look, we haven't even dated, really. And we can't, really. Because you are married. And I am pretty sure that means you aren't in the market to date. So how would we even know, if we were a good match for each other anyhow?"

"Do you think we are?" I ask timidly.

"Yes. I do. But I think we have a lot to learn about each other. I also think you have some soul-searching to do, little lady. You need to take some time to really find what you think will make you happy. And if that's me, great. But if that's not me, then that's okay, too. As long as you are happy."

Click.

Fiona: December 2015
Visitation

I decide I want to try out yoga this morning on the outside patio. They have a scheduled class at 9 am. Before leaving our room, dressed in my workout gear, I ask Trisha if she wants to join me.

"Hey, want to come with me to check out yoga this morning?" I ask before realizing, she is still half-asleep, her pink foam rollers still in her hair.

"Um, nah. I'll pass today. Maybe tomorrow."

"See you later," I say, heading out the door.

I run into Jade in the hallway and she is all dressed up in her workout clothes as well. Go figure, Miss Peppy is ready to tackle the day with a chipper attitude and morning yoga session.

"Oh great! I take it you are heading to yoga class, too?" she asks me with a huge smile.

"I sure am," I say, inwardly debating whether I should fake a stomach bug or not.

I know Jade is a nice person and I should be thankful for her friendship right now in my life, but I still can't help resenting that perfect, upbeat personality she has at all times of the day.

"This class is so refreshing!" she assures me on the way outside.

"Great, I look forward to it," I say, regretting having decided to try it.

We begin the class right on time and to my surprise Jade doesn't talk for the entire class. She is like a total Yogi Pro and super flexible. I struggle to keep up, but she winks at me and gives me the thumbs up several times during the class. After it is over, I do feel a bit refreshed, as she said I would.

"Not bad for your first class, Fiona!" Jade says encouragingly.

"Yeah, right," I answer, and roll my eyes.

"It takes years to master yoga. I have been doing it for almost five years now. It is such a stress reliever for me."

"Yeah, I do feel better," I tell her while walking back towards my room.

"So what time is your counseling today?" Jade asks me.

"Oh, I'll have to look, I don't remember."

"Do you have any visitors coming today? Sundays are visiting day, you know," she reminds me.

"Oh, right. No, I don't think so. I just got here yesterday and all."

"Right. Well, I will just catch up with you later, okay?" Jade says, and cowers off, as if I have somehow managed to upset her again.

I return to my room and Trisha isn't there. I take advantage of my alone time – something I have become accustomed to over the past month – and I begin to obsessively read all of my letters to Chloe again. I fall asleep eventually and when I wake up Dr. Hall is standing over me, repeating my name.

"Fiona, Fiona…"

I want him to leave. I hate the way these people treat me as if I didn't have any right to privacy. He's looking less polite and less handsome by the minute.

"Fiona, you have a visitor, waiting to see you in the visitor center, sweetheart."

I sit up and hide the letters as best I can.

"Oh. I do?" I ask, confused. I am not expecting anyone. It must be either my mom or my brother Mikey Junior, I assume.

"I'll be right down," I tell Dr. Hall. He walks out of my room.

I look at myself in the mirror and see I have sleep lines on my cheek. I must have been out cold. I put a little chap stick on and use my hands to smooth back my short hair; to try and not look like I was sound asleep just a few moments ago. Although, maybe the rough-and-tired look I have on right now is just what I need to convince whoever is waiting for me that I am sick and mental.

I walk down to the visitor center and see lots of family members visiting with their loved ones. Something I was not used to seeing at the state center. There it was rare for anybody to come on visitor day.

All of a sudden, I see her.

Chloe is standing in the corner of the room, all alone, wearing a polka-dotted dress, with her blonde hair, all wavy and big, just the way she knows I like it. She is twirling her loose curls, anxiously around her fingers, before we make eye contact. She smiles a close-mouthed smile at me and lifts her hand in a slight wave.

I walk over to her, hurrying.

"What are you doing here, all the way in New York City?" I ask her, shocked as hell.

"I had to see you Fiona. I haven't seen you in…in a month! I haven't even talked to you in…"

I put my index finger over her mouth to hush her.

"I know. I'm sorry. I am…I am not doing well," I say, remembering I need to convince her that I am still sick enough to stay here…forever.

"Well of course, you aren't doing well, Fiona! You are locked away. I mean, at least this place seems nice. But what do I need to do to get you out of here for good, baby?" she asks me, very determined now.

"I don't know, Chloe. I am pretty sure, I am going to be here a while." I look down at my feet. I have never been good at lying to Chloe.

"I did what you asked. What do you mean, Fiona? You said…I did what you asked me to. I shredded the papers," she says loudly.

"Chloe, keep your voice down," I say sternly, remembering suddenly what I asked her to do that first day: the day I was admitted into Living Waters a month ago. "Thank you. I knew I could count on you," I tell her, smiling at her sincerely.

"Fiona, I'm going crazy without you. All of us are. The boys miss you, too. Your house…"

I realize Chloe and the boys are still living in my house, without me in it. Back in Florida.

"We just need you back home with us," she says sadly.

"Well, I don't know when I'll be released, Chloe. I'm sorry."

It is so hard to see her like this. Hurting. Am I hurting her more by keeping myself locked up in here? I am so torn about what the right thing to do is. Being with me is detrimental to her emotional health. I know it is. And if I am outside, if I get out of here, how will I stay away from her? I can't. So this is my only answer. Keep faking insanity and stay here. Permanently. Or until I think of a better plan.

"Well, it was nice of you to come," I say in a lifeless, unemotional voice.

"It was nice of you to come? Really, Fiona? How about 'I miss you, Chloe. I love you so much.' What the fuck, Fiona. What have they fucking done to you?" She's shouting, drawing attention to us.

"Shhh…" I try to get her to calm down.

"Look," she tells me, "I am staying at your dad's house for a few days, which your brother is now living in, not that you care. But if you aren't going to give me answers, I will find them myself."

"Chloe, wait!"

"I'll be back here tomorrow, if they allow it. Try to remember who you are, Fiona. Don't let them change you."

She walks out of the double doors without looking back.

I can't help feeling like somebody has punched me in the stomach. As I begin to walk back to my room, I feel faint. I see Trisha is in there reading something on her bed. I try to avoid her and walk to our bathroom, but of course, she notices the decorated human walk into her room.

"Hey, Fiona. Have any visitors today?"

"Nah," I say, and proceed to the bathroom.

I close the door and look at myself in the mirror. The sleep lines are gone, but I notice how disheveled I look. I could use a serious haircut. I wish we were allowed a buzzer: I would just do it myself. I can't believe Chloe came all the way to New York to see me. She must have left the boys with Trent back in Florida. She is staying with my brother at my dad's house. What is she trying to find? Does she know more than I think she does? I remember everything I asked her that first day on the phone. How I asked her to shred those papers from my dad's office when she got a chance. I don't know how she did it, but she says she did. I trust she is telling the truth. I think about all the secrets, I uncovered before my dad died. Everything I…read. I wonder how much Chloe read. Before she shredded them. She is probably going to go there and read everything she can find now. Hell, by tomorrow morning she will know more than I do. Great. What have I done? What have I started?

Chloe: July 2015
Fluid

Fiona and I decide to do another 'date' at her house, since there are no tiny dictators there to boss us around. I am feeling guilty, sick in the pit of my stomach, like I'm some evil person who will eventually burn in hell for her actions. Her magnetic pull is too strong, though, so I go anyway.

I get there around six and she's dressed in a sleeveless white tee with basketball shorts. I notice that the sleeveless shirt shows off more tattoos: more than I thought she had.

"Mind if we get takeout?" she asks as I walk in.

"Not at all," I answer.

We order sushi from a restaurant downtown and pick it up together half an hour later. While we are paying for the food, I notice there are several people staring at us. There is no question tonight that Fiona is a lesbian. Her boyish outfit just screams it. I look right at one of them and take Fiona's hand in mine proudly. She looks at me and gives me a curious but inviting smile. Her skin is so feminine and soft. I forgot what it was like to hold a female hand like this. She doesn't let go of my hand until we get back in her car.

After dinner, we look through old photo albums of her as a teen. She had long straight hair then, but the same perfect skin, minus a lot of the tattoos, and bright blue eyes. She dressed like a tomboy but had more of a feminine look than the androgynous one she has now.

"Did you always know you were a lesbian?" I ask, still staring at her teenage self.

"Absolutely," she says. "I've never even been with a guy."

"I wish I was like you. So confident in what I wanted. Maybe you are right, maybe I am stuck in purgatory."

"I didn't really mean all of that, you know. I wish sometimes I was more like you. Then I would have more prospects, ha, ha."

"Yes, that's true, I guess, when you look at it like that, ha!"

I tell her all about my past relationships: about Andy, and Janie, and my parents being so disapproving of the "gay lifestyle." She gets it. She gets it all. She understands me. I can see it in her face. I feel so completely comfortable with her.

"Do you think of yourself as more of a guy?" I ask.

"I don't really think of myself as any gender. I know I am female; I was born that way. I have lady parts and I don't mind that. I have never wanted to 'transition' to a male or anything, I just feel more comfortable with less makeup, shorter hair and I'd rather wear a dapper suit than a fancy dress. Actually, you will never see me in a dress, k."

"Ha, ha, yeah – I can't picture you in a dress."

"This tattoo right here." She pulls my hand across her collarbone and places it on the word "fluidity" that is inked across her skin. "This tattoo is my gender. Fluid. That's what I am."

She holds me while we watch a movie and sweetly kisses me goodbye on the cheek before I leave.

When I get home, everyone is already asleep in the house. Thank God. I run the bath water and rip all of my clothes off, in some kind of manic episode I must be having. "I can't do this – I can't do this." I am in too deep. I am starting to feel things I have never felt before and it's all-encompassing. Living in this house with my husband is no help at all. It only makes this more confusing. Sadder. That's what I am – I am sad. I'm not happy at all about any of this. I am no victim. I am a cruel, heartless bitch. Who would do something like this? Trent is right: I did take vows, and those vows are going to shit. I want Fiona. I want her all to myself, so badly that the inside of my soul aches. But how am I going to explain myself to anyone, especially my family? I decide that I can't; that this just can't be. I am straight. I convince myself that I am no longer bisexual, I am not a lesbian, I do not have feelings for Fiona and I will stay with my husband.

After a long bath I go to sleep.

The next day, Trent and I go to an emergency session of counseling that I've begged the therapist for out of sheer desperation. I don't contact Fiona for another week. She calls me at the end of the week and leaves a message after I decline her call.

"Chloe. You doing ok? I know this isn't easy on you and I get it. No pressure over here on my end, but I just want to check on you and see how you're doing, love. You know, I read something the other day. A quote that made me think of you. 'How does one become a butterfly? You must want to

fly so much that you are willing to give up being a caterpillar.' When you are ready to fly you call me, ok?"

Damn her. DAMN her perfect words and how perfectly they flow out of her beautiful lips.

I suppress all of my emotions just like I always have, and I continue with the counseling for four more weeks and don't contact Fiona at all. She doesn't call.

Fiona: December 2015
Unsettled

I lie wideawake, while Trisha continues to snore loudly in her bed beside me. Her hair is in her usual foam rollers. She looks like a Barbie made in the eighties. I can't turn my mind off. I decide I want to smoke a cigarette. I rummage through my suitcase and all I find is an empty pack. I know Trisha smokes, so I grab one of hers and head out to the hall in my slippers and robe. I am not familiar enough with this place yet to know how the hell to get outside in the dark while everyone else is asleep. I have no idea what time it is, but I find an exit door all the way at the end of the hall. It looks unlocked, so I push on it lightly. It doesn't budge. I push harder. It swings open and a violent alarm starts to sound throughout the whole building. I cover my ears.

"Oh Shit," I say out loud. "Wrong door?"

Dr. Hall sees me first, standing by the open door, and he runs up to me. "Fiona? What are you doing? Were you trying to escape?"

"No," I say. I absolutely was not trying to escape. "No, I just wanted to smoke a cigarette," I clarify.

He shakes his head at me and I notice everyone is out of their rooms now, staring at me.

"I swear," I say a little louder.

I didn't even consider the possibility of an alarm or of anyone thinking I would escape. I am realizing now that I am the only one who knows that I don't want to escape: that I want to stay here locked up for now.

"Fiona, I am going to have to ask you to come with me to my office and we can talk, okay?" Dr. Hall says to me.

I follow him to his office and everyone starts to disappear back into their rooms.

"Sit down," he suggests as we walk in. I notice he has lots of pictures of his family hanging on the walls. They are the picture perfect, J. Crew-catalog family.

"So. Tell me why you would want to leave here so quickly, after just being admitted?" he asks.

"I told you, I didn't want to – " I start to think about how this could actually work in my favor. How I am trying to seem mental and this is exactly what someone that was crazy would do. Think they could escape, somehow, in the middle of the night. I decide to confess.

"You're right. I was trying to leave," I lie.

"But why, Fiona? I noticed you did not show up for your counseling session yesterday either," he reminds me.

I guess that was when I was sleeping on my bed, before Chloe showed up. Whoops.

"We need you to be compliant, Fiona. If you want to get better and get out of here," he informs me.

Perfect, I think. My lack of compliance is perfect.

"I am sorry," I say convincingly, "I just want to go home."

No, I don't. Well, not really.

"I know, sweetie. We want you to, too. But first, you have to go to the counseling sessions and stay in your bed at night. I am sorry, but I am going to have to assign you a sitter for the next few days. They will be with you all of the time, except of course, when you need to use the restroom or cleanup. If you can prove to me over the next few days that you are compliant again, then there will be more freedom again, okay Fiona?"

"Okay," I say.

This sucks. I don't want some stranger spying on me all day.

"Goodnight, Fiona," Dr. Halls says, and he allows me to go back to my room until morning.

I wake up and there is a woman – who looks like a butch cop, actually – standing in the corner of my room. Trisha must already be up. Rare, I think.

"Um, excuse me," I say. "Who are you?"

"I am Collette. I will be your sitter until further notice," she informs me.

Right. The sitter.

"Ah," I say, "I see. Well, I need to use the restroom and 'cleanup', if you could excuse me," I say, giving her a false smile.

She walks out of my room and stands right outside the door. I walk to the bathroom, splash cold water on my face and change clothes before venturing out of my room to be monitored all damn day. I notice, as I walk down the hall towards the cafeteria, that everyone is staring at me. They look either frightened or concerned for my mental state. I assume, it must be a reaction to my alleged 'escape' last night. I play to their fears.

"I am not going to try and escape today, I promise!" I say while walking towards the Barista.

Everyone simply turns away, as if they weren't making assumptions at all.

Jade walks right up to me, a few minutes later, as if she is unaware of anything that happened last night. She acts no differently towards me at all.

"Hey. No yoga this morning?" she asks.

"No…long night," I say, trying to discover whether she knows about last night.

"Oh, yeah, I haven't had a good night's sleep here yet," she says with a smile.

I still have no idea if she knows about my attempts last night, but I continue to order my coffee and take a seat at the closest table. She sits down next to me.

"So what time is your counseling today?" she asks.

My counseling. I have no idea, but I guess I need to figure that out, considering I missed it yesterday and all.

"I need to go look, actually. I missed it yesterday." I begin to walk towards the elevator, feeling a bit rushed.

"I'll come with you," Jade says, following me to the elevator. I notice my sitter is trailing behind. Jade doesn't ask, why I have this bodyguard with me. I find that odd.

Jade waits for me to check my counseling schedule, which is pinned up to the bulletin board in my room.

"My counseling is at ten," I announce.

"Great. Mine is at the same time."

Of course, it is.

"So, what is your 'real' story, Fiona?" Jade says suddenly.

"What do you mean?" I ask.

"I mean, why you are really here? You tried to kill yourself, but why? You took a bunch of pills, right? But why would you do that? What's the real reason you are…unstable?"

I can't believe she is asking me this. We aren't friends. I have known her less than forty-eight hours. What does she think I am going to tell her? I don't owe her any explanation of who I am.

"That is really none of your business."

"I saw you last night," Jade says casually. "I saw you had a cigarette in your hand. I know you weren't trying to escape. You wouldn't do that. You aren't dumb. You just wanted a smoke, right…? But why would you play into it? Why would you want to be in trouble? I think…you want to be here. Maybe you have an unstable home environment and this is actually a safer place for you? Am I close?" she asks.

How meddlesome of her! I cannot believe she is berating me like this!

"I have no idea what you are talking about," I respond, trying not to act as if I am threatened by her keen observations.

"Look, I was a Psych minor in college," she explains. "I can read people pretty well. And you…you are smart. You want them to believe you are insane, but you aren't. You may be able to fool everyone else, but you can't fool me."

Why does she care? What difference does it make to her if I am sick or not?

I suddenly feel ill. If I can't fool Jade, I am not sure Dr. Hall will be convinced much longer.

"But see, that is a sickness in itself," Jade pipes back up. "Wanting to appear ill. Maybe you just like the attention…"

"I do not like attention!" I yell angrily. I can't hold back my emotions anymore. I am starting to come unwound. "You need to stay out of my head! You don't know what you are talking about. You know what I think, Jade? I think you are so fucking lonely that you have nothing better to do than stalk me and follow me around like a desperate little puppy looking for a companion. Get out of my room."

It was harsh, I know. But she needs to know, she can't pry on my psyche anymore. She needs to back the fuck off.

I have a terribly unsettled feeling inside after being so cruel towards poor Jade. Until today, she has been nothing but nice to me. But I can't get distracted, worrying whether I am going to step on any toes or hurt anyone's feelings. That is not why I am here. I realize now that I do not need friendship. I need to just stick to the plan. I march out of my room and head to Dr. Hall's office so he can pick my brain. I just hope he is not as smart as Jade.

I need to talk to Chloe. I need to call her and get everything settled. I need to know if she has found anything while rummaging through my father's office, as I assume she has been doing. Please let this counseling session go smoothly and quickly, I pray.

Chloe: August 2015
Taking Flight

August is by far the worst month in Florida. It's so hot; it's so rainy. I look up at the sky and it looks like a storm is coming. The clouds are almost black and it feels eerily calm. I feel eerily calm. Trent and I have a counseling session this afternoon.

My phone rings and it is Lana. I have been avoiding my friends again. I always do this when something bad is going on because I know they can tell by talking to me that I am not myself. I feel like enough time has passed and I can answer her call today and explain that we were having marital issues, but now we are perfectly fine again.

"Because we are," I, for some reason, say out loud.

"Hey, Lana."

"Heeeeey. I miss you. Have you been avoiding me again?"

"Yeah, sort of. Just working out the kinks of my marriage."

"Well, I am glad you are back to your happy self and we can talk again. You know it's great that you stay together for the kids. That's very big and selfless of you."

Click. I hang up on her.

I couldn't do it. How could she say something like that? I didn't say any of those things! Was I that transparent? Had everyone known the truth about me all along? That I was staying in my marriage for all of the wrong reasons? The sky was looking darker and darker.

Trent walks in the door wearing his usual baseball cap, and snug jeans, mid freak-out. "So, kids are at my mom's. You ready to go see the therapist, sweetie?" he asks.

"No. I'm not!" I say, flustered.

"Okay, do you need some more time to get ready?"

I realize I haven't blown dry my hair yet and it is dripping down my back, making a small puddle by my feet.

I look at how desperate Trent looks to me now. He has more facial hair than usual. A sign that he is neglecting to care for himself, in my eyes. He is only concerned with making me happy lately. But why? I don't deserve it, or him.

"No, I mean I can't do this, Trent," I blurt out. "I can't stay married to you. The kids will adjust. They will have to adjust. I won't keep them from you, I would never keep them from you. Please know that. I'm so, so sorry. I can't live this lie anymore. I want to be happy. I have to go, I'm sorry."

I run so fast to my car that I am still out of breath when I reach Fiona's house. What if she has a girlfriend now? It has been almost five weeks since I last talked to her. A lot could have happened in that amount of time. She could be married, in all actuality. I look up at the sky and notice it's just starting to rain. I hurry out of my car and sprint up to her front door. I knock loudly and wait for what feels like an eternity.

"Chloe?" she asks in an alarmed voice as she opens the door. "Are you okay? Is it pouring already? Why are you so wet and…breathy?"

I remember that in my impulsiveness, I have forgotten to dry my hair, which is still dripping wet, and I am probably looking like a soggy mess right now.

"Hey," I say, still completely out of breath. "I had to see you. I know it's been awhile since we've talked and I am so sorry for waffling back and forth and for putting you in the middle of all of this and for anything else that I can't really think of right now because my thoughts are so incredibly unorganized, but I want to learn to fly. I'm ready to learn to fly, hypothetically speaking, that is. If you are still ok with that, I'm ready now."

"Hey, hey…" She puts her arms around me for a second and then grabs my face firmly with her soft, feminine hands. "It's going to be okay. Take a deep breath, okay?"

We walk inside, out of the storm, which is now raging.

"Are you sure, you want to be with me, or try to see where this is going?" she asks.

"Completely. There's no turning back now."

"Would you like to dry your hair?" she asks somewhat sarcastically.

"What, is this not a good look on me?"

"You're beautiful, Chloe. I just want you to feel comfortable."

I believe her.

"Here, use my bathroom. Dry your hair and then we can talk or watch a movie if you'd rather. Whatever you want."

"Okay."

I come out a few minutes later and she is sitting on the couch laughing at some commercial. Her smile is so beautiful. She is perfect, I think.

"Hey, feel better, sexy?" she asks with a smirk.

"Much, thanks."

"Come sit with me, I won't bite," she says while motioning me to her.

"Promise me you won't break my heart, Fiona." I say as I sit down next to her on the couch.

"I promise."

"I am really into you," I say while inching closer to her. "It scares me a little."

"Why? How can you love someone completely any other way? You have to give yourself to that person. Every inch of your being has to be an offering. If you fail at love, so be it. There are second chances, there are other loves. Nothing is ever the same for a lifetime. Life is messy, Chloe; that's the beauty of it all."

I feel compelled to touch her, so I take her hand in mine and our eyes meet instantly. I can tell she is about to kiss me like no one has ever kissed me before and I don't want to ever forget this moment, so I try to freeze time just for a second. She kisses me passionately with both of her hands on my face and then runs her delicate fingers through my hair. I smile at her and she flips me onto my back on the couch. I am so turned on and so in love at this moment that I never want it to end. I have never felt this way before in my entire life and I start to realize, I am in way over my head.

I decide, it's best, I stay at Fiona's tonight. I want to give Trent time to process the reality of all of this. Or maybe I want to give myself that time, too. I call him. He doesn't answer so I leave a message and say my goodnights to the boys on the message, too.

"Here, take this. It's the least dikey shirt I own to sleep in."

She hands me a Bert-and-Ernie shirt where Bert has his arm around Ernie while they sit together on a couch.

"This is the least Lesbian shirt you own to sleep in? Everyone knows Bert and Ernie are gay."

"Whatever, they're best friends. It's super comfy, I promise." She insists.

I hesitate before deciding not to go to the bathroom to get changed and I simply slip my shirt off over my head and stand there for a second in my bra and cut off shorts. Fiona immediately looks down. I put the Bert-and-Ernie shirt on and she shows me to the guest room.

"So, you can sleep in here if you want. Or on the couch if you'd rather watch TV. No TV in the guest room yet, sorry. Oh, which reminds me. My mom is coming to town in a couple days."

"She is? Oh, what for? Just to visit...?" I ask.

"Well, I kind of left on bad terms with her, and left my dog there in New York, so she is going to bring him to me and stay a few days at my place. It's okay if you sleep here still, if you need to. As long as you are comfortable sleeping in my room."

"Yeah, okay. We'll see. She won't be thrown off by all of this?"

"She's known I was gay since I was fifteen, Chloe. It's no secret."

"No, I mean me. Like, being married and all of the gory details."

"She doesn't have to know all of that yet," Fiona says, "But I assume at this point that won't be a problem for too much longer, right?"

I hadn't really sat and thought about all of the logistics myself. I guess Fiona is right. I can't just stay in limbo when I know what I want. The next step is to officially file for divorce. It's the only thing that makes sense. I mean, I know Trent and I have been having problems for the past few years, but they were different problems from the normal marital problems. And looking back at my marriage I realize now that I was pretty damn unhappy for about half of it. He hadn't done anything wrong. And I'd like to still believe I hadn't either. What would our reason for filing be? WIFE BECAME A LESBIAN AND LEFT HER DEVOTED HUSBAND AND CHILDREN FOR A FEMALE. This was starting to sound a lot like I was the reason for the divorce. Trent would still be with me if it weren't for me wanting to leave.

"Chloe?"

I realize, I have been in my head for the past few minutes. "No, that won't be a problem for very much longer; you're right. I guess I need to meet with an attorney and with Trent sometime this week."

"Take all the time you need. I know what we have isn't going anywhere."

She was right. These feelings weren't going anywhere.

"Hey Fiona," I say as she is walking to her bedroom, "How do you feel about maybe taking the kids somewhere with me tomorrow during the day?"

"Like the park or something?" she asks.

"Yeah, they love the park, if you're up for it?"

"Sure, meet me there at noon and we can go on my lunchbreak, is that cool?"

"Okay."

"Goodnight Chloe. Don't think too much. Try to get some sleep."

"Yeah, you too."

I wake up to the smell of freshly brewed coffee. This is something new: not having tiny hands poking me. I walk out to the kitchen and see Fiona is all ready to jet-off to work. She is pouring her coffee into a travel mug that has a Ninja Turtle face on it.

"Heeey, morning, sunshine." She kisses me on the cheek.

"Morning. What time do you have to be at work?"

"Mmm, right about now."

"Ha…Okay, well, let me just grab my things and I'll leave with you. I need to get home before Trent leaves for work anyways, to be with the boys."

"Nah, no rush. Here's my spare. You keep it so you can come and go when you need. Just put it under the front mat when you leave."

I snoop around for just a few minutes before I rush home. The only alarming thing I find is a strap-on in the drawer next to her bed. Now I feel a little uneasy having told her, I was this experienced lesbian. I have never used a strap-on. I'm not even really sure how to use one. Maybe I am more inexperienced at this girl-on-girl thing than I thought.

Fiona: December 2015
Interrogation

I walk in to Dr. Hall's office right on time today. Right at 10 am.

"Fiona," he says with a smile. "I am so glad you could make it today."

I sit down in a comfy-looking chair, right across from his desk and try to relax.

"So, how are you feeling today, Fiona?" he asks me.

"I am feeling numb," I say. It is the only thing that comes to mind.

"I can try to get your antidepressants lowered if you think that is a problem," he offers.

"Thank you. That would be nice."

"So, other than attempting to leave, how are you liking your stay here so far? Has the staff helped make you feel at home?"

"Sure," I say shortly. Not caring to offer any positive feedback at this point.

"Well, these counseling sessions are designed to give you an opportunity to communicate to me what you think you need help with in order to get better and get back to your normal life. Does that sound good?"

I nod my head in agreement. Although, getting out of here is not the plan, he can't know that.

"Great. So, tell me a little bit about your family, Fiona. Are you close with your…?" I can see him look over my charts and realize, I only have my mother and brother now. "…mother?" he asks.

"Define close."

"Do you believe you have a healthy relationship?"

I am not sure, what I believe anymore.

"We do now," I respond.

"As opposed to when, Fiona? When you were little? When you were a teenager? What caused discord for you two, back then?"

I hate shrinks, I think to myself. They know all too well exactly what to say to get you talking…

"She expected a lot of me, in a lot of ways," I say, trying to be as indirect and vague as possible, on purpose, of course.

"When you say she expected a lot of you – can you elaborate on that Fiona? What did she expect from you?"

"She expected me to hide things from my father; she expected me to act a certain way around him. She also expected me to put on a smile. No matter what."

"No matter what? That doesn't seem fair. She wanted you to act happy, when maybe you weren't always. Am I right?"

"Right" I say.

"What did she ask you to hide? Your…sexuality?"

"That, yes."

"Ah. Well, that had to be really hard for you. Pretending all of the time."

"It wasn't easy."

"But your dad found out anyway, I assume?"

"He did. When I was about fifteen."

"And it looks like you were sent here. Around that time? To the Meadows, correct? Your charts state that you had what is defined here as a 'mental breakdown' after attempting suicide at such a young age."

That time, I had. I had tried to kill myself.

"I…I took a lot of pills. Yes."

"And they weren't your pills? Whose pills were they, Fiona?"

"I don't remember."

"Well, I can imagine going through so much and struggling with your identity at the young age of only fifteen had to take a toll on you. I am not surprised that you turned to drugs and alcohol. It is a common crutch for a teenager in your position, with your family background and wealth as well."

With my wealth? Is he honestly insinuating that rich people are crazier?

I have no comment.

I raise an eyebrow to show my concern for his remark.

"All I am saying is that back then, when you were younger, it makes sense that you would need to numb the pain with something tangible like pills, but now…I am not sure I understand your reaction to your…to your father's death," he says, looking right at me now. "Why would you try to kill yourself this time, Fiona? You had come so far, sweetheart. It seemed you were in a really good place before he was sick. I just want you to be able to get back to that place. What can I do to help you remember how happy you were then? Because you know your father wants you to be happy."

"Ha! He wants me to be happy? Right. Because he is such an honorable and generous soul. Please. Are we done here for today?"

"We have a few more minutes, actually," Dr. Hall says.

"Well, I am not feeling well. And I would like to use my phone call for the day."

"Fiona. I want to help you, sweetie. I want to remind you that you are capable of being happy and healthy. Because just a few months ago, you were. Remember?"

I do remember. That is the problem. I miss Chloe, I miss her boys, I miss my mom and Mikey and the tattoo shop, and I even miss fucking hot, humid Florida. I miss the sunshine. I miss my life, but I am toxic to the people around me. I am a ticking time bomb just waiting to explode. I don't want to blow up everything Chloe has. I don't want to create a chaotic disaster anymore. I need to be isolated.

"Well, I am good at suppressing: an expert, actually."

I start to walk out of the room.

"Fiona. I will see you here tomorrow, same time."

I nod and leave his office. I hate shrinks.

I walk over to the front desk and ask to use my phone call. Chloe said, she was going to come by again today, but I haven't heard from her. I need to call her and find out what she knows and what is going on.

"Chloe, it's me," I say as she answers her cell phone.

"How are you today, sweetie?" she asks me in her sweet, feminine voice.

I instantly feel soothed.

"I am okay today. Just…tired," I explain. "Chloe, I need to know if you read any of the…documents, before you shredded them. Or if you know…anything? Anything at all that you want to talk about?"

"Yes," she says.

"Yes what?"

"Yes, I read them," she says.

"All of them?"

"All of them."

"I see."

"Look, Fiona. I am so…I am so sorry. I had no idea. He really had me convinced that he was a better man than you thought. I should have believed you. I mean, I could tell how badly he must have hurt you, but he was so…manipulative, I guess. So good with his words, and convincing. And to think all of this time he was hiding…that…"

"It's okay," I interrupt her. "I need to know who else knows. Do my mom and Mikey know?"

"No. I didn't tell anyone. Just me."

"Good. Let's keep it like that, okay?"

"What do I need to do, Fiona? What can I do with you in there?"

"Nothing. I can handle it."

"I don't understand, Fiona…"

"Trust me. I have it all under control," I assure her.

And I do.

After attempting to convince Chloe that I do in fact possess the ability to keep my father's secret life under wraps while being locked up, I march back to my room to bum a cigarette from Trisha.

"Hey," she says. I give her a 'Do you mind?' look, grabbing her cigarettes off her bedside table and placing one behind my ear.

"Go ahead," she tells me. "I'll join you."

We walk out the exit door, which does not apparently sound a loud alarm during the daytime.

"You look shaken up," Trisha observantly announces while puffing on her menthol.

"I am. A little," I bravely admit to her.

"Do you want to talk about it?" she asks me, sounding all too familiar, like a shrink from my past.

"Ugh. You sound like a shrink," I blurt out, annoyed.

"Sorry. I hear a lot of them speak, I guess," she says innocently, a smirk spread across her glamorous face.

"I know, right?" I feel as though all of us in here are of the same breed. All of us have probably seen numerous counselors and psychiatrists our entire lives. We get each other, which makes for a familiar feeling. A little homier than elsewhere, I suppose.

I quickly forgive Trisha for inquiring – so professionally – whether I want to talk about it or not, and suddenly decide to fill her in on some things.

"My fiancée has been on the outside doing some…some cleanup for me." I feel as though, the way I worded that may sound like I had her cleanup a murder scene or something, so I clarify. "I mean, she has been helping me clean up my father's house. He recently passed away," I say for what feels like the first time out loud.

"I am so sorry, Fiona."

"What from?" she asks me.

"A neurological disease called A.L.S."

"Oh yeah, like the Ice Bucket Challenge thing?" she asks.

"The what?"

"The Ice Bucket Challenge. Where people dumped ice on their heads to raise money and awareness for A.L.S. last year?"

"Right," I say, still having no idea what she is referring to.

"Man, that sucks. I knew a guy that had that. It was pretty rough."

"Yeah. It was…hard."

"So your dad lived in New York?"

"Yeah, I grew up here, actually. We weren't really close, though…until he got sick."

"It always seems to happen that way, right? Someone gets sick and feels they got to reach out to their family, mend fences and all…but that's good, right? That you guys got close, at least at the end?"

"It was nice, yes," I say, wondering if it actually was nice or not. I mean, I made the mistake of getting a little too comfortable in his house while he was sick, and that is how I came across all of the secrets he was keeping in the first place. That would have never happened, had I stayed a safe distance away, but I had to whisk in and take care of him for that couple of months. Now I am left trying to keep his private life just that. Private. And why should I? Why do I care now what people think about him…? I shouldn't care. He didn't care about me. Not really; not even at the end.

"Well, so you are stressed because your fiancée is left cleaning up his house or something, while you are in here, not able to help?" Trisha asks me, still confused about what the big deal is, I assume.

"He had…He had a lot of valuable documents that I am pretty sure he wouldn't want people to uncover, ever. I had her shred some of them. But I feel confident that there are other…secrets…she may uncover, and I am not there to help her keep them hidden. It seems silly, I guess, but for some reason I don't want the rest of the family in on all of this. It would…crush them." I realize I am disclosing a lot to Trisha, this mean girl who somehow has become my biggest confidant in this place.

"Ah. I see. Secrets, huh? Sounds juicy. Well, don't worry yourself to death, Fiona. I mean…"

I can tell Trisha feels awkward all of a sudden, having used the word 'death', thinking I tried to kill myself yet again.

"Look, I didn't try to kill myself," I admit.

"I didn't think you did," she says.

Does everyone know, I am a fraud?

"All I am saying, Fiona, is that there's only so much you can hide. Things always have a way of…showing themselves. Their true selves, with time."

She is absolutely right. I know that, first-hand. How naïve of me to think, firstly, that I can fool anyone in here for much longer into believing I am insane when I am clearly perfectly fine; and secondly, that my father's secrets will never leak out. They are inevitably going to leak out, no matter what I do to try to stop it. Is it even worth my angst? I am not so sure anymore.

Chloe: August 2015
Finalized

We walk into the tattoo shop and I can see the boys' eyes get really big all of a sudden.

"Mommy, is this a doctor's office? Why is everybody getting shots?" asks Kaden.

"It's not a doctor's office, sweetie. This is where my friend Fiona works. She is a tattoo artist. She is going to go to the park with us today."

"Did she draw the bug on your arm?"

"She sure did. Isn't that cool, Kade?"

"Yeah. Can she draw Spider Man on my arm?"

"With a pen, yes."

Fiona is just finishing up someone's tattoo, so we wait by the door.

"Alright, man, see you later," she says to some guy who looks a lot like Marilyn Manson.

"Hey little dudes," she says to the boys as she takes off her apron. "You ready to do some sliding?"

"Yeah, okay," Kaden says.

Max just clutches my leg tightly.

Fiona is great with the boys. She pushes Max on the swing and plays pirates with Kaden while chasing him around the playground. Kaden thinks her tattoos are the coolest things ever. She has a lot of cartoon-looking ones so he probably thinks of her as a walking, breathing, and coloring book.

I keep the boys in their car seats, get out of the car and shut the door for a minute to say goodbye to Fiona before she goes back to work.

"Thanks for doing this, Fiona."

"Of course, baby. I know the way to your heart is going to be through those tiny little dudes right there. I'm kind of a big kid myself, so it was fun getting to hang out with them. They are really cool, and so is their mom."

"Aw. Now I'm blushing," I say.

"See you tonight after work at my place?" she asks.

I figure it will take Trent a few days to get himself set up in an apartment so I'm sure I will stay with Fiona a few more nights. "Yes, ma'am."

She bites her fingernail. "Can't wait."

I leave for Fiona's house after we all eat dinner together as a 'family.' Trent and I are pretty good at acting semi-normal around the kids. He's actually handling this very maturely. He hasn't blown up at me in front of them at all. I lie and tell Kaden and Max I will be staying at my mom's for some days this week. I'm not really ready to explain to them that Fiona and I are a couple.

"Why, mommy?" asks Kaden. His big, blue eyes look concerned as they stare up at me.

"Well, sometimes grownups have slumber parties, like kids do. And Grandma and I are going to have some this week, ok?"

"Psh…slumber party. I bet it's a slumber party alright. Woo-hoo!" Trent mumbles facetiously.

I retract my comment about him being mature. But I can't blame him.

When I get to Fiona's she is on the phone.

"Yes, a – huh…right…I know. I know, mom. Christ, it will be fine. Tell him to just call me if he needs to talk about it…Fine. Yep. Talk to you later…Love you, too."

She hangs up and turns to me, "Sorry about that, girl."

"No, it's okay. Is everything alright with your mom? She still coming in a couple days?"

"Oh yeah; yeah, it's all good. She will be here tomorrow night, actually, so I need to sort of clean up some tonight while you are here if that's okay. She's kind of a perfectionist."

"Of course. Tell me what needs to be done and I will help you out."

"No, you don't need to do that. Take these shiny shoes off." She starts slipping my glitter sandals off one at a time. "And relax, girlfriend. Want me to run you a bath?"

"Run me a bath? Well, that sounds delightful, when you say it like that."

"Ha-ha, okay. You can use my tub. It's bigger," she says while leading me into her bedroom.

She fills the water up high, and she's clearly added a lot of bubble bath because the bubbles are nearly pouring over when I walk in.

"Whoa, how about some water with those bubbles."

"Sorry, I got a little carried away."

She kisses me on the cheek.

"So. You haven't really told me much about your family. Other than that, you and your mom were having an argument when you left New York," I say, getting into the tub. I notice her stare at my bare skin for a second before she looks down at her lap.

"Yeah; yeah we were. Uh…it had more to do with my father than my mother. They're divorced, by the way. They have been since I was around ten."

"Oh, okay. What's your father like?"

"Ohhhh…my father. Well, he is a narcissistic asshole, who I haven't talked to in over a year."

"Well, tell me how you really feel about him?"

"Ha, ha, I'm sorry. Yeah, we don't really get along. He doesn't really accept my lifestyle, if you know what I mean."

"But, your mom seems cool with it – you said – right? I thought they'd known since you were fifteen or whatever."

"No, I said my mom has known since I was fifteen. She made me hide it from my father for years. They were divorced. He's a workaholic and I didn't see him much, so it wasn't that hard to hide from him. He's known for a few years now. I have a brother too, by the way. He and my dad are pretty 'tight.' My brother works for him, at his company. He's kind of in training to take it over one day."

"What kind of company?"

"He's in the coffee business."

"Like, he makes the coffee? Or owns a shop?"

"He owns some shops."

"Well, that's cool. You never had any interest in that? Seems like you love coffee."

"I am an artist, Chloe. I'm not a businesswoman. He's tried to push it on me my whole life. Actually, I think now he would be embarrassed for me to take over any of the company, because of how I look."

"I'm sorry. I don't mean to pry."

"It's alright, baby. You just enjoy your bath. I'm going to go start cleaning."

I think about my family and how I haven't told them anything about what is going on with Trent or about Fiona. I need to call my parents and fill them in, but I am so afraid of their reaction. I also don't want any outside influences to change my mind. I have made up my mind and don't need any more confusion from the people around me. I decide I will just call my mom tomorrow and tell her everything.

I get out of the bath, dry off and walk out into the living room to find Fiona with headphones on, jamming out while she cleans counter tops. She sees me.

"Hey, how was your bath?" she asks.

"Fabulous."

"I'm almost done cleaning."

I pick up a dust rag and dust the living room for her, even though she asked me not to. Being a homemaker is all I have known for some time now. She finishes up with the cleaning and goes to her bedroom to change clothes. I follow her.

She confidently strips down to her bra and panties.

"So, I'm thinking about getting a new tattoo soon..." she says to me while still in her underwear.

Where? Is there any space left? I think as I try not to stare at her boyish yet beautiful body covered in colorful artwork.

"Oh yeah, what of?" I ask in an interested tone.

"I can't decide, exactly. I have always wanted something religious, like scripture or a really great quote on my thigh."

I didn't know she was religious at all. She is still in her underwear.

"That sounds neat."

I notice, she has a very realistic-looking dog, drawn on her shoulder blade. He's scruffy but really cute.

"Is that your dog, drawn on your shoulder?" I ask.

"Aw, yes, that's Marvin. I can't wait for you to meet him tomorrow. He's sho shweeeet..." she says in the most gooey, girly voice, I have ever heard come out of her mouth.

"Yeah," I answer. "I can't wait either."

"How about you Chloe? You going to let me brand you some more one of these days?"

"Maybe. I bet that would get you all hot, wouldn't it," I say, walking closer to her.

"Oooh, well, it sure would, baby doll."

She grabs me and throws me onto her bed and we make out like teenagers for a good half hour or so.

I wake up the next morning with my head on her chest. She is still half-naked. I guess, I fell asleep on her last night.

"You were so cute; I couldn't move you. Sorry," she says, yawning.

"It's okay. I better get going, though. Got to get home to the boys. Oh, and I forgot to tell you that Trent and I are meeting with an attorney at five today. To get a contract all written up."

"That's about the time my mom should be getting here. You are staying with me tonight, right?" she asks.

"Yes, if that's still okay. Trent says the apartment will be ready for him to move into in a couple of days."

"Yeah. I just have to go pick up my mom from the airport after work, so we'll be back here around six, probably. We can pick up dinner on the way home and all eat together if you want. I don't dare cook for my mom."

"That sounds great, baby. And you are a fabulous cook, by the way," I say, clutching my keys.

"Have a good day, Chloe. Good luck at your meeting. You're a strong woman: you know that."

"Thanks, Fiona. I hope so."

The meeting with the attorney is brutal. Trent cries, I cry: it's pretty gut-wrenching. I knew, I was making the right decision. I don't question that. But I still love Trent. He's the father of my children. Am I making the right decision?

"Give her anything she wants," he says at one point.

"Alright," says the attorney. "Well, with you both being very civil about this, all that's left is for you both to sign and file when you're ready."

"Good. Then it's finalized. Goodbye, Chloe. I'll see you tomorrow morning," says Trent with tears still in his eyes.

Fiona: December 2015
Secrets

I lie in bed and can't stop thinking about all of the letters. All of the love letters I read. The letters my father wrote. It was his handwriting. His signature. His name at the bottom of each and every single letter. The receipts, the trips, the secrets: so many secrets. How could he be so judgmental of my life? How could he have lived a lie for his entire existence? I don't know him at all. It is a shame, really. To know now that his whole life was a lie. Well, for lack of a better word. I wouldn't call his life so much of a lie as I would call it a simulation. A fake existence made up of fake feelings and actions every day. I remember the day, I found the love letters in his office. He was taking one of his long naps. Chloe and I weren't talking and I was desperate for something to take my mind off of the hardships of my own life at the time. So I wandered around his huge house and ended up in his office. I made the mistake of prying a little too well and came across the bundled letters in a drawer. I read the first one. A love letter to Alex. I remember wondering, why the letter seemed so secretive. So, what if he met someone in Columbia named Alex. They fell in love. As I kept reading, the letters became more and more detailed. More descriptive of who Alex was.

Alex was a man.

My father – the man who was so unaccepting of my gender identity and my sexual preference – was in fact in love with a man. He was…gay.

I know, I will never get to hear this from him, and I know, how hard he worked at covering this up. And for some reason, I feel inclined to keep this huge secret. From my mother, from Mikey, from the company, or his legacy as he knew it would change. His legacy – my family's legacy – would change. And that might crush my mother and Mikey. I need to protect them. I need to feel important again, and not just like a wrecking ball. It was hard enough for my mother adjusting to my sexuality as a child, but to know that her one true love wasn't who she thought he was – wasn't who she thinks he is – would be devastating to her.

I decide I need to see Chloe. She mentioned coming to The Meadows again, and I know she is still in town at my father's – at Mikey's house.

I barely sleep.

I wake to the sound of Trisha, humming some Mariah Carey tunes while reading one of her fashion magazines on her bed. At least, the rollers are already out of her hair this morning.

I rush out of the room, still in my pajamas, to make my phone call to Chloe. I feel a sense of urgency all of a sudden, as though I have to inform her of everything at once.

"The phones are all tied up," the front desk attendant tells me. "You'll have to wait a few minutes."

I stand right by the desk, waiting, in order to not lose my place in line. I glance over and see Jade, who tries to avoid me for the first time ever. I decide, I need to make things right with her. I did lose my mind and scream at her in rage after she figured out who I really am. But what I am really trying to accomplish here? Her being so onto me didn't sit well with me at all, and neither does her upbeat personality, at times.

"Hey Jade!" I say, yelling across the room so I don't lose my spot in line. "Can we talk?" I ask her as we make eye contact.

"Sure," she says, and walks over to me by the front desk.

"Look," I begin, "I am really sorry about the other day. You are right. I mean, you are smart. I guess I am not fooling anyone," I say a little more quietly now, so the desk attendant doesn't hear me.

"Well, I wasn't trying to pry," Jade says sincerely. "I just want you to be able to talk to me. Or maybe I just wanted to be able to feel like I could talk to you, too. Like we were friends. But I guess you don't seem to want to make any friends here, huh."

"No; that's not it. I was just caught off-guard by the whole thing. I appreciate your friendship and I am sorry for being so cruel."

"It's okay. I forgive you," she says with a big smile. "Yoga tomorrow?" she asks.

"Yes, yoga. Nine o'clock, right?" I make sure.

"Yes. See you there, friend."

"Miss?" says the front desk attendant. "You can make your phone call now, honey."

"Thanks."

I immediately dial Chloe on her cell phone.

"Hello?" She answers on the first ring.

"Chloe, it's me. I thought you were going to come by the Meadows again yesterday? Or today? We need to talk," I explain quietly.

"Fiona, I'm sorry. I got caught up with…things. What's up? Is everything okay?"

"Listen, Chloe. Can you come by today? I would like to talk in person. To get everything out in the open, if that's okay. How soon can you come here?"

"I will be there in thirty minutes," she assures me before hanging up the phone.

I decide now that if I am willing to sacrifice Chloe's happiness in order to selfishly involve her again in my turbulent life, I need to look approachable again, at least. My hair has been rocking an electrocuted kind of look the past month or so and I probably smell like the bottom of a foot. I hightail it to my room to freshen up. My sitter, Collette, can barely keep up.

"Listen, I have a visitor coming soon and I need to shower and fix myself up. Can you give me a little privacy?" I ask her fervently.

"Of course," she says, and stands with her back to my door in the hallway.

I take a quick shower and don't bother to shave my legs, but I make sure to use soap and shampoo. My hair looks awfully long these days, so I style it differently, with it longer towards the front of my forehead, very punk-rock like. I use what gel I have left to keep it in place. I put on eyeliner and mascara, something I haven't done in quite a while. I grab my stick of deodorant and wipe a streak under each armpit before sliding on a sleeveless tank top and some tight, whitewashed jeans. I tie up my chucks and run out into the hall, realizing Chloe should be here any minute. My sitter follows close behind and places herself in the corner of the visitor center: to give me some privacy, I assume. Chloe walks in seconds later.

"Chloe!" I call out, waving shyly at her.

She smiles from ear to ear when she sees me.

"Fiona. You look like…yourself. You look beautiful, baby," Chloe says, and gives me a huge, embracing hug, her delicate arms sliding around my waist.

"Let's sit down, Chloe. We need to talk."

"What is this about, Fiona?" Chloe anxiously asks me.

"When I told you that I wasn't trying to kill myself that day at the hospital, before Living Waters and all…I meant it. That was the truth. I know it was selfish to take all those pills of my father's after he died, and I can see how it looked bad, but I would never intentionally try to harm myself again – especially now that I have you, Chloe. I love you. I just don't want to hurt you. My life is…straight chaos. Especially right now. With everything that you and I have read…over the past month. Who knows, what is going to happen now, Chloe? So for the past month I have been pretending to be more insane than I actually am. I have played a part, to keep myself locked up in these places.

Because I want to protect you. I don't want to drag you into this more than you already have been. You have come too far in your life to regress. To get wrapped up in the chaos again. You deserve better...You deserve..."

Chloe interrupts me. "I want you, Fiona. I love you. I told you I am not looking for the perfect fairytale of a life anymore. I am pretty sure that doesn't exist. But how many times do I have to tell you to stop pushing me away? I did it to you once – I know that. But this thing with you being separated from me in here has gone too far. We need to get you out of here, baby. We need to sort these things out together as a team. Because that is what we are. My boys and you and me, we are a fucking family, Fiona. Don't you get that? We are engaged!"

She is right, we are engaged to get married, and she didn't propose to me thinking, I was going to be stuck in here forever, unable to marry her. She proposed so that I would get out of here and we could get married.

"You are right, Chloe. I am so sorry." I take her in my arms and kiss her passionately now.

"Ahem!" I hear the attendant say from behind me, but I keep kissing Chloe, disregarding the noise around me.

"Can you start to prove to them that you are sane? Because we both know you are sharp as a tack, Fiona," Chloe insists.

"Yes. Absolutely," I say, and this time I mean it more than ever. "Chloe. Those letters you read – did you understand what they were?" I ask. It's the first time I've spoken of it.

"Yes. I understood. I mean, I understand," Chloe says with a serious look on her face.

"And you strongly believe that...that...my dad was..."

"I believe, he was gay; yes, Fiona. It actually makes perfect sense to me now."

"Me too," I say, feeling some sense of relief to have said it out loud. Now it is all in the open.

"Listen, Fiona. You need to put on your big-boy pants and get the hell out of here, okay?"

"I'm on it."

Chloe hugs me goodbye and informs me, she will only be here two more days before she has to get back to the boys in Florida, and to Mugged.

We decide that is probably not enough time to get myself released, so she's going to arrange another trip up as soon as she can work it out back home.

"I will call you tomorrow," I assure her before she walks away from me towards the door.

"You better," she jokes.

"I love the shit out of you, Chloe Fields."

"I know you do. And I love you, too."

She turns her beautiful face away from me and it takes everything in me not to run to her and escape for real with her this time, straight out of the front door. For the first time since I arrived here, I want the hell out.

Chloe: September 2015
Metamorphosis

"Hey!"

I let myself in. Maybe I shouldn't have done that, with meeting Fiona's mom for the first time and all. I'm not really sure what Fiona has told her.

"Chloe! Hey! So, mom…This is Chloe."

"Veronica Lennox," says her mother, shaking my hand very professionally.

She has loads of gaudy jewelry on her arms, and is dressed so…uncomfortable-looking.

"Nice to meet you," I say with a big smile. "And this must be Marvin." I give the dog, a big pet and he licks me relentlessly.

"Yes, Chloe, meet Marvin Gay," Fiona says in a big, proud voice.

"Ahh…Marvin Gay. Wow, you really are a Lesbian, aren't you?"

Her mom laughs and smiles at me. Maybe I've broken the ice a little. "Well," says Mrs. Lennox, "Shall we eat?"

"Absolutely," I say. "Starving."

"So, Chloe. You have lived here all of your life, basically?" her mom asks, taking a sip of her wine.

"Yes, I have. I never really made it out, hah…but it's a great place to raise a family. I have two little boys."

"So I have heard. That's wonderful. I have been waiting anxiously for my Fiona to have a family of her own. She's always loved children. Haven't you, Fiona?"

"Yes, mom. I have. Chloe's kids are awesome."

"So, you are recently divorced?" she asks, so nonchalantly.

"Oh, well, it's not quite set in stone yet, but yes, we are getting divorced. My husband and I."

I won't call him my husband much longer, I realize.

"Mom." Fiona gives her mom a stern look.

*"It's okay, Fiona. I figured these questions would come up...eventually."
I didn't think they'd come up so soon, considering Fiona had made a point of
saying her mom didn't need to know all the details yet, but apparently, she did.*

"Well, I am very happy for you and my daughter. You seem like a sweet, responsible girl. I know how much responsibility it takes to raise a family, myself. You must, too. I only hope this is not a phase for you. Being with a woman. I'm only confused because you seem to have jumped back and forth a bit."

God, what else has Fiona told her? So much for 'no gory details.' She knows all about my past!

"I can see how you would be concerned, Mrs. Lennox."

"Call me Veronica, please," she interrupts.

"Veronica. I can see how this all can be a bit confusing. I guess, having been a dancer for half of my life, I can maybe explain it like this. Imagine that I am a very flexible ballerina. I don't really look at whether someone is a man or a woman. I just see the person. And I see Fiona. This...beautiful soul who makes me feel so content in my life and so complete. So, I guess I am just flexible in who I am with. But my core is always there."

Fiona looks up from eating and stares deeply at me. Her eyes look bluer than they have ever looked. She smiles at me and shakes her head.

"Isn't she amazing, mom?" she says with a childish grin spread across her face.

"Yes, Fiona, she sure is," Veronica says, and smiles a sincere smile at me from across the table.

We spend the rest of the evening, sharing stories about our families and Veronica tells tons of hilarious ones about Fiona trying to play a Princess in the school play, and how she always knew Fiona was a lesbian growing up.

"Well, I'm going to head to my room and catch up on some sleep, dears," Veronica says eventually.

"Goodnight, mom. I'm really glad you're here. And thanks for bringing my baby Marvin back to me."

"Alright, sweetheart. I love you. Chloe, it's been so nice getting to know you."

"You too."

"That went great," Fiona says to me, and shuts the door to her room. Marvin jumps right onto the bed like he owns the place.

"Yeah, I guess. You didn't tell me you were going to fill her in on so much about my life?"

"I'm sorry, Chloe. She asked a lot of questions on the way back from the airport. I'm a terrible liar so it just kind of all came out. It took the heat off the issues she and I have had recently. You aren't upset with me, are you?"

I was a little upset with her. A warning would have been nice before I was interrogated at the dinner table.

"No, it's okay. I was just caught off-guard, that's all. I wasn't really prepared to answer questions about us."

"Well, you did fantastic. And that speech about being 'flexible'…wow. That was something. I hope you told your mom that same thing."

I hadn't. For some reason it was so much easier to explain myself to her mother than my own.

"Yeah. I talked to her about it."

"Well, my mom wants to hit the town tomorrow. Do you think Trent could watch the boys for a few hours so you can come with us? I want to show her the tattoo shop and grab lunch or something."

"Sure, of course. That sounds nice."

Fiona and I lie intertwined in bed for a while before falling asleep. Her skin feels so nice next to mine. I'm terrified to admit it, but I know I have fallen madly in love with her.

The next morning, I hurry home and spend some quality time with the boys before I have to meet Fiona and her mom downtown. We bake blueberry muffins and I decide it would be a nice gesture to bring some to her mother, so I wrap some up and take them with me.

We go to the tattoo shop. Her mom seems very unimpressed with the whole thing. She has a distasteful look on her face the entire time, but manages to fake a smile at Fiona. To let her know she is trying, I assume.

"So mom, I was thinking, we could grab a coffee at this coffee shop Chloe and I really like. The Bean Hut. They have sandwiches and croissants and stuff, too."

"Sure, sweetie. Sounds delightful."

We walk a couple blocks to the coffee shop, none of us saying much. As we get closer, Fiona's expression changes. She runs up to the window of the shop. There's a sign on the door.

"CLOSED. Will be reopening under a different name and owner as MUGGED in October. We apologize for any inconvenience."

"Did you know about this!!!?" Fiona screams frantically at her mother. "This is why you are here!"

Fiona takes off angrily, basically running down the street back toward the car.

"Fiona – I had no idea!" her mom shouts after her.

"What's going on?" I ask, confused, as her mother and I begin to head toward the car.

"Her father. That's what's going on."

Her mom and I walk quickly back to the car in silence and find Fiona sitting with her head in her lap in the front seat, her knees curled up to her chest.

"Fiona, I had nothing to do with this. I'll call your father when we get back to your house and talk to him about it."

"How did he know I loved that coffee shop? How does he always find a way to take something I love and crush it and stomp all over it?"

"What does your father have to do with the coffee shop closing?" I ask, still confused as to why Fiona has reacted this way.

"He owns Mugged, Chloe. All of them. He started the company. That's his shop that is going to replace The Bean Hut. There's no way, he didn't know that I worked right there. He's a manipulative son of a bitch."

"Wow, I had no idea. So he owns all of them?"

I am starting to realize Fiona must be filthy rich. There are tons of Mugged coffee shops all over the North East. I see them everywhere. This will be the first one in this town, though.

"This must be his ploy to haunt me here, too," says Fiona to her mom. "Make his mark here and remind me I can't escape him no matter where I go."

"Oh, Fiona you are being overly dramatic, honey. I am sure he had no idea that it was so close to your work and all," answers her mom dismissively.

We drive home in awkward silence. I try to hold Fiona's hand in mine but she barely clasps it at all.

"I need a minute," she says, and closes the door to her room behind her when we get to her house.

I sit in the kitchen with her mom, not knowing what to say.

"I guess I need to phone her father and get all of this straightened out," Veronica says eventually, with a sigh.

"Do you really think he did this to hurt her? To like come here and take over her territory or something?" I ask.

"I'd like to believe he has more of a heart than that, but you never know. He's of a different breed, love. My son, Junior – he works for his father's company now, in New York. Their father tried to get Fiona to work for him too, at one point. She had no interest. I told him pressuring her would only drive her further away from him. They had a rocky enough relationship as it was. He didn't really know what to do with her as a child. She was the little girl that he always wanted. He was so excited when we found out we would be having a little girl. Most men want a son, but not Mike. He always wanted a girl to spoil and treat like a princess. A daddy's girl, I assume. But Fiona was not that. She was a tomboy, and that was confusing to Michael. He already had a son to play ball with. He wanted her to be girly and wear bows. He didn't really know how to connect with Fiona...Well, and then when he found out she was a lesbian, he basically disowned her for a while. He has made numerous attempts to reach out to her and apologize, but she won't talk to him. That's why this would be poor timing for him to do something like this. Right when he is trying to really mend their relationship. It just doesn't make sense," Veronica says. "You know, Mike was an art major in college, not a business major. Fiona gets her incredible artistic talent from her father."

I don't really know what to say about all this, so I offer her a muffin, since we ended up not having lunch.

"Here., I made some blueberry muffins with the boys this morning. Have one," I say as I hand her a muffin.

"Thank you, sweetheart."

She takes a bite and gets a pondering expression on her face. "They could use a touch more vanilla, sweetie," she says with a smile.

"Mom, God, please don't criticize Chloe's baking, too," Fiona says as she walks into the kitchen.

"I did all of the baked goods and sandwiches for Mugged when Michael and I were together. Sorry, I can be a bit opinionated about people's cooking."

"Do you think dad has some master plan to try to convince me to run this Mugged, mom?" Fiona asks.

"I don't know, sweetheart. Do you want me to step outside and call him?"

"Sure, that's fine," Fiona agrees, sitting down next to me at the table.

"I'm so sorry, Fiona." I take her soft hand in mine. "Maybe your dad just wants some way to be close to you," I say hopefully.

"I don't know, Chloe. He has hurt me pretty bad my whole life. This is just the icing on the cake, you know? He wants me to be something I'm not. I don't want to run one of his coffee shops. I liked The Bean Hut. I liked that it wasn't tied to him. Everyone in New York knows me as his daughter. I came here to get away from that. Then he just goes and opens a shop three blocks from my work!"

"Well, maybe you should just talk to him about it. Tell him how you feel. I mean, don't you want some kind of relationship with him? Your mom said he has really been trying recently."

"I don't think, I'll ever have the sort of relationship I want with him. And that's hard for me to accept."

"I know what you mean."

And I do.

"Well, I'm sorry to have blown up like that. I don't like that you saw that side of me. I don't like letting him get to me."

I squeeze her hand tighter. "It's okay. I forgive you."

At that moment, I realize I am someone Fiona confides in. I am her girlfriend. She trusts me. With everything. She tells me things that are hard to open up about. I feel there for her, as she is for me. There is no big spoon, little spoon anymore. We are complete equals. I am starting to transform. I feel so peaceful in this moment, like a weight is being lifted off my shoulders.

Veronica walks in abruptly and breaks my train of thought.

"Okay, I talked to your father, Fiona!" she exclaims. "He says he had no idea how close the new Mugged was to your shop. I really believe him, Fiona. He was pretty upset about the whole thing. He does need someone to run it, though, and now he is hoping you may be interested in doing it…part of the time…or finding someone for him, at least."

"I am not going to run that shop for him, mom. I am starting to build clientele at the tattoo shop. People are having to make appointments to get in with me now."

I blurt out, "I can do it. I mean, I love coffee. And I really need a job. I have to help support my boys now. I don't necessarily have any experience, I know, but I'm a quick learner."

"Chloe, don't be ridiculous. You do not want to work for my father in any way, shape or form, honey. Trust me. You just don't. And he would probably be the one training you. He or my brother, Mikey Jr."

"Now, that's not such a bad idea, Fiona. Your father needs someone quickly. I didn't mention this to you, but he and Junior are coming here next week to get things up and running. He will want to start training someone soon. October will be here before we know it."

"Oh. My. God. I cannot believe you two are actually considering this. You are making a big mistake, Chloe. I promise you." Fiona walks to the couch and sits down, placing her hands on her lap. I follow her and sit down next to her.

"Look, I don't know everything that has happened with your father in your life, but I can tell it has had a big effect on you and I'm so sorry for that. But your family would be doing me a big favor in letting me have this chance at a really profitable job. If you can try to look past all of the tension between you and your dad and just give me a chance, I think this could be a really good thing, Fiona."

She looks at me with her beautiful blue eyes and I can tell she is about to say something completely selfless…

"Okay. You're right. It's for you. I will talk to him. See if he will give you a chance at the job. But he's going to work you to death. I hope you know that, Chloe."

"Thank you, thank you, thank you, Fiona!" I give her a big kiss on her lips, right in front of her mother, not even thinking, it may make her a little uncomfortable.

Her mom clasps her hands together in agreement. "Well then, we have a plan, ladies. Fiona, are you sure you feel comfortable calling him about this? I can talk to him about it if you want."

"No, I'll do it. I need to face him. But only for you, Chloe: only for you."

I can tell this is hard for Fiona. I know I have to make things right between her and her dad somehow. Maybe I can bring them together. Things are beginning to transform in my life. I'm about to be divorced. I have a girlfriend. And now I will hopefully have a job to help support my family for the first time in my life. I feel so light and weightless in the midst of all of the chaos.

Fiona is saving my life, I think.

I sleep like a baby and wake up to the sun shining brighter than ever.

Fiona: December 2015
Willpower

I have a hard time focusing on anything besides a new plan to convince Dr. Hall and the nurses that I am completely fine and not a threat to myself anymore. I need to get out of here. I can no longer shield Chloe from my turbulent life. She is a part of it and she willingly has subjected herself to everything that comes along with being with me: with being married to me. It seems apparent that I have not done the best job of convincing the patients – Trisha and Jade in particular – that I am as insane as I wanted them to believe, so maybe it will be easy to prove I am well. I have counseling with Dr. Hall in a few minutes, so I make myself look more cleaned-up than before and head out to his office. Colette follows closely behind.

"Fiona! Glad to see you made it here on time again today," Dr. Hall exclaims as I take a seat across from him at his desk.

"Yes. It has been a good day," I announce with a sincere smile.

"You do look rather glowing today. Your hair looks nice, Fiona," he compliments me.

"Thanks. I could use a haircut, actually."

"Well, we could probably arrange something. So tell me, what has put you in such a marvelous mood today, sweetheart?"

"I saw my fiancée a little while ago and I realized I need to get better for her. That I love her and that she needs me to be well." It is the first honest-to-God, truthful thing I think I have said to him since arriving here.

"Well, that is fantastic, Fiona. Realization that you want to get better is a great first step."

A first step? I don't like the sound of that.

"Actually, I am feeling much, much better. I would love to have those antidepressants lowered like you agreed to do, and work out a plan to get home," I say hopefully to him now.

"Let's take it day by day, but I think that sounds like a great plan."

"Well, can you let Colette know, I won't be planning any escapes and that she is free to do whatever it is she normally does – when she isn't stalking my every move, that is?"

He chuckles a little. "Okay. I can call off your sitter for now. You have been very compliant with her the past few days, it seems. I know you want your freedom back. We can arrange that. But, let's talk more about your family for now. Can we do that today, Fiona?"

"What do you need to know?"

"What do you think would be helpful for me to be aware of for your recovery?" he asks me.

"I am a lesbian, you know…" I announce, stating this blatantly obvious fact out loud to him.

"I know," Dr. Hall says, nodding his head slowly. "And this has been a great source of conflict with your family; maybe your father in particular. Am I correct?" he asks. "You said he didn't accept you for who you were and that you were expected to pretend a lot…to pretend you were something you were not."

"Yes. When my dad shipped me off to these places, it wasn't always as bad as he made it seem. I mean, I wasn't as drug-addicted or alcohol-addicted as I was just…confused. To him, I mean. I wasn't confused at all, really. He just thought I was. I have always known who I am, and it was only because of my father that people thought I was struggling with my identity. He sent me to rehabs for them to change me. I think he believed the medication they gave me would alter my brain into liking men. Well, it didn't. And he wasn't happy with the results, time and time again. But he went to his grave with lies and secrets far greater than anything I was forced to hide, and for far longer, too. He doesn't get a chance to explain himself now, to his loved ones. That is his loss, and only God knows his soul and whether it was in the right place all of those years. So I will leave that part alone, and end simply by saying this: I am not insane. I promise. I am completely happy and content with myself and who I am. I have a fiancée who loves me and I plan to marry her when I get the hell out of here. I did not try to kill myself, or to escape from here the other night. I just didn't think anyone would believe the truth. But the truth is…I want to go home. I need to go home. I am not a threat to myself or anyone else. I need to make things right in my family and be there for them. We have all been through a lot over the past year. So if you could please just trust my sanity, I would like to be discharged, sir. Oh, and taken off the lithium. It is ruining my creativity and my thought processes."

"Wow. That was quite a monologue, Fiona. Have you considered theatre as a hobby?" he asks me, and I can't quite tell if he is making a joke or not.

"I miss my job. I miss drawing and creating artwork for people, sir. I am one hundred percent well," I reiterate.

"I think it's wonderful that you have such passion for life all of a sudden, Fiona. And that you miss your art. We have a wonderful art room here. Have you checked out all we have to offer?"

I interrupt him now, quite displeased with his lame response. "Listen to me, please. Do not keep me here. I will have my mother get me out of here, no matter how nasty it has to get if you decide to keep me here against my will. Do you understand?" I say now in an arrogant and angry tone.

"I do understand, Fiona. But there are a few things you need to get sorted out before I feel it is in your best interest to just up and leave suddenly, okay? Please trust that my goal is to get you healthy and then get you home with your loved ones. But you need a little bit more time, I believe. Now, I know your mother and your family are very powerful here in the City and that they do what you wish, or try to get you what you need. But please note that I have many documents stating your unstable ability to cope with your reality right now. So do not be surprised at the outcome. It appears you are done talking to me for the day…"

I absolutely am done – with him.

"Thank you for your precious time," I say, irritated, and storm out of his office.

I realize now that I haven't helped my situation by acting insane for so long. Admitting to something I didn't do, like when he thought I was trying to escape when in fact I was only trying to smoke a damn cigarette. These drugs are making my judgement foggy. They are keeping me 'in line', I guess, but they are making me forget my real passions outside of this place. They have been making me feel more content in here than I actually am. My real purpose is out in the real world again. With my family. Doing what I love best…tattooing.

Dr. Hall pokes his head out of his office as I am heading back to my room.

"Fiona, don't forget we have group today in the conference center in an hour, sweetie," he reminds me.

"I'll be there," I assure him.

I feel helpless in here now. I feel there is so much to be dealt with at my father's house that I literally can't do it while being locked up in here. I decide I want to call my mother and try to get her to get me out of here immediately. She does have a lot of pull at these types of places. On my way to the front desk I see Dr. Clark, my psychiatrist from my childhood and from Living Waters.

"Dr. Clark. What are you doing here?" I ask.

"Fiona. Oh hi," she says, somewhat startled, as if I've caught her doing something illegal. "Oh, I just needed to deliver a few patients charts to the office," she explains.

I am still skeptical about whether she has inherited my trust fund from my father, something I will have to address when I get out of here. She is a sneaky-looking thing to me now. I decide to ask for her help anyway. I am desperate at this point.

"Dr. Clark, do you think you could talk to the director here about getting me discharged?" I ask her hopefully.

"Discharged? Already? Last I heard, you tried to escape from here in the middle of the night, sweetheart."

Apparently, these shrinks all talk to each other and break HIPAA regulations with no regard to the patient's privacy.

"Are you allowed to know that?" I ask her, perturbed.

"I am your primary psychiatrist, Fiona. I have privileges to your information and records."

She has a lot of privileges, it seems, and I am going to become aware of all of them pretty soon.

"I see," I say. "Well, thanks anyway."

She looks a bit torn as I walk away towards the phone. I look back at her and she has the saddest look on her face. I don't know what to make of it.

The phone is free, so I call my mother on her cell in the hope of getting through to her.

"Fiona! It is wonderful to hear your voice. I have been meaning to come see you…I am sorry I haven't been by," she explains.

"It's okay, mom. I need your help, though. I am feeling so much better and I am ready to come home. To go back to Florida. Can you get me out of this place, mom?" I ask her, and wait for what I hope will be the ideal response.

"Fiona. Are you sure that is the best idea, honey? You haven't even been there a full week yet."

"I was at Living fucking Waters for a month, mom! A month! With lunatics. Let's be serious. I am nowhere near the caliber of craziness of the people in these places."

"Well, I do see your point. But I just want you to accept all the help they are willing to give you. If you are worried about the money there is no need to…"

I interrupt her speech. "No. I don't care about money, mom. I care about being with Chloe. And my family. I haven't had time to even readjust to dad being gone, mom. Because I was immediately placed in a mental institution, remember?"

"I know. Well, I can talk to Dr. Clark."

"Don't bother with Dr. Clark," I tell her. "She is a lost, fucking cause."

"Oh, well, okay. I will do what I can, then, sweetie."

"Thanks, mom. I appreciate it."

"Of course, sweetie," she says. "I am always on your side."

She is. Although we are so different, she has always fought for my freedom and independence.

Although my mom has now agreed to call and attempt to persuade them to let me out of here, I am not so sure it will work this time. I tried so hard to convince them I was insane that now – once they've finally come to believe it – I have to convince them of just the opposite. That I am completely well, capable of taking care of myself and able to live without all of these drugs, too. I am not so sure any antidepressants should be prescribed with lithium. The nurse assured me that the type I was on was completely safe to take with the lithium, but ever since then I have felt as if my whole thought process has changed. I am starting to think that the drugs have actually caused me to be a totally different person. Someone who lacks passion and complies with things they don't even agree with. That isn't me at all and I need to get the hell off of these damn drugs before I morph into some sheep that only follows the masses. Lord knows I am not a sheep.

I walk briskly over to the nurses' station and remind them that Dr. Hall gave the okay for me to be taken off of the lithium to start with.

"Let me check your charts," the first nurse says to me, unaware of any changes and looking rather puzzled by my request.

I tap my fingers nervously on the counter, waiting for them to give me permission to not have to swallow my daily, mind-numbing drugs anymore.

"I see no changes in your daily routine listed on your chart here. I can phone the director and get the okay to mark it on here. Give me one moment, miss."

Of course, he didn't tell them; he forgot last time as well.

A few minutes later, she informs me she has spoken to him.

"The doctor says he wants to wait a few days before altering your medication. He suggested; we separate it into two doses so you do not have to take it all at once. That may cause less drowsiness and less of the 'numbness' he says you have complained of."

"Are you kidding me? I am being forced to take Lithium? For what? What exactly is it for, anyway? In my case, that is…Do I have a clinical illness I am unaware of being diagnosed with?" I loudly shout at the poor nurse, who has absolutely no control over this decision, I realize.

"Miss, I am sorry…I just…"

"It is not your fault," I try to apologize. "Thanks anyway for your help."

I can't believe these places. Even the ritziest of clinics, one my mom is paying tons and tons of money for me to get better in, is denying me a basic human right to choose what I put into my body. It is like Monsanto is regulating the pharmaceuticals here. Shoving Goddamn GMOs down my throat or something. I am so frustrated. I decide I need a cigarette. My mother hasn't been here to give me any money for commissary, so I end up having to bum one, yet again, from Trisha.

I storm outside and start to puff on my cigarette, trying to calm my nerves, which are raging. Being in here, unable to leave, makes me feel like a child or a teen all over again. I remember being in here when I was fifteen, feeling this same way. Except then I never intentionally tried to stay, only leave. I remember crying into my pillow at night, wishing my mind didn't think the way it did. That I wasn't this suicidal girl who was trapped in a family so unaccepting of her. It was only after I was on my own and not under my father's roof at all that I gained independence and began to embrace my unique and eccentric characteristics. I found my passion for art was a useful tool for making a living. It wasn't just something I was good at, but something I loved and enjoyed doing, too. I believe that my mind, in all of its craziness, is what has given me the ability to be a creative and talented artist. Without the bad there would be no good. There would be nothing to pull from for my artwork. I feel inclined to draw for the first time since I have been in here. I mean, draw in here, that is. I decide, after I put out my cigarette on the cement, that I will go and check out the art room the director mentioned.

Back inside, I walk down the long hallway, searching for the art room. On my search, I come across an office with a glass window on the door. I have never seen it before. I see Dr. Hall and Dr. Clark in the room together. They are giggling together and I notice myself make a disgusted face. I can't stand Dr. Clark anymore: she has been so sneaky ever since my father passed away. I am not sure I even like Dr. Hall, the director here, anymore either. All of a sudden, I see Dr. Clark take Dr. Hall's hand in hers and I can tell there is something going on between them. It is making my stomach turn. I think back to all the picture-perfect family photos of Dr. Hall with his family and wife – the ones he has on the walls of his office.

"Ugh. Disgusting," I say out loud. I try to dismiss what I've just seen and keep walking in search of the art room. I start to realize what this means. If they are in cahoots with each other, I may be in serious trouble, trying to get my mom to get me out of here by talking to Dr. Hall. He isn't going to do anything that Dr. Clark suggests he doesn't do. Who knows, she is probably just using him to keep me locked up in here. I am sure it is in her best interest, since she has her hands in my father's money now.

I finally come across a room, labeled "Art Therapy Room", so I decide to walk in and see what they have to offer. I need something to take my mind off this hellish day I have had.

Jade is the only one in the room when I walk inside.

"Fiona!" she immediately greets me excitedly.

"Hey, Jade. What are you working on?" I ask her, noticing she has a paintbrush in her right hand and an easel in front of her.

"Oh. Just some abstract art therapy, I suppose," she tells me.

I take a closer look at her painting, and although it is abstract it is clear to me what is going on in the painting. It looks as though someone is falling from the sky, maybe even out of an object: a plane maybe. I can't really tell what from, but they are clearly falling. On the ground below are lots of human looking figures screaming from beneath this falling person. It is actually quite morbid, but I love it. I suddenly realize what an amazing artist Jade truly is.

"Wow. Your painting is stunning," I say admiringly.

"Oh, thank you. I don't know…It is just therapeutic for me right now," she explains.

"Does it represent the fall you took? I mean, the injury where you broke your back?" I ask, feeling a bit nosy afterward.

"Yes. I assume it does. It just sort of happened. The painting, I mean. Not the 'accident.'"

"Well, the accident just sort of happened too, right?" I ask her, trying to make a joke, but realizing this is not light-hearted at all.

"Right. It just happened," she says, looking down, avoiding eye contact with me.

I know that look. The look when someone doesn't want to risk getting caught: when they are a terrible liar, like I am.

"Jade?" I say. "Is there anything you would like to talk about?" I ask, sounding just like a damn shrink now. Shit, they're rubbing off on all of us, I guess.

"The accident wasn't so much of an accident," she admits, still looking down at her ballet flats.

"I see. Well, it is a little ironic, isn't it? You are in here partly for the wrong reasons, just as I am. I actually did not try to kill myself, but you did," I say, and smile at her, hoping she will get the humor in this, as I do.

She begins to laugh. I can tell she gets my humor now. She knows I have no ill-intentions toward her. She knows I would never judge someone in her position because I have been there.

"Fiona?" she asks after regaining her composure. "Do you think that there are people with normal minds? I mean, what defines normalcy anyway? People like you and I, who have…well, tried to call it quits on ourselves. Do you think we will just keep repeating the process over and over again? Causing the people around us to worry about us…forever?"

"I absolutely do not believe in a normal mind. Those people who think they have the perfect life – you know, the ones with the professional photographers who snap family photos of them almost every weekend just so they can post them on social media to make everyone think they are happy – those are the ones with the real fucked-up problems. Those are the people whose kids turn out to be serial killers from all of the lack of independence growing up. All of the clubs and tennis matches they were forced to be in. Thank God, we aren't those seemingly perfect people, am I right?"

She laughs again and dabs at her eyes a little, wiping away the tears she is now starting to shed. "I haven't told anyone, what I just admitted to you," Jade admits.

"I won't tell a soul," I promise her, knowing how important it is to her for no one to know the truth.

"The people on the ground in the painting are all of the ones that I could have hurt," she says.

"But someone caught me. I know, I broke my back, and I could be paralyzed or whatever, but I lived for a reason, Fiona. I want to truly believe that. I have to."

"I agree with you. I would like to think I did, too."

And I think about how I have never thought about it in this way before, not until now.

I go grab a paintbrush and another easel and begin to paint beside Jade. I paint Chloe. I paint her face, with her long, flowing locks of hair framing it. I give her a solemn look on her face. This is the first time, I have painted her without looking at a photo of her to go by. I try to capture her expression of solitude, but I realize it is hard to do this, having not seen her much over the past month or so. I am beginning to forget the details of her face. I paint next to Jade and neither of us speaks. We just continue painting in silence until it is time for dinner.

Chloe: September 2015
Like Father Like Daughter

We leave the tattoo shop, hand in hand. I feel some kind of pride at being with Fiona, like I have finally conquered love. Her phone rings as we are getting back into her car.

"It's my dad," she says in a stunned voice.

"Well, answer it," I say loudly.

"Okay. Okay. Hello?" Fiona timidly answers, and puts him on speaker phone so I can hear while she drives.

"Fiona. It's Michael. Your father. I'm so sorry it took me a little while to get back to you. We have been swamped at work."

He definitely sounds like a businessman.

"It's okay. I'm glad you called me back."

"Of course. It's so good to hear your voice. It's been way too long, Fiona. Your mother told me how upset you are about the new shop taking over The Bean Hut. I had no idea you frequented that coffee shop, or that it was so close to where you are working now. I apologize for any inconvenience I have caused."

Fiona rolls her eyes. "It's okay, dad. I guess it was just coincidence."

I know Fiona doesn't believe in coincidence.

"Well," she continues, "Has mom told you, I am dating someone new? Chloe."

"Yes, she has mentioned it. I'm happy for you, honey," he says sincerely.

"Well, she could really use a job right now. She is recently divorced with two small children and I thought you might consider her for the new shop? She could run it for you…"

"Does she have any experience? You know my schedule doesn't allow for much training time. I will be there next week and then again, the week before it opens. That's it. Mikey Jr. will be with me both times, in case I have to fly home abruptly."

"She has experience, yes," Fiona lies.

I don't have ANY experience. What is she talking about? I haven't even had a job since before Kaden was born!

I give her a terse look.

"She has two children, like I said – two boys actually, lots of energy. She makes coffee every morning while balancing one on her hip. She also is great at carrying multiple sippy cups at one time while talking on the phone. I know she can make a mean grilled-cheese sandwich and she's very prompt and responsible. Oh, and a wonderful housekeeper. Very tidy." Fiona smiles at me confidently.

"Ha! I see your point, Fiona, but can she run my store? I also need help with graphics and wall art. I am trying not to hire multiple people for these things."

"I'll do your graphics and wall art, dad. Just give Chloe a chance at the job. She won't let you down," Fiona promises earnestly.

Michael sighs loudly through the phone. "Okay. She can have the job, but if she makes one error or misses one training because her kid is covered in head-lice she's out. Got it?"

I smile and bite my lip to stop myself from squealing loudly.

"And, Fiona?" he says. "We should sit down and talk while I am in town. Just me and you, kid."

"Yeah, okay, dad. We'll see. Thanks for letting her have the job."

"I'll email you this week about the graphics and what I am leaning toward for the artwork and design. We will be in touch soon. Have a good day, Fiona," Michael says very professionally.

"Bye, dad."

I shriek: "Ahhhhhhhh!!!! I am employed!"

"Christ, Chloe! My eardrums are bleeding! I've never seen someone so happy to be employed by my father."

"Well, I am. I most definitely am. Thank you! I need to call around and get the boys on a waiting list for a daycare, and an aftercare program, just in case. I have to look up the ratings…"

"A waiting list? There are waiting lists to learn your ABCs now? Jesus. I have a lot to learn," Fiona says as she is getting out of the car. She walks around to my car door and opens it for me.

"Whoever said chivalry was dead must have been with a man," I say. And we both laugh.

We walk inside to find Marvin has ripped up an entire roll of toilet paper and it is scattered around the whole house.

"Marvin, you bad little animal, you," Fiona says, barely raising her voice. "Guess my house isn't doggy-proofed yet."

"Yeah, no kidding, or toddler-proofed. Pretty soon you are going to have to worry about that one, too."

Oh God, maybe I shouldn't have said that. Am I assuming too much, thinking we may all move in together at some point? My kids, too.

"I mean, I'm just kidding…"

"No," she interrupts, "You're right. I may need some help with that here soon. From this experienced mother right here." She puts her hands around my waist. "So you probably shouldn't get your finger wet with that new tat there, and I probably shouldn't get my arm wet either. So maybe we should take a long bath together instead of a shower? What do you think?" She winks at me and I can feel all the tiny hairs raise on my arms.

"Not a bad idea at all," I agree.

She starts to take off one article clothing at a time: first her shirt, then her bra, then her shorts. She is standing in only her panties now.

I awkwardly take off all of my clothes pretty much all at once and she laughs a little, like I am some amateur at this. She climbs into the tub with her back pressed against it and her legs spread for me to come sit between. I climb in and mold into her wet skin. She wraps her one arm around my thigh. Her fingers start to caress me slowly and I don't stop her this time. With just one finger I feel such pleasure and intimacy with her in this moment. I turn my head back and kiss her passionately while my feet start to flex in climax.

"Wow," I say, flustered. "So that's what I have been missing, huh?"

She laughs and turns me around to face her in the tub. I have my legs pulled up to my chest now.

She looks deep into my eyes and doesn't even flinch. "I love you, Chloe."

"I know. I love you too, Fiona."

We take a long bath together and only get out once our skin is completely pruned. I do Fiona's makeup and we get ready together for our double-date with Viv and her girlfriend, Winter.

"Where are we eating?" I ask Fiona while applying my mascara.

"Oh, this great sushi place downtown by my work called Koto. Have you eaten there before?" Fiona asks.

I have eaten there with Trent several times.

"Yes, I have. It's great. Good choice."

The four of us have a wonderful dinner. We talk about tattoos…a lot. I have by far the least amount at the table. Winter has almost full sleeves and who knows how many under her clothing. But they make me feel completely comfortable and at home despite our differences. The dinner is delicious and I decide I want to pay for Fiona's and my meal, since I basically have a job and all.

The waiter lays the check down and Fiona tries to snatch it out of my hand.

"No, I would like to pay. My treat!" I announce proudly.

"Well, alright baby. Aren't you a great date?"

I place my credit card in the sleeve and the waitress comes back a few minutes later with a strange look on her face. "Miss," she says while handing me back my credit card, "Your card was declined. I'm so sorry. It could just be the card. Do you have another one you would like me to try?" she asks nervously.

"Hm," I say, confused. "Sure, here's my debit…" All of the sudden I realize what has happened. "Actually, no. Not without my ex-husband's name on it, I don't," I say.

Fiona gives me a stunned look as it starts to sink in.

"Did he really cut you off without warning?" Fiona asks angrily.

"Apparently so. I'm so sorry, Fiona. I will pay you back when I can," I say, and feel so embarrassed.

"You need to call and confront him, Chloe. You guys have kids together. What if you were with the kids and not me and couldn't pay for the boys' meal? That's ludicrous of him!" she shouts.

I can tell, Fiona is really angry at this point, but it's kind of cute her sticking up for me like that.

I try to process the situation and say, "Okay, I'll call him in a few minutes, after we leave."

We say our goodbyes to Viv and Winter and I apologize for the dramatic turn of events.

"Hey, you know what, it was as good of a time as any, right?" Viv says, and gives me a hug goodbye. "We've all been there," she says.

We have? They have?

I call Trent to confront him while Fiona drives us home.

He answers, "Hey, Chloe."

"Hey! So you just cut off all of my funds, Trent! What if I had been with the kids!?" I immediately yell at him over the phone.

"Calm down, Chloe. They weren't supposed to take your name off the credit card until next week; not right when I called. I mean, what do you expect, though? I'm not funding your dinner outings and coffee dates with your girlfriend anymore. You know you get half of my savings. It will be transferred into your account next week when they were supposed to stop your credit card. I'm sorry for the mishap. Do you need me to loan you money until Monday?"

"No!" I hang up. "Ughhhh! I don't believe him. He did it on purpose," I say, still raging.

"Well, I got you covered until as long as you need, baby. Don't let him get to you. These things are bound to happen, though. You guys aren't going to be civil all the time."

She's right. This is going to be a regular thing now: us fighting about money and parenting and every other little thing.

"I know, Fiona. I love you so much. Thank you. I know this will all get easier eventually. Just promise me, you won't flake out on me before that day comes, okay?"

"Let's be serious, Chloe. Have I flaked out on you yet? It hasn't exactly been smooth sailing to even get to this point. I'm not going anywhere. I promise. Why don't you come over tomorrow morning and I will plan something special for the two of us?"

"Hey," I say as I walk into Fiona's house the next day.

"Heeeey, baby! You ready for our adventure today?" she asks excitedly.

"I think so. Adventure huh?" I ask.

"Yes, I think you will like it," she says with a great big smile and just looks mysteriously at me for a long time. "Well, let's go," she finally says.

Fiona literally blindfolds me a few miles away from our 'destination.'

"I can't believe, you are making me wear a scarf around my eyes, Fiona," I say in a somewhat aggravated voice.

"You promise you can't see, Chloe? It will ruin it! Tell me the truth: can you see through it?" she asks.

"I can't see a damn thing. You are going to have to carry me into wherever we are going."

"Deal," she says.

I hear her turn off the car.

"We are heeeere…" she exclaims as she shuts her car door.

She comes around to my side of the car and holds my hand so I can get out without tripping. She leads me all the way inside, somewhere, and I can hear a lot of people talking, and probably staring at how ridiculous we are.

"Alright, can I take it off now, Fiona? Come on."

"Nope, not yet. Waaaiiiit… Hey, here you go," she says to someone. It seems like she is paying him for something.

"Alright, this way," the man says, and I feel a rush of air whisk by my body. Someone is leading us back outside.

"Okay, Chloe. You can take your blindfold off," Fiona finally says.

I remove the scarf from my eyes and look around. All I can see are hundreds of colorful butterflies flying around me. It is the most beautiful scene,

I have ever seen. Flowers with butterflies perched on their blooms are next to me, and a fountain for them to drink from is in the distance. I look up and notice there is a covering over the area, keeping the butterflies inside this magnificent paradise we are standing in.

"What is this place?" I ask Fiona.

"It's a butterfly sanctuary. Do you like it? Isn't it beautiful?"

"It's amazing, Fiona!" I say with tears in my eyes.

She kisses me and I can feel the tears start to pour out of my eyes now. I can't control my emotions. I'm embarrassed for crying, but something inside me feels so liberated in this moment. I am an emotional wreck.

"Oh baby, it's okay. I love you so much. I'm glad you love this place as much as I do. I thought you would, my beautiful butterfly," she says so lovingly to me as the tears still flow rapidly from my eyes.

"Oh, Fiona. It's perfect. Everything about it is perfect. You are perfect. I love you so much."

I stare at Fiona, wishing I could stay in this moment forever. All of the colorful butterflies floating by her flawless face; her smiling at me. It is as if no one else is here except the two of us. I kiss her passionately for a long time, not caring who is watching. No one else in the entire world could possibly matter right now. I try to take in every inch of my surroundings. I spin around in a circle looking up at the sky. I decide to extend my arms and just close my eyes for a second. Without being able to see, I can hear so much clearer. I hear the birds and the wind; I hear little children, fascinated by the flying creatures. The weather is perfect.

This is the best day of my life; I think to myself.

I stare at Fiona during the entire car ride home. I can't help but notice how distinct her jawline is. Her eyebrows are perfectly groomed. Her teeth are brilliantly white and straight. Her skin is glowing and smooth. Are there no flaws she possesses? Is it possible to be so in love with such a perfect human being?

"So, Chloe. I talked to my mom," she says, interrupting my stalking stare, "And she says my dad and brother will be coming here in a few days. On Tuesday. He wants to start training you. I told him I would teach you as much as I know from growing up in the midst of the shop – before they get here. Can you make arrangements for the boys Tuesday?"

"I have already talked to a daycare who is going to watch the boys any days I need during the summer. So yeah, I just have to let her know what days the week, before. But I'll make sure I have arrangements for Tuesday."

"Well, they will be here for a week, and knowing my dad, he will want you there every day."

She wasn't kidding about the workaholic part.

"Okay. I will figure something out, then."

"I had such a good day with you, Chloe," she says while touching my hand.

"Me too, Fiona. Thank you. Thanks for giving me the best day of my life."

I talk to Trent the next day, about Tuesday. The daycare says, it is too late-notice to take the boys, so I am in somewhat of a bind trying to find someone to watch them. Trent eventually says his mom will watch them Tuesday through Thursday if I need her to. Thank God. I can't already have issues finding childcare when I haven't even started this job yet, I think.

"Thank you, Trent. I'll be back to the house by six for you to drop the boys off with me," I say, and hang up the phone.

I can't find out where Fiona has wandered off to. I finally find her in her bedroom looking through a box of old memorabilia.

"What are you looking at, baby?" I ask, sitting down beside her.

"Just old photos of me and my dad. Look at this one." She hands me a photo of her on her dad's shoulders, wearing a Yankee's baseball cap. She looks like a little boy, but I can tell it's her by her distinct jawline and bright blue eyes. Her father seems tall and he is very slender, like her. He has her same fine bones – even though his face is masculine, of course – and the same amazing blue eyes. I am curious about this man I have heard so much about, but I decide not to ask in case it upsets Fiona.

"You were a cutie," I tell her. "How old were you there?"

"Oh, I don't know. My parents were still together, I remember. Maybe I was like five or six. They look pretty unhappy in most of the pictures after I was about seven. I can tell my dad is genuinely smiling here. He looks really happy."

"Are you nervous about seeing him in a couple of days? I mean, since it's been so long?" I ask.

"Not really. Well, maybe a little. I only hope he is pleasant to you. I don't want him to ever hurt you the way he has me. And with you working for him now, that could easily happen, Chloe."

"I'm not worried about it, Fiona. I am a strong woman."

"Yes you are, baby. That's for sure. A strong and sexy woman who I happen to have all to myself. And right now, we are the only two people in this room. With this fairly large bed that is made up way too neatly. What do you say we...mess up the sheets a bit? I don't like things wound so tightly," she says in a tantalizing voice that happens to make me want her very, very badly.

"I think that's the best idea you have ever had," I say with my lips close to hers.

She attacks my lips with hers uncontrollably and touches every inch of my skin wildly. She frantically removes each piece of clothing that is draped over my body and throws it all on the floor next to the bed. She takes off all her clothes and presses herself over my naked body and inches her fingers down past my thighs, then inside me. We make love for over an hour. Her lips never leave mine and her body never strays away from my skin. Her face looks so desperate for me the entire time, like she can't ever get enough of me. My heart is racing, knowing that this is the love, I have been craving my entire life and that I have it now. I have Fiona, and she has me.

I realize I must have fallen asleep on Fiona after our wild lovemaking. She is still out cold so I try to carefully remove my arm from under her without waking her. I fail and she opens her eyes slowly.

"Well hello, you wild animal, you," she says, still in that sexy voice, I love so much.

"Hey," I say quietly.

"Are you sure, you are out of practice with this lesbian lovemaking thing? Because that didn't feel like some out of practice shit to me," she says, and gives me her infamous wink.

"It just feels pretty natural with you, Fiona. Like I have been with you forever. Maybe we were both butterflies in our past life together," I say. I immediately feel cheesy.

"Maybe we were," she says, standing up. She is still completely naked. I don't mind.

"So, I was thinking we could spend what's left of this perfect day going over some things to prepare you for training with my dad on Tuesday."

"Yeah, okay. Probably a good idea."

"Well, there's going to be a lot of paperwork and all, but basically I can tell you what really pisses him off – what he is particular about and the kinds of coffee we sell. I've never actually worked for him, obviously, but I pretty much know the routine from overhearing him scream at employees over the phone my whole life."

"Grrreeaat," I say sarcastically. "Sounds awesome!"

"Hey. I tried to warn you, but you are a pretty convincing woman who has me pretty much wrapped around your little finger. But anyway…Our main specialty item – the one we sell the most of – is the white espresso. It's not sold at too many places, so people drink that shit up…"

Fiona tells me all about the different coffees, the sizes, what kinds of sandwiches they usually sell, how her dad hates tardiness and uncleanliness, and basically scares the hell out of me for the next hour or so. When she is finally done 'training' me for meeting her father, I ask her about the artwork she agreed to help with.

"So, have you and your dad talked much about the artwork you are going to do at the new shop? I mean, does he want you to like paint the walls or just pick out pieces to hang?" I ask

"He wants me to paint a mural on the main wall. Maybe hang a few things on the others and then do some online graphics and stuff. I have an idea for the mural, but I'd kind of like it to be a surprise."

"Okay. Sounds right up your alley."

"Yeah, it will be nice to actually paint something again, I think. I mean without a tattoo gun in my hand."

"I'm excited to see the finished product. Well, I better get going back to the house. I told Trent I would be there by six. Do you want to come over later? Maybe after the boys go down?"

"I think I'm going to stay over here tonight and work on some stuff. Clean up a little, too, before my dad comes to town, if that's okay with you."

"Of course. I'll call you tomorrow. I love you."

"Love you too, baby."

Today Fiona's father and brother are coming to town. I'm terrified. I need to call Fiona after I take the boys to Trent's to see what the plan is. He is going to take them to his mom's in a little while, since he has to go to work.

"Boys, come on. Let's get your shoes on!" I yell across the house.

I get their tennis shoes on and load everything into the car. I'm not a pro at this workflow thing yet. I feel really rushed.

We get to Trent's and he walks out to my car to grab the boys from me. "Go on in boys, I need to talk to mommy for a second, okay?" he says as he lets them out of their car seats. He turns to me once they've gone. "So, I talked to a realtor," he says. "He thinks the house will get some bites right away. It's a good time to sell, apparently."

"Oh, okay, well, good." I am feeling frantic, not having talked to Fiona yet about when to meet her at the coffee shop.

"Okay, well," says Trent, "I just wanted to let you know that I gave them your phone number so you can set up what times you are free for showings and all."

"Great. I'll let you know if I get any calls. Have a good day, Trent. I'll be back here to pick up the boys sometime this evening. It may be after dinnertime, though."

"Okay. See you then," he says. "Good luck at 'work,'" he adds with a smirk.

"Thanks," I say, and peel out of the parking lot.

I immediately call Fiona from the car. "Hey, I'm headed downtown to the coffee shop! Am I late!?" I say breathlessly.

"Calm down, Chloe. They aren't even here yet. You are fine. See you soon," she says calmly.

Phew! I can relax a little on the way there.

I get there and Fiona's dad and brother still haven't arrived. Guess he doesn't hold himself to the same timely standards.

I am pacing back and forth outside the coffee shop.

"Did they say they were almost here?" I ask, concerned.

"There they are." Fiona points down the street at two thin businessmen dressed exactly as I imagined they would be: in spruce black suits and ties. Michael Lennox is tall, just like I suspected from seeing his photo. His son Mikey is half-a-head shorter.

"Fiona!" Her dad hugs her and smiles at me from over her shoulder. His eyes really are the same incredible blue as hers. They look tired, though, with dark circles under them.

"Dad. You look different. You look really thin. Are you on one of those hardcore paleo diets or something?" she asks him.

"No, no. Just been busy with work. No time for real meals, I guess. And you, you look beautiful, darling. I like your hair like this." He touches her hair softly with his hand.

"Thanks, dad. Mikey Jr.! You look the same. Dapper as usual," she says, giving him a high five.

"Thanks, Fi," says her brother. He doesn't have the elegance and good looks of his father and sister, but he has a serene air about him that is comforting and attractive.

"So, this must be Chloe. Nice to meet you," Mr. Lennox says, and shakes my hand firmly.

"You too, sir. Thanks for letting me have this opportunity to run one of your shops," I say very professionally, and I can see Fiona shaking her head behind her father.

"Shall we check out the inside?" Mr. Lennox says, unlocking the front door.

It looks so desolate inside. It is kind of sad to me. Fiona and I had one of our first dates here, inside this shop, and now everything is just gone.

"Nice amount of space in here. More than I thought," Mr. Lennox says proudly. "Fiona. Do you have the sketch of the mural you are thinking about doing on the back wall, sweetie?"

"No. I'd like to just freehand it. I want it to be a surprise. If you trust me enough to do that."

"Well, I guess so. I know you are a very talented artist like your father," he says with a wink very similar to Fiona's infamous wink.

We spend a few hours going over a lot of protocols. Safety procedures, how to ask customers what they would like, how to work the register, and I practice carrying trays just in case I have to serve some tables on a busy day. It's a lot for me to take in, but I feel like I am doing a competent job.

Throughout the day, I watch Fiona and her dad, trying to hide my fascination. They look so alike! Could a man who looks and moves so much like this gorgeous, incredible woman that is his daughter really be so awful? How could he be so cruel to a child that was almost his mirror image?

"Well, I think that's enough for today, ladies and gentlemen. Don't you think?" Mr. Lennox asks.

Thank God, I think to myself. I haven't had lunch and I am starving. Other than not giving us a lunch break Fiona's dad doesn't seem all that bad, though.

"Fiona. Why don't Mikey Jr. and Chloe go pick us up something to eat from that deli around the corner? My treat. You and I can stay and talk for a few, while they are gone, okay?" he suggests. "Just charge it onto my company card, Junior."

Mikey and I walk down the street to grab some lunch, leaving Fiona alone with her father. I feel a little guilty, like I should have intervened and shouted, "NO! She can't stay with you, Michael! It's not safe!"

Oh well, too late now.

"So…" I try to make conversation with Mikey Jr. "You think you will run your dad's company one day. When he doesn't have the energy for it anymore?" I ask. He rolls his eyes rather cavalierly and doesn't slow his brisk pace, his head held high. He has a certain confidence about him that I envy.

"Oh yeah. I've always wanted to. He basically started training me the moment I was born. It's all I know. I majored in business at NYU."

"Oh, okay. It seems like you know the business pretty well already," I say.

"So, how's my sister been?" he asks, changing the subject. "I mean, after she left so abruptly, I haven't really talked to her much." I notice how blue his eyes are: almost as blue as Fiona's and his dad's. But not quite.

"Oh, she's great. The tattoo shop thinks really highly of her. She has a lot of regulars and mainly only takes appointments now."

"She definitely got dad's artistic talent, that's for sure. I remember she drew this picture of me once and it looked freakishly real. She was always really good at portraits."

"Oh yeah. Why did your dad not pursue the arts? I mean, what got him interested in opening a coffee shop and all? Wasn't he an art major?" I ask.

"I think he just realized, he didn't want to be a starving artist anymore. He says my mom made him feel really deflated, back when Fiona and I were little. Because they didn't have any money to do anything or go anywhere. So he just got lucky, I guess. Right place at the right time. The coffee shops just took off in the city. Everybody loves their coffee, right?"

"Yes. Absolutely. Guilty," I say with a smile.

We order some sub sandwiches and take them back to the coffee shop. As we walk back in, Mr. Lennox is holding both of Fiona's hands in his across the table. Looks like it was a decent conversation to me.

We eat our subs and don't talk too much during lunch. Fiona has a disconcerting look on her face the whole time. Fiona and I say our goodbyes to her dad and brother shortly after. Then she walks me to my car.

"So, I'll see you here tomorrow, same time?" she asks me before I get into the car.

"Sure. Will I not see you tonight?" I ask, confused. We usually spend our evenings together every night now.

"Actually, I still have some stuff I need to work on for my dad and I think I am going to stay up all night and knock that painting out at the shop tonight alone. He lent me the keys to close up when I'm done," she says, holding up the keys.

We haven't spent the last couple of nights together. Should I be worried?

"Okay. I miss you," I say in a childish voice, and put my arms around her waist.

"I miss you too, Chloe. We can spend tomorrow night at my place, okay? I promise. Trent has the boys tomorrow, right?" she makes sure.

"Right. Sounds good," I say. "Wait, Fiona!" I yell as she is walking to her car. "What was it your dad and you talked about while Mikey Jr. and I went to get lunch?" I ask.

"Oh, it was nothing," she insists. "Just healing old wounds."

"Okay. I'll see you tomorrow." And I drive off.

Fiona: December 2015

Exit Strategy

Jade and I rush off to Yoga this morning, attempting to make it there on time. By 9 am. I don't get much out of the class this time, as my mind won't settle. I keep thinking about Chloe, and my mother, and Dr. Hall and Dr. Clark, and what I saw yesterday in that office. My stomach begins to feel unsettled again. After class I explain to Jade that I need to make a phone call and that I am not feeling well. I rush off to the phones by myself. First, I call Chloe.

"I talked to your mom," she informs me right away. "It isn't looking good, trying to get you out of there right away, baby." She sounds concerned.

"Yeah, I bet," I answer, knowing that the two psychiatrists are working against me now.

"Listen, Fiona. I leave tomorrow morning for Florida. Maybe your mom and I can come have lunch with you today. So I can say goodbye."

"Okay. I will see you then," I tell her, and rush to my room to shower.

I stand in my bra and panties, alone in my room. Trisha must be socializing in the common area. As I get close to the mirror to put on my mascara, there is a tap on the door.

It's Jade.

"Oh, sorry," she says after walking in, seeing I am not clothed.

"It's okay. You can come in," I assure her.

She walks in hesitantly and tries to look the other way as she talks.

"I want to leave, now," she blurts out.

"Ha. Yeah, me too," I agree.

"No, I mean. We should leave. Together," she says. I look at her, wondering whether she is crazier than I thought.

"I wish we could, Jade, but you know how well that went for me, when they thought I was trying to escape against their will," I remind her.

"Right, but we could work together. Create a plan…"

"Jade." I look right into her bright blue eyes. I shake my head 'no' with an apologetic look on my face.

She notices my painting from yesterday, which I have hung on the wall next to my bed.

"Is that your girlfriend?" she asks me curiously.

"Yes, my fiancée, Chloe. She is actually coming here any minute with my mom to eat lunch with me," I explain, still trying to get ready with her distracting me.

"She is really pretty," Jade says.

"Thank you. The painting doesn't do her justice," I admit.

Jade walks over to me and gets very close. I am still standing in my bra and panties. She places her hand on my face and presses her lips against mine. She looks into my eyes. I do not kiss her and she doesn't exactly kiss me either. Just holds her lips there on mine. I give her a puzzled look, wondering what the hell she is trying to do right now. I squint, but I stay very still. Shocked, I guess, in the moment.

"I'm sorry," she says, and races out of my room as quickly as her feet will take her.

I stand in shock for a long while. I am pretty sure Jade is not a lesbian, but I have never heard her mention anything about a boyfriend or significant other. We haven't really covered those bases, now that I think about it. I can barely focus enough to get dressed before wandering into the visitor center to meet Chloe and my mom for lunch.

I am surprised to see my mother is alone in the visitor center when I arrive.

"Where is Chloe?" I immediately ask.

"She had something she had to take care of in Florida," my mom mysteriously informs me.

"She couldn't have called?" I ask, rather pissed off.

"It was something with the boys, Fiona. She had to catch a flight home quickly. I am sure she will call."

"Well, is everything alright? Are they okay?" I ask, worried now.

"Yes. I believe everything is fine, honey," my mom calmly reassures me.

I wonder what could have happened.

I try to enjoy lunch with my mother, having not spent time with her in quite a while, but my mind is all over the place. I keep thinking of Chloe and the boys, wondering what could have happened. And that awkward moment I had with Jade, a few minutes ago, hasn't helped anything, either. Then the image of the doctors pops back into my head. Gross.

"I talked to Dr. Clark," my mom eventually mentions.

"Chloe told me it didn't go well, huh?" I say.

"She is just still concerned with your mental state, Fiona. With you having tried to...well, you know. After Michael died. And your attempt at escaping sure hasn't helped anything, honey."

"I didn't try to escape...Ugh! Never mind. I know, mom. I'm sorry. Just keep trying, okay? I promise you I am fine. I would be a lot saner if I wasn't still in here, though."

"I know, sweetie. Just hang in there, okay? I love you. I need to get going. Mikey Junior needs some help going through your father's office things. It is quite a process. He has so many papers," my mom informs me, and I start to feel faint, wondering if they will find the letters that reveal all of my dad's secrets.

"Oh, well, if you want to wait, I can help you when I get out of here," I say, trying to encourage her to put it off, but knowing it isn't likely.

"Well, that's nice, Fiona, but we don't really know how long that will be at this point, sweetie, and we need to get going with it all," my mother says.

Once again, I feel so helpless. I have no control over what they'll find or read. It is a terrible and overwhelming feeling of anguish.

"Thanks for having lunch with me today, mom."

"Of course, sweetie. I will talk to you soon, okay?"

"Yeah, okay."

After my mother leaves the cafeteria, I decide to step outside onto the balcony for some fresh air. I remember we have group soon, and think about how I will have to see Jade there. Maybe I should talk to her and just confront her about what happened, I think to myself. I hesitate, suddenly thinking of Chloe, and wonder what happened that made her cancel and leave for Florida. I feel dizzy, and realize cutting the Lithium in half hasn't helped me feel better at all.

After letting the cool breeze brush my face I head over to group, a little early.

I am the first one to arrive at group, so I sit with my legs crossed on the carpet, waiting for more people to arrive.

Trisha arrives with a clan of other glamorous girls and sits next to me.

"Hey, roomie," she says, very high school like.

"Hey, Trisha," I respond.

Her friends just stare at me, like she did the first day. Jade arrives a few minutes later and sits on my other side. She doesn't make eye contact and I can sense she is feeling a bit nervous, but clearly not nervous enough to completely avoid me.

"Hey, Jade," I say, trying to calm her nerves a bit and let her know I am not upset with her. Although, I am a bit confused.

"Oh, hi, Fiona," she responds, as if she hadn't noticed she was sitting right beside me.

Eventually everyone is present and Dr. Hall begins group with a warm hello.

"Welcome everyone," he greets us. "Today I am very excited for group. We are going to try something new and play a little game. The object of the game is to use your senses to really get to know someone. I think making connections with each other, and friendship, is a very important part of the healing process. So, everyone stand up. And grab the person next to you. They will be your partner."

Jade smiles at me awkwardly. I smile back in acceptance.

"Okay, ladies. Face each other and close your eyes. I want you to study each other with your eyes closed. Try to find things that make it clear who the other person is. You will have two minutes to get to know each other with your eyes closed, so try to take in as much detail as you can because there is a little game we will play afterwards," Dr. Hall explains.

Jade and I face each other with our eyes closed, just as Dr. Hall has asked us to do.

"Okay, you may begin," he announces.

I reach out my hands and end up bumping Jade's hands with mine. "I'm sorry," I say.

"It's okay. You go first," she says.

I reach out once again and touch Jade's face this time. I feel her high cheekbones and try to remember how far they are from her eye sockets. I touch her hair, her lips and her ears next. I feel she has circular earrings on in her first hole, then the second earring above feels like a rhinestone stud or something. I try to remember what it feels like. I realize I am taking up way too much of the two minutes.

"Sorry, you go," I say quickly.

She barely has enough time to feel anything before Dr. Hall calls time.

"Your two minutes are up, ladies," he says loudly as he looks at his watch.

"Now I would like everyone except one person – " He grabs a random girl from the circle. " – to line up. One at a time, you will get five minutes to go down the line. I will guide you, with your eyes closed, while you carefully try to find your partner. I hope you took note of memorable things and how they felt," Dr. Hall informs us.

One by one, everyone goes. Some partners get their partner right, but the other one gets it wrong. Soon it is my turn to go. I close my eyes. I can hear everyone changing positions in line so that I will not know where Jade is in the lineup. I walk down the line, feeling carefully the different features on everyone: their hair, their earrings in particular. Eventually I come to someone who I believe to be Jade.

"Two more minutes, Fiona," Dr. Hall announces.

I touch her lips and feel certain it is her. I feel her circular earrings first, then the sharper set, the rhinestones. I can hear her take a deep breath and I say out loud, "Jade. This is Jade."

"Good job Fiona, it sure is," Dr. Hall confirms.

I open my eyes and look at her blue eyes. She doesn't smile, just stares straight into mine.

"Okay, Jade. Do you think you can find Fiona?" Dr. Hall asks.

"Yes," Jade confidently answers. As she closes her eyes, I wander to the very end of the line.

She quickly feels everyone before me in line, seeming to immediately be able to tell it is not me. When she finally gets to me, she only has fifteen seconds left, since I am the last. She touches my hands. Then she touches my lips. That is it.

"Fiona. This is her," Jade says, with two seconds to spare.

"Excellent!" Dr. Hall says.

We end up being the only pair who both pick each other correctly out of the line.

"Okay, ladies," Dr. Hall says. "Since Fiona and Jade are the winning pair, they will each get a free copy of the daily devotional that we have been reading here in group. Great job," he says as he hands us each a copy of the book.

"Now, can anyone tell me what the point of the game we played might be?" he asks.

"I can." I raise my hand slightly.

"Okay, Fiona, what do you think?" he asks me.

"Well, being an artist, I sometimes close my eyes to really imagine what I am about to draw before I sketch it out. I mean, I can picture it better with my eyes closed. The details, that is. It forces you to be more aware of what is actually right in front of you. It actually allows you to see things more clearly, I believe."

"Yes, Fiona. That is a great interpretation. Also, did you know that closing one's eyes has been studied by many researchers and that they concluded, it is sometimes a quick way to soothe fear and anxiety in what could be stressful or unnerving situations? Concentration levels have been proved to increase with one's eyes shut, rather than open, when examining something as well. So it is amazing you were able to find your partner so quickly, after really studying them with your eyes shut Fiona. Everyone, I want you to remember this exercise in your daily lives when you may feel anxious. I want you to close your eyes, take a deep breath and listen, or feel. It has proven beneficial for many neurological disorders. I look forward to trying another fun and therapeutic game with you all tomorrow, here at group. Have a wonderful rest of your day."

Chloe: September 2015
The Mural

The next morning, I once again arrive at the coffee shop before Fiona's dad and her brother do. As I am getting out of my car, I notice Fiona is already here. I see her sipping a coffee at one of the outside tables, still dressed in the clothes she wore yesterday, but wearing a paint-spattered smock on top. It looks like she hasn't slept. She must have stayed up all night working on the wall mural. I walk up to greet her. She has paint all over her and her eyes are incredibly blood-shot.

"Hey, baby, did you stay here all night?" I ask.

"Yeah. I did."

"Wow. Well, can I look at the wall? I'm dying to see it! Or do you want me to wait for your dad?"

"No, go on in," she says. "I'll be right there."

I walk in, look up at the wall Fiona has spent the whole night painting and I'm immediately taken aback. It's a portrait of her as a child, with her dad. He is crouching, a Mugged coffee cup in one hand. His other hand rests on Fiona's face and he is smiling. They are surrounded by butterflies. They must be at a butterfly sanctuary similar to the one she took me to. Every detail is exquisite. I want to go up and touch her. Little Fiona. She looks so delicate and serene, and her father so content. The butterflies are colorful and look real. I feel like I am back in that butterfly garden with her all over again.

She walks in from outside.

"So, what do you think?" she asks.

"Fiona. This is amazing. You are so talented. I think your dad is going to love it."

I run up to her and hug her tightly. I get paint all over my shirt, but I don't care. I have missed touching her, the past few days.

"So you went to a butterfly sanctuary with your dad too, huh?"

"Yeah. He, my mom and Mikey Jr. were there that day. It was his idea. He and my mom were still married at the time. I remember he had just opened the coffee shop and had been working every day. I made him feel really bad about not being around, so he said he wanted to surprise Junior and I, and this is where he took us. It was a long way from the apartment where we were living at the time, so it was really special. He took the whole day off from work and spent it with us. I thought it was a perfect picture for the wall. I hope he does, too."

Mr. Lennox walks in the front door. He is wearing almost the same exact suit as yesterday, only navy instead of black.

"Good morning, ladies, sorry we are late…"

He stops, noticing the mural.

I watch as he starts to relive that day. I can see it in his face: how awed he is by her work and by the memory she has incorporated into it.

"Oh, Fiona. My little girl. I remember that day like it was yesterday. That's me and you, kid," he says with tears in his eyes. "It's perfect." He then proceeds to take a hanky out of his suit pocket and discretely wipes his eyes.

Fiona runs up to him and jumps into his arms, almost as if she is that little girl again. They hug for a long time.

"Wow. Fiona. It's amazing," Mikey says.

"Thanks, bro."

"That was a good day," Mikey agrees, smiling.

"Well, there are a few final touches, I need to make on the wall, but other than letting it dry, it's almost complete," Fiona says.

"Alright. Let's get down to business." Mr. Lennox clears his throat, back to his usual tone.

We spend the morning writing up menus, practicing folding napkins and creating web design on Mikey Jr.'s laptop. We pick out what tables and chairs we like and order them for the shop.

"Well, I better get to work," Fiona says as she closes the laptop. "These half days are killing my clientele. I've had to cancel a few appointments already this week. I'll see you at my apartment after six tonight, right, Chloe?"

"Yes. I'll see you around six," I confirm.

Mikey Jr. follows her out and I am left alone with her father for the first time. I help him pick up a bit and then he offers to walk me to my car.

"Sure," I say, and he grabs his things and we head for the parking lot.

"You seem to be really grasping everything well, Chloe. I think you are going to be a great fit for this shop," he says as I am getting into my car. I can smell his aftershave as he leans over me.

"Wow. Thank you, Mr. Lennox. You have done me a huge favor letting me have this job. I know it was a risk for you, so I promise not to let you down. I'll do whatever it takes."

"I know that feeling, my dear. Not wanting to let your family down. You have a lot of drive, like I did at your age, Chloe. That's a good quality to possess. It will take you far in life. Who knows, maybe you and Junior will both take over the coffee shops when I retire."

"Let's not get ahead of ourselves," I say, and start the car engine.

"I'm glad Fiona has you, Chloe. She's going to need you," he says and walks away. "See you tomorrow!" he shouts from a distance.

I wave goodbye as I drive off. I can't help but wonder what he meant by, "She's going to need you." Was she prone to crisis situations? I haven't heard any out of control stories about her at all. She looks a little rough on the outside, but she isn't wild or reckless. I don't think she has been arrested or anything. Maybe I should ask her some questions tonight. I realize I have a couple of hours to kill before Fiona will be home from work. The boys are staying with Trent's mom today, so I decide to surprise Fiona with a nice dinner. I drive to the supermarket and pick up some steaks and fresh vegetables and salad ingredients. I also grab a bottle of red wine. I still have the spare key, so I cook it all up before she gets home.

"Hey, Chloe. It smells fabulous in here," Fiona says as she walks in.

"Surprise! I wanted to cook you a good meal. I know you are probably exhausted from being up all night and I haven't seen you in a couple nights, so voilá!" I say, revealing the spread on the table.

"Mmm...meat!" She licks her lips.

We eat and drink wine for a while and talk a lot about the coffee shop and how it's coming along.

"I am so sleepy, baby," she says. "Want to snuggle up with me and watch a movie in bed for about ten minutes before I pass out?"

"Sounds romantic," I say.

I clean up the kitchen for Fiona and then make my way to her bedroom, where she and Marvin are already snuggled up under the covers. "Come lie with me, gorgeous," she says.

"So your dad seems surprisingly friendly to me," I say while lying down next to her under the covers.

"He has been on his best behavior, that's for sure," she agrees, and curls up in my armpit, like Marvin usually does. I can't help but notice how sad she looks. I try to convince myself that maybe it's just because she is so tired.

"Are you sure everything is okay, Fiona?" I ask anyway.

"Yes, of course, baby. Everything is perfect. I love you."

It takes her about two minutes to fall asleep.

When I wake up in the morning, I hear Fiona, already awake and talking to someone on the phone. I think it is her mother, judging by the conversation.

"Yes, He told me…I know. Oh, I'm glad he likes it…No, I'm not upset with you. I understand…Of course…Yes, please do. Love you too. Bye." She hangs up.

"You're up early." I pat her on the butt.

"Good morning. Want some coffee?" she asks, handing me a Mugged coffee cup to fill.

"Sure. So, was that your mom on the phone? How is she doing?" I ask instinctively.

"It was. She's good. I was just telling her how things were going with my dad."

It didn't sound like that was what they were talking about to me.

"Are you going to grab anything to eat, or should we head to the coffee shop?" she asks quickly.

"Um…no, I'm not hungry. Coffee is good."

We head to the coffee shop. Fiona seems very distracted on the way there. She doesn't say much to me and looks straight at the road during almost the entire ride. When we arrive, she gets out, shuts her door and walks around to my side.

"My lady." She grabs my hand.

Guess she was fine, I think. Maybe just a little tired still from lack of sleep.

She doesn't stay long at the shop with me today. I think that on previous days she stayed all day only to help me adjust to her father. Today she insists she has a busy schedule at work and heads out mid-morning.

I feel more comfortable around her dad and brother now. They have been nothing but nice to me throughout the week and I feel as if I am getting the hang of things. Around four o'clock we decide to call it quits. We agree to meet one last time – just for a few hours in the morning – to wrap things up before they leave town the following day.

Mr. Lennox catches me staring at Fiona's mural on the wall before leaving. "She's pretty talented, huh?" he asks me.

"She sure is. I can't believe she painted this in one day. It's amazing to me."

"I like to say she gets all of her talent from me, but she has far surpassed me in her artwork. I could never paint that so exquisitely," he admits.

"She did both of my tattoos, too." I show him my wrist and index finger.

"I'm not surprised she convinced you to let her paint your skin," he says, rolling his eyes.

"I love her, you know. I love who she is. I wouldn't change a thing about her," I say confidently to him.

"I love her too. And no matter what she has told you I wouldn't change a thing about her either, Chloe. Not a thing. I know I wasn't the best father to her when she was young, but we have both come a long way. She wasn't always the easiest daughter, either. She had a lot of struggles with her identity. She wasn't always as confident and comfortable in her own skin as she is now. But I always loved her. Whether I did a good job of showing it or not, I did love her. I want to make up for that lost time, somehow. I wish I could, at least. I'm glad to have been able to be here with you girls for the week. It's been wonderful." He puts his hands on my shoulders.

"Me too, Mr. Lennox. I'll see you tomorrow morning. Have a good night."

I pick up the boys from Trent on my way home. I don't know if Fiona is staying at the house with me or not. We forgot to talk about it last night before she passed out from exhaustion. I get the boys inside, and then call Fiona on her cell phone.

"Hey, baby. You coming over to my place after work? We are here now. I'm cooking up some food if you're hungry," I say.

"Sure. I'm almost done here. See you in thirty."

I am glad she is coming over. I feel I'm being kept at a distance by her, ever since her father arrived. Maybe it's just a big adjustment, her being around him again for the first time in over a year. At least I hope that is all it is.

Fiona walks right in the front door.

"Hey, little dudes!" she says as she shuts the door. "Hey, gorgeous girlfriend." She kisses me on the lips.

Woo. I guess we are no longer sheltering the kids, I think. And I guess she isn't being that distant anymore.

"You seem chipper," I say to her.

"Just glad to be with you guys and with family all week, I guess."

"That's sweet, baby. I'm glad you had a good day."

"Mommy?" Kaden asks. "Can I have ice cream, since I ate all my dinner?"

"I'll serve you some ice cream, Kade. I feel like being crazy and eating my dessert first tonight," says Fiona, and takes out the ice cream.

I watch how much Kaden loves her. How comfortable he is with her now. They have become so close over the past month. I serve Max a little bowl of ice cream too and we all sit and eat as a family.

Fiona and I oversleep the next morning. I wake up to my phone buzzing. I look at the time and realize we are going to be extremely late for the coffee shop. The kids must have slept in. I answer the phone.

"Hello?" I say in a scratchy morning voice.

"Hi. Mrs. Stearns?"

I still haven't gotten around to legally changing my name back to Chloe Fields. "It's Fields now. Chloe Fields," I correct the woman on the line.

"My apologies, Ms. Fields. This is Susan, your ex-husband's realtor," she says.

"Oh, hello."

"Good morning. I am sorry to call so early, but I was wondering if you were going to be home in the afternoon for a walk-through. I have a lovely couple, wanting to see your house today around three o'clock."

"Oh, perfect. I should be here, yes. I mean, I will be here."

"Great. We will see you at three then, Ms. Fields. Have a good morning."

It is strange hearing someone call me by my maiden name again.

"Fiona. We got to get up!" I shake her a bit.

"Ughhh. Okay. Okay, I'm up," she finally says.

We rush around for the next thirty minutes trying to get the boys dressed and ready to drop off at Trent's while trying to get ourselves ready and out of the house as well.

I realize on the way to Trent's that this will be the first time he has met Fiona.

"So, I realize you have never met Trent. I didn't really think that through when asking you to stay over last night. I'm sorry," I say on the way to his apartment.

"Why, you think he's going to freak out or something, Chloe?" she asks.

"No. It's just weird, I guess. I don't know, never mind."

"I think it is harder for you, Chloe. Because you have a big heart, I think you are worried it will upset him. Am I right, doll?"

She is pretty spot-on.

"Yeah, maybe a little. I've hurt him enough, you know."

"That's understandable, Chloe. But it will be fine." She squeezes my hand tightly and doesn't let go.

We pull up to Trent's and he doesn't come outside. Maybe I should just bring them up to the door and avoid the whole dramatic situation, I think to myself. No, they have to meet eventually.

"Mind coming to get the boys out of the car, Trent?" I ask. "We are in a hurry," I add.

"Guess not. Be out in a minute," he says, sounding somewhat frustrated.

"Hey boys!" Trent says as he unfastens their seatbelts. He doesn't even look at Fiona.

"See you later, Chloe." He starts to walk away, back towards the apartment.

"Wait!" I yell. I was not going to let him get away with not acknowledging Fiona at all. "This is Fiona," I say loudly. "My girlfriend."

"Well, hello, Fiona," he says in a flippant tone. "I am Trent. The ex."

"Nice to meet you, man," Fiona says from inside the car. And Trent continues to walk back inside the apartment.

"Whaaat the hell, Chloe," Fiona immediately says as we drive off.

"Ugh, I know. I'm sorry I exploded like that. I am just sick of everyone in my life pretending that we aren't together or that you don't exist. I had to say something. He can't get away with that shit, you know?"

"Aww. Baby. Was that your way of standing up for me? That's kind of cute," she says with a wink.

"Shut up, Fiona. This is a big issue for me. I mean, I know my parents were nice to you and all, at their house, but they basically refused to acknowledge that we are a couple. I am not afraid to admit that I am a lesbian anymore. I want to, like, shout it out!" I roll my window down and yell out of the window. "Hey, Middleton, Florida! Guess what? Chloe Fields is a raaaaaaging lesbian now! You happy?"

I look over and Fiona is cracking up beside me. All I can do is start laughing with her and pretend I am not neurotic, but completely sane. She loves me for being a little crazy, at least. Thank God.

We finally pull into the coffee shop parking lot and I see her father and brother have actually beat us here this morning. We must be late.

"Hey, dad," Fiona says as she is getting out of the car. "I'm sorry we are late. Rough morning." She looks at me and shakes her head with a smile.

The meeting with Trent was pretty funny – looking back at the situation now – but I am really upset that the people in my life still treat me like a confused, sixteen-year-old little girl. I am a grown woman who has a real-life girlfriend. Is that so hard to acknowledge?

I have a hard time concentrating at the coffee shop. Fiona doesn't stay long, again. She heads off to work around ten and tells me she will meet me at my house after work tonight. Around two we finish up at work and I realize her dad and brother will be leaving tomorrow morning, so I probably won't see them again for some time.

"So, is Fiona going to swing by your hotel or anything after work to say goodbye?" I ask while gathering my things.

"Junior and I are going to stop by her work and say goodbye in a few minutes," answers Mr. Lennox. He takes a picture of the wall mural. "I want to text her mother a photo of Fiona's painting," he explains.

"Yes. That's a good idea," I say.

"Well, Chloe. We will be back in the last week of September to set up the shop, decorate and get things ready to open. Can you find someone for your boys to stay with that week? It will be a busy one."

"Of course. And thanks again for giving me this job. It's a huge blessing for my family."

"I couldn't have found a better manager myself," he says with a grin. "You're a good kid, Chloe. Promise me you will take care of my Fiona. Okay?"

"I will."

He gives me a big hug and doesn't let go for a few minutes. Being this close to him, his aftershave is almost nauseating. It's kind of nice. He seems like such a nice guy. I don't see what all the hype has been about him. Maybe he has really changed over the past year.

I hurry to Trent's mom to grab the boys, and barely make it back to the house before the realtor shows up. The couple seem very interested in the house. They say they want to discuss things for a few days but will call back if they are interested in making an offer.

Fiona gets to the house around six.

"Where are my little dudes?" she asks as she walks in. She is holding a big bag. She opens it and takes out several older looking toys.

"These were my ninja turtles and he-men from when I was a kid," she says, handing them to the boys.

Of course, she had all boys' toys.

"Where did you get all the old toys from, Fiona?" I ask.

"My dad dropped them by the shop on his way out today. When he said goodbye."

"That's odd. Isn't it? He just happened to have all of your old toys with him?"

"I don't know…He didn't really say why he had them with him, I guess…" she says strangely. "But they are super cool, aren't they, boys?" She sits down and plays Ninja Turtles with the boys for a while before we eat dinner together.

That night Kaden falls asleep hugging one of Fiona's old Ninja Turtles. I catch her taking a picture of him and texting it to her dad. I walk up behind her and touch her arm.

She jumps. "Oh! You scared me."

"Sending that picture to your dad?" I ask.

"Yeah. I'm sure it will remind him of me as a little kid. I never let go of that turtle. Carried him with me everywhere. It's like a walk down memory lane," she says, nostalgic.

"Yeah, I bet," I say, noticing she has fallen into a trance. "Well, it seems you and your dad really mended fences this week."

We walk to the bedroom together, so closely our bodies are touching, and I can't help but notice how detached Fiona is the entire way.

"Yeah. I guess we did. Maybe I have you to thank for that, huh?" she asks.

"Oh, I don't know. I'm just really thankful for you right now, Fiona. For giving me an opportunity to really take care of me and my boys. And for giving me the chance to love you."

"Baby. You can be so stinking' cute sometimes. You know that?" She kisses me and we hold each other for a long time before letting go. There's something in my soul that knows we are bonded together for life.

"Fiona?" I ask as we are starting to fall asleep later. "Will you paint a picture of me with my boys? Like the one you did on the coffee shop wall?"

"Yes, of course, baby. I'll paint you anything you want."

And we drift off to sleep together.

Fiona: December 2015
Privacy

I quickly start to walk back to my room after we are let go. I need a minute to process everything, I just experienced. Jade sure seems to know me. I am shocked she found me so quickly after only having thirty seconds or so to study me in the first part of the game. I feel like she must have cheated. Maybe peeked out of one eye, without anyone noticing. Oh, well. I decide to go read through my devotional. I want to be by myself for a minute to relax before I call Chloe to find out what has happened back in Florida. Before I can make it to my room Jade runs up to me, breathless.

"Hey, Fiona, wait!" she says hurriedly, in a breathy tone. "Look, I don't know what I was thinking. Being so intrusive with you in your bedroom earlier, okay? I don't want to ruin our friendship. I really value you as a friend here, Fiona. I am so sorry."

"Look, I get it. It's okay. We are all lonely. It makes sense. Don't sweat it, Jade," I say with a smile.

"I'm not gay," she blurts out before I walk into my room.

"I know you aren't. I mean, I didn't think you were."

"Okay. Just making that clear," she says. "Want to paint together later?"

"Yes. I'll meet you there in an hour and we can paint before dinner. How does that sound?"

"See you there," she says before running off down the hall.

I sit down on my bed and flip through the free devotional, I was just given by Dr. Hall. I think about what a hypocrite he must be. Cheating on his wife while preaching about Jesus and about being faithfully and godly. For some reason, every time I think about him with Dr. Clark, I feel queasy. I read a few excerpts from the devotional and decide to close my eyes just for a few minutes. The lithium still seems to make me really drowsy.

When I wake up, I have a puddle of drool on my bed next to me and my face has to be peeled off the comforter. Trisha is now sitting on her bed, reading her usual fashion magazine.

"Have a good nap, bum?" she asks me with a smirk.

"Oh God, I was drooling. I am disgusting, I'm sorry."

"Ha, ha, yeah. You were out cold," she says. "Dr. Clark came in here looking for you, but decided not to wake you when she saw how asleep you were."

"She did? What did she want?" I anxiously ask.

"I don't know. She said you were expecting her and grabbed something from a box under your bed," Trisha informs me.

"Wait! What?" I immediately slide out my box of personal things from under my bed and notice all of my letters are gone, along with some other important documents of my father. "Shit!" I say.

"What?" Trisha asks, concerned.

"That bitch!" I yell. "I'll be back later."

I run out of my room and down the hall in search of Dr. Clark. She has now illegally confiscated my personal letters to Chloe, along with some other seriously informative files of my dad. This is a disaster. "I knew she was a sneaky little shit," I say to myself.

I remember I am supposed to call Chloe, and also that I am supposed to be painting with Jade right now. I realize I am right by the Art Therapy room, so I poke my head in and see Jade alone, painting on an easel. "Hey. You made it," she says to me cheerfully.

"Hey. Something has come up. I have some things to take care of," I inform her. "I am sorry. Can we paint tomorrow together?" I ask, still with a look of terror – I am sure – plastered on my face.

"Fiona? Are you okay?" she asks, probably realizing how flustered I am. "What is going on, Fiona?"

I feel so alone in all of this that I impulsively decide to tell her what is going on. Something I would not normally tell someone like Jade. Someone I hardly know.

"Dr. Clark – you know, the other psychiatrist that comes here sometimes…Well, she is my primary psychiatrist. Since I was little. And she is a cunt." Wow. I cannot believe, I used such a nasty word, and out loud at that.

"Geez Fiona. What the hell did she do?"

"She has stolen my personal belongings, not to mention that she was basically fucking Dr. Clark the other day in some secret office or room down the hall!"

"Wait, what? Isn't he married?"

"Yes. He is apparently a man-whore."

"Do you want some company, Fiona? Are you looking for her?" Jade asks me, concerned.

"I need to find her, and I need to call Chloe," I explain.

"I'll come with you. If that's okay. You seem really upset," Jade insists, and follows me down the hall towards the phones.

Luckily a phone is free, so I immediately dial Chloe's cell phone number, praying she will answer quickly. She doesn't pick up.

"Ugh!" I yell, and then realize everyone is looking at me like I am insane. Great; that will only work against me.

"Fiona. Why don't we go sit down and relax, talk a bit in your room or something?" Jade says. She takes my hand and leads me away from the phones.

We get to my room and Trisha isn't there. Jade sits down on my bed with me.

"What is going on, Fiona? Please let me in," she begs.

I take a minute before I respond, and a few deep breaths.

"My life is a mess right now, Jade. My family – my world – is falling apart. I faked being insane to protect them, you know. But this place, these people…The doctors and nurses are making me go crazy. Invading my privacy. Taking away my freedom. It's enough to make someone actually go insane, don't you think?" I ask her, hoping for an ally in how I am feeling.

"Absolutely." She takes my hand. "It is hard enough to come to grips with the fact that you have no control over your mind, or your mental health, but to succumb to these dictators is infuriating."

"Yeah, well, Dr. Clark is out to get me, I feel. My father used to pay her lots of money, it seems – from what I have found – to keep me locked up in these places. And I am pretty sure whatever trust fund used to be mine from my father is now in her hands. And the letters she stole from under my bed today tell a lot. Not to mention all of the documents. This isn't good, Jade. This is really, really bad, actually."

"It is going to be okay. I will help you get what you need back from her somehow. I will help you get out of here. I will stand up for you."

"Thank you, Jade. I don't deserve your friendship. After how I have treated you. I am sorry," I plead.

"It's okay. We will just blame it all on the meds," Jade jokes.

"Right. Damn lithium is making me insane," I tell her.

"Lithium? What the hell are you doing on lithium? How much?" she asks me, and I remember she was a psych minor.

"I don't know. I think when I asked initially, they said it was for my aggressive and manic tendencies or something. All I know is, it is making me way more insane than I was off of it."

"Yeah, I am sure. That is a pretty hardcore drug. Unless you are a diagnosed bipolar with extreme manic episodes. I am not sure I agree with them putting you on that drug at all. It doesn't make sense."

"Well, I wouldn't be surprised if the doctors got together and this was all in their master plan somewhere." I start to think hard about what I have just said and realize what strings they are able to pull, being doctors and all. They literally could completely alter my brain and how I function by putting me on all these drugs. Sure, it would be completely unethical and illegal, but they clearly don't care at all about morals or ethics. Especially Dr. Clark.

"I really need to get a hold of Chloe somehow," I say to Jade with emphasis.

"I know, Fiona; I know. You will. Try her one more time before dinner, okay? Just sit here with me for a minute," she suggests. "You know, I have never questioned my sexuality until now, Fiona." Jade admits. I start to feel uneasy with where this is going. She'd better not start this verbal diarrhea shit again, I think to myself.

"I know you are engaged," says Jade, "And I am not trying to be a homewrecker by any means, but your fiancée is sure one lucky lady." She's staring deeply into my eyes.

I suddenly think back to the first dinner I had with Chloe at my house, in Florida. How she confessed her love to me while she was still married to Trent. And I was receptive. Because I knew she was special and I didn't care what I had to do, or who I had to hurt to have her. Maybe I was selfish, looking back now. I feel like Jade is completely out of line, but at the same time I can relate to how she feels because I knew damn well Chloe was married and I still fell in love with her. I let myself love her when she was off limits to me.

I don't really know how to handle this invasion of privacy that I am feeling from Jade. I feel like she is trying to get too involved in my life. It is making me feel incredibly uncomfortable, but at the same time I really do like her, and as a good friend, now.

"I know we are both lonely, Jade. And I am not upset with you, like I said, about earlier, but this can't go anywhere besides where it is right now. I mean, we are good friends. And I am so grateful for that, but we can't be more than that. I can't be more to you than that. I couldn't even if I tried," I say truthfully.

."I know. I just find you so intriguing: so unique, so eccentric. I have never met anyone like you. It is hard for me to understand it myself, but I want you to know I think you are amazing," she adds.

"Well, I think you are, too." I take Jade's hand and squeeze it firmly, letting her know we are okay.

"Hey, I am going to go try and call Chloe again, like you suggested; before dinner, real quick," I say, and stand up.

"Yeah. Okay. Save me a seat at dinner, OK?" Jade says before walking out of my bedroom.

I walk to the phones by myself, finally feeling like I have a little privacy to phone Chloe. She answers this time.

"Thank God,"

I announce after she greets me with her usual "Hey, baby."

"I know. I am so sorry, Fiona," Chloe begins. "I feel terrible that I didn't get to see you one last time before coming back to Florida, but Max had an accident at school yesterday. He fell and broke his arm. It was really traumatic for me, being all the way in New York when I found out, so I felt I needed to rush back and be there with him. I am sorry."

"Oh man, I am so sorry, Chloe. Poor little dude. I bet he was tough, though, wasn't he?" I ask, feeling really awful for the little guy.

"Yeah, he was. I actually stayed at Trent's last night, Fiona. I know it may seem crazy, but he didn't want to be away from either of us so I didn't know what to do…I promise nothing…"

"Chloe, it's okay. I get it. I understand. I just miss you, that's all. And I have a lot to talk to you about."

"Is everything okay? Any luck with getting the hell out of there?" Chloe asks me.

"Actually, quite the opposite. Dr. Clark stole a lot of documents and letters from me. From under my bed." I begin to realize that I have never mentioned I wrote Chloe more letters since being in here. When we weren't speaking for those few weeks while my dad's health was failing, before he passed away, I wrote her love letters. I am not sure if she ever read them or not. They are still at my dad, I assume. But I told her about those letters. I haven't mentioned these. She might actually be concerned with my mental state if I tell her, I once again wrote her a bunch of letters, possibly ones she may never read. It seems illogical, now that I think about it.

"What letters, or documents are you talking about? What did they say?" Chloe asks.

"Well, the documents were receipts of my father's. Things he purchased. Places he went. The letters were…to you, actually. I just never sent them," I try and explain.

"How come?"

"I don't know. It was more therapeutic for me than anything else, I guess."

"Well, did they say something that would allow her to have any ammo towards you? I mean, they don't make you sound irrational or crazy, do they?

Who cares if she reads them? Let her judge our love. I don't care," Chloe declares.

"I don't care about that either, Chloe, but it is more about the things I mentioned in them about my father. And about my past. There were some pretty detailed ones. I don't even remember all of it now, to tell you the truth. I just want them back. I don't want her to have anything of mine anymore. It is so fucking unfair."

"I know, baby. I know," says Chloe, trying to calm me down. "I will try my hardest to get back up there as soon as Mugged and Trent will let me."

Trent? I assume she means, when Trent is able to watch the boys for her, but it is the way she just said it.

"Hey, Chloe?" I decide to ask her. "Is Trent still dating that girl, Aubrey? The one I made a fool of myself in front of?"

"Oh, no. They broke it off, a while ago," she informs me.

For some reason, I start to have an uneasy feeling in my gut. I feel as if Chloe is awfully close to Trent again, all of a sudden, and I would be lying if I said it doesn't make me a little nervous.

"Oh. Well, I thought she seemed nice. That's a shame," I pipe up.

"Yeah. I guess you don't really know people sometimes," Chloe says.

She is right. Having been so wrong about so many people in my life, I am starting to realize she is absolutely right. I feel though I do not know anyone in my life anymore. It is like that saying: You can't judge a book by its cover. I remember analyzing Jade that first day. Thinking she was this happy-go-lucky nerd who had it all figured out, but coming to find out she is as messed up as I am. She is just better at hiding it, I suppose. Then of course, there was my first impression of Chloe, that day she sat in my chair for the first time at the tattoo shop. She seemed so girly and innocent. So straight. But she wasn't. She isn't. She has skeletons in her closet, too. She had obstacles, and hard times and flaws, and all of the things that prove she is in fact human. But my dad had to be the biggest shocker of all. My seemingly homophobic, judgmental, egotistical, and narcissistic father was apparently in love with a man. For years. I would have never guessed it. So, at this point I am afraid to make any assumptions about who someone might be or the battles they may be fighting inside. You never really know, do you?

"Fiona? Are you still there?" Chloe asks me after a long bout of silence.

"Yes. I am here," I finally manage to respond.

"Well, I better get going. Trent made us all dinner. I love you. Take care of yourself, sweetie," Chloe says, in a tone that I am not too familiar with, from her.

"Yeah, you too."

Chloe: October 2015
Strength

"Baby?" I ask timidly. "Are you ready to talk about what is going on with your father?"

Fiona stares down at her barely eaten food for a long time.

"You're right," she says after clearing her throat. "He is sick. He was diagnosed with a neurological disease over a year ago. I didn't know about it until he was here last month. He told me that day at the coffee shop, while you and Mikey Jr. went to get us lunch."

I have no idea what to say.

"What is the disease?" I finally ask.

"Something called A.L.S.," she says. "I don't know that much about it. He keeps telling me he is going to be fine, so I haven't asked much. Maybe weight loss is just one of the symptoms."

A.L.S.? I knew a couple of people who died from this disease. I am pretty sure the life expectancy isn't long, after being diagnosed. Has Fiona not Googled it? If my dad had been diagnosed with a disease, I would Google the shit out of it! Why has she not Googled? And why did she not tell me a month ago?

"Fiona. I am so sorry." I stand up and sit on her lap with my arms around her. "You haven't Googled A.L.S.? Why didn't you tell me when you found out, baby?"

"You had enough on your plate, Chloe. My God, you were still going through a lot of changes. I couldn't add to that. I'm sorry. I should have told you, though."

I lie in bed that night with an uneasy feeling in the pit of my stomach. I know I should tell Fiona everything I know about the disease. I know she doesn't know it is fatal. That it is serious and that he is not going to be fine.

But I don't know how to tell her without hurting her. Why did he lie? Shouldn't her father just be up front with her? I am in a big dilemma.

The next day at the coffee shop, I have a really hard time making eye contact with anyone. I try to work on tasks, I can do by myself. Eventually, Fiona has to head to the tattoo shop and I am left with her brother and dad. Mikey Jr. decides to go run an errand for us so I stay behind with the intention of confronting Mr. Lennox about the situation. We finish up a few mundane things before I ask him.

"Hey, Mr. Lennox? Can I talk to you about something, sir?"

"Of course, Chloe." I see his hand has a bit of a tremor. A symptom of his disease. "Fiona told me about you being sick. That you have A.L.S."

He looks up from writing a check. "Yes. I have had it for about a year and a half now, dear. Hasn't seemed to put a damper on much." He smiles at me.

"She has no idea that it is a terminal illness, sir."

I immediately feel like I am out of line.

"Steven Hawking has had A.L.S. for almost fifty years, Chloe. I think I will be just fine, dear, but I appreciate your concern."

"Steven Hawking is a rare exception. I have known two people who have died within two to three years after finding out they had it. She needs to know the truth, Mr. Lennox. She needs to know that it will inevitably debilitate you and you won't be able to speak, or move, or…"

"That's enough, Chloe!" he shouts.

I realize how upset he is and how incredibly meddlesome I have been. "I'm sorry. I'm so sorry, sir. I just…This is going to…Fiona is going…" I have tears flowing down my cheeks now.

"I know." He puts his hands on my shoulders, calm now. "I know, dear."

"If you don't tell her I will," I say sternly.

"Why don't we all have dinner out tomorrow night?"

"Alright," I say. "I'm really sorry, Mr. Lennox."

"I know, Chloe. I know."

It is hard for me to contain my emotions around Fiona, when she gets home from work. I want to tell her how I am feeling and what happened with her father, but I know he is planning on talking to her at dinner tomorrow. I try to not bring it up during dinner. I talk about the new store and business stuff to avoid the subject. She tells me about a really neat tattoo she drew on someone today.

"Hey, Chloe, by the way," she says after describing the tattoo in detail, "Did my dad mention, he wants to take us to dinner tomorrow night?"

I am caught off-guard. "Oh, yes. He did," I say awkwardly.

"Okaaay…Do you know why? He seemed a little jumpy when he asked me? Kind of like you are now, Chloe?"

"No, he just said he wanted to talk to us about something, that's all." I try not to make eye contact with her.

"Spit it out, girlfriend. You are a terrible liar."

"Honestly, I don't know what he is going to say, exactly. I think he just wants to talk to you about the A.L.S."

"THE A.L.S.? Like it is some personified thing, ha, ha." She tries to laugh it off.

She is handling this so bizarrely, I think.

"Alright, Fiona, look. You want a heads up?"

"Sure – "

"Your dad is really sick," I interrupt her. "He's not 'fine', like you guys keep saying. Well, he may seem fine now, but he won't be. I knew two people who had A.L.S. They both died from it within three years of finding out they had it. One of them died after only two. It completely debilitated them. It was terrible. My friend's father couldn't speak, couldn't walk, and basically was a vegetable at the very end. I'm not telling you these things to hurt you, Fiona, but you act like everything is going to be fine and it's not. Your dad probably won't even be able to work much longer. I mean, my friend's dad ended up having to get this special wheelchair that could sense where his eyes looked to know which way to move, because he couldn't move his – "

"Chloe! I get it! Stop, please…Just. Stop. I know he isn't going to be fine. I Googled. After you made me feel like an idiot for not researching it before. So I know what the statistics are, okay? But my dad is a really tough guy. He promised me he wouldn't give up."

"I'm sure he won't, Fiona. He is really strong and I get that. I just don't want you living in denial. It isn't healthy and it doesn't make things easier in the end. Trust me. I know."

"Yeah. Well, can we cross that bridge when we get to it? Right now, I would just like to enjoy this lovely evening with my gorgeous girlfriend. And tomorrow we can eat with my dad and face the truth, if you want. OK?"

She looks so small and innocent to me right now. So vulnerable. I have never seen Fiona this way. My heart aches for her.

"Absolutely, baby. Absolutely." I kiss her intensely.

That night, we make love and Fiona completely breaks down. She cries almost the entire time. It isn't weird to me, or off-putting. Just sad. Gut-wrenchingly sad. I want to hold her and never let go.

We show up right on time for dinner the next night. We are both exhausted from a long day at the coffee shop. It is opening day tomorrow and I can't help but have butterflies in my stomach. Fiona's dad is fashionably late, of course, so we decide to sit down at the reserved table and wait for him. We don't say much to each other before he arrives.

"Ladies!" he says loudly while walking up to the table. "I am sorry, I am late." I notice his gray suit looks a tad baggy and he appears more unkempt than usual.

Fiona and I stand up and give her dad a hug.

"Mikey Jr. will not be joining us tonight. He is doing some last-minute things to get the shop ready for tomorrow."

The waitress walks up to take our drink orders. Fiona's father orders for us. He asks for three glasses of water with lemon and a bottle of Chardonnay.

"What are we eating tonight, ladies?" He asks.

Isn't he going to choose our dinners for us, too?

"Um, I think I'll do the filet," Fiona decides.

"Ah. Good choice. And for you, Chloe?"

I haven't eaten at this sort of fancy restaurant as often as they have, so I have no idea what to order.

"Maybe a salad?" I say hesitantly.

"The Cob Salad is wonderful here," he assures me.

He gives the waitress our order a few minutes later.

"Dad…" Fiona starts up the conversation we are all anticipating anxiously. "We know you are sick. And we know you can't fix this. You can't buy yourself out of it, and no matter, how strong you are, it's going to inevitably break you," she says with her head down.

"Fiona. I wanted to tell you the severity of the disease, but until we get to a point where it is evident, I feel no need to let it define me."

"I understand," she says, and looks up. "It's just…you have always been so strong. And I know we haven't had the best relationship. Or a relationship at all, for that matter, but it's my turn to step up to the plate, dad. Let me take care of you. Let me help you with the business. When you need it. Chloe, too." She includes me in the conversation now. "Chloe is so nurturing and we know you don't have a wife to – "

He interrupts her mid-sentence. "Thank you, girls, so much for the kind words."

I haven't even said anything yet, I think.

"But I have Mikey Jr., who lives locally, and my doctor is in New York. There is only so much you two can help with because of the distance. Right now, why don't we just focus on the fact that Mugged is opening tomorrow? Let's celebrate life." He holds up his wine glass to initiate a toast.

"To Mugged," I say, and hold up my Chardonnay.

Fiona raises her glass with only a half-smile. "To Mugged," she says.

We neglect to talk about his disease the rest of the dinner. It is pretty clear that although he admits the severity of it now, it still isn't an open topic of conversation. We order another bottle of wine and I feel tipsy for the first time in a long time.

"Well," I say as I stagger out of the restaurant at a slant. "That went well."

"You okay, Chloe? You seem a little drunk, baby."

I am sober enough to notice her giggling at my buzz.

"I am sooooo fine," I say as I attempt to locate my car keys.

"Here, Chloe. Let me help you, sweetie." She grabs my purse and finds my car keys right away. "I will be driving the mom wagon tonight, okay?"

She buckles me in and I mumble a bunch of nonsense to her. I feel like I have some profound things, I need to get out, but as I am saying them, they clearly are more entertaining than profound.

"So you are a nervous drinker, huh?" she asks me on the drive home.

"Nah," I say while trying not to toss my cookies.

"Chloe. Thanks for protecting me," she says seriously.

"What do you mean?"

"It's just…I have never had anyone defend me to my father like you do. He really likes you and for some reason you are good at being this mediator between us. You are like this angel that watches over me. And maybe him, too. Do you believe in God, Chloe?"

Is this really the deep conversation she wants to have, while I am inebriated?

"I went to a Christian private school as a kid, Fiona. God was kind of shoved down my throat a lot."

Classy way of putting it, Chloe, I think to my drunk self.

"Well, I believe in God. I have to. I feel like my dad is starting to repent, you know, like people do before they die – "

I interrupt her. "He's not going to die any time soon, Fiona."

"No. I know. But he is trying to really be a better person. And I think he has a good heart underneath all the layers of bullshit. So do you think he will go to Heaven, Chloe? Like, how people get second chances. You think God will give him a pass?"

I am suddenly starting to feel sober again.

"Fiona. He most definitely will get a pass. He is so strong. So is his heart, and his love for you. God sees that."

Fiona: December 2015
Paralyzed

After hanging up the phone, I realize the distance between Chloe and I is apparent. She is still at Trent's house. Eating dinner with him and the little dudes. Like they are one big happy family again. I really like Trent, and I feel if Chloe weren't gay, she would definitely have found the perfect match in him. But she is gay. Isn't she? She is engaged to me now. Something about the whole situation is off-putting to me. I try to push the thought of her being with Trent right now out of my mind and focus on myself for once. On getting out of here.

I have no appetite, but I decide to head towards the cafeteria for dinner anyway. Jade is sitting at her usual table when I get there and waves at me to come sit down next to her. Honestly, I would rather be alone. I miss my privacy. I miss solitude. At least at Living Waters I had privacy. Everyone besides Marjorie kept to themselves. They were too crazy too socialize. Here, on the other hand, I have a slew of friends fighting for my attention. I am not sure either situation is ideal.

I sit down next to Jade and immediately scarf down my dinner in order to be done with the chore. I hastily rush off after dinner, barely saying goodbye.

I need to find Dr. Clark.

While pacing the halls, I eventually come across her sly face, looking down at a clipboard while walking towards me.

"Where are you headed?" I ask her, and she startles almost immediately after looking up from her charts.

"Oh, Fiona. You scared me, dear," she admits, stunned.

"Listen. We need to talk," I say very confidently.

"I am in a bit of a rush, Fiona. Would you like to schedule a session tomorrow?" she asks me.

"No. I need to talk now," I say firmly, not taking no for an answer.

"Okay. Shall we head towards Dr. Hall's office, then?" she cautiously agrees.

I follow close behind her as her heels clank on the cold tile floor. I try to think of what I will say when we reach the office, but I have nothing.

"After you." She unlocks the door and holds it open for me to walk through first. I take a seat across from Dr. Hall's desk, just like I would do at the daily counseling session. I confront her almost immediately.

"Listen, I know you stole some of my personal items…from underneath my bed," I declare.

"I have no idea what you are talking about, sweetie," Dr. Clark says while giving me a fake smile.

"I don't play games," I say. I stand up and walk close to her, right up to her face. I can almost feel her breath on my lips now.

"Neither do I." She doesn't back down.

"I don't know, what kind of agreement you and my father have had all of these years," I say, letting it all spill out now, "but I am not in agreement with it and he is no longer in charge. If I have to hurt you to get back what is mine I will!"

And before I can even take a breath, after finishing my train of thought, I feel a sharp jab, similar to the start of a new tattoo in progress, although this time my whole body becomes paralyzed. The sudden sensation is terrifying. I am fully awake, I think, but I can no longer move a muscle. The only thing I have control over are my thoughts and the flutter of my eyes.

"Fiona," Dr. Clark starts to explain casually, as if she hasn't just stabbed me with a paralyzing drug. "You are exactly right, sweetheart. Your father is no longer in charge. I am." I feel spooked watching her, unable to move an inch. "Don't worry. The injection I just gave you was just a large dose of Dilaudid. Once it wears off, you will be able to move again. Listen closely, though, Fiona. If you refuse to comply with my arrangements for you – which I will inform you of in just a moment – I will see it fit to keep you doped-up on Dilaudid at all times, if I must. Is that clear?" she asks me. "I will take your blinking as a yes."

I sense she is finding great pleasure in my immobility.

"Fiona. Your father was a generous man. Do you know that I counseled him as well? Of course, you didn't. How silly. Well, he was an anomaly, you see. Such a strong personality: wise and intelligent. A jack of all trades, really. But we both know, he had some secrets, don't we, Fiona? I know you went pilfering through his personal things, so why is it that I am not allowed to do the same with your things, sweetie? It is only fair, isn't it?"

Her voice sounds eerily haunting while I'm all doped up.

"Well, we can just call it even, then, okay? Now, I am not sure what your plans are for your future, but I am going to go ahead and let you know my plans for your future. I plan to keep you here a long, long time, Fiona. Possibly even…forever, if I need to."

The last sentence resounds loudly and it is all I hear.

Forever.

As I come out of whatever paralyzed state Dr. Clark cast me into, I am sure I exude fear. I bend each of my fingers and toes to make sure I am able to move each and every muscle again. After sitting in the chair in Dr. Hall's office for what has felt like an eternity, I stand up and begin to walk – or rather, stumble – back to my room.

Is it possible for Dr. Clark to truly keep me here, drugged and captured, against my will?

What kind of twisted system is this anyway?

What kind of system allows such a thing? I remember, in group, the other day, a patient discussed her experience with the Courts. She mentioned being held in jail for three weeks while being heavily addicted to heroin. She had been arrested for crashing her car while high as all hell, and her bail was too expensive for her family to afford. So after starting withdrawal from the heroin her body began to shut down, probably from the profuse vomiting. The jail hospital had to admit her, she said. Strapped to her bed, of course. She was so dope-sick from withdrawal that she spent most of her jail sentence in the hospital; on our tax dollars, that is. All I could think about during this story was how our legal system is absolutely ass backwards. It makes no sense. And here I am locked in a prison myself. Unable to get out.

Corruption. That is what this is.

I finally make it back to my room, in shambles. Trisha – I know – can sense the fear in my eyes, and the wear and tear to my body from the overdose of Dilaudid.

"Fiona," she says, astonished. "You look like hell. Why don't you lie down? Have you not been sleeping well?" she asks.

"I have been sleeping just fine," I assure her as I take a seat on my bed while managing to just barely fake a smile.

"Oh well, maybe the lack of sunlight, then, is just showing on your face today," she decides quite harshly. I must look ghastly, I assume.

"Trisha," I say after a while. "Would it offend you if I could ask for some privacy, just for a little while? I don't mean to kick you out of your own room, I just need…a minute," I desperately ask her.

"Sure," she sincerely agrees. "I'll be back later."

She calmly walks out into the intimidating halls.

I sit for a moment in complete silence, wondering what my next plan of action should be at this point. Confronting Dr. Clark has brought a shocking turn for the worse. It has been clear to me for some time now that she was out to get me: to keep me 'sick.' But I had no idea, she would take it this far. Injecting me with paralyzing doses of potent drugs in order for me to comply is absolutely psychotic. And why do they need me in here so badly? Why do they want me to stay locked up? She is the one who needs to be locked up. Forever. Although, my body is able to respond to my mind's demands again, I feel just as paralyzed as I sit alone, unable to come up with any ideas on how to leave.

Chloe: October 2015
Acting Out

"Hey, Chloe? Can I talk to you for a moment?" Kaden's teacher asks after we get the boys fastened into their car seats.

"Sure." I shut the door and stand outside of the car with her so they can't hear.

"We have had a couple of issues with Kaden, both yesterday and today."

"What kind of issues?" I ask.

Kaden has never acted out in school before. He has always been that kid who is on his very best behavior in front of other people. This is shocking to me.

"Well, some kids were picking on him so – rightfully – he stood up for himself. But he was quite heated and ended up really hurting the other child. The child flipped backwards over a chair. Yesterday Kaden only shoved him, so I tried to leave it alone, but today he snapped. I'm sorry. I guess I should have told you yesterday, but I just didn't want to…I mean, with it being the first day…"

She is starting to sound really muffled to me now, like on Charlie Brown. Waa Waa…is all I can hear.

"Yeah, okay. Well, thanks for telling me. I will talk to him," I say, and start to get back in the car.

"Um…Miss Fields. The other parent is very upset, so I actually had to schedule a parent-teacher conference for tomorrow. Is five okay?"

"He isn't even quite six yet," I say, astonished.

"It's protocol. I'm sorry. I'll see you tomorrow."

"Wait. What was the kid picking on him about?" I ask as she starts to walk away.

She hesitates before saying, "He was making fun of him for having two mommies."

I get into the car and just sit there with the ignition off for a while. Neither of the boys says anything. We just sit in silence. I eventually ask if they want to go get some ice cream. Kaden seems confused. He is old enough to know he has done something wrong and I don't think he was expecting ice cream to be the punishment. Fiona calls me a few times while we are at the ice cream shop, but I don't answer. We just eat our ice cream together. Me and the boys.

"So, I heard about what happened at school, Kade," I finally say as we are finishing up. "I'm glad you stood up for yourself, buddy. But, you know, you really hurt that other boy. It's okay to tell him he is being mean, or that he needs to stop, but being physically violent isn't okay. You know that, right?" I ask him.

"I know, mommy," he says in his sweet little innocent voice.

"Well, I am sorry he made you feel embarrassed for having two mommies, and I am sorry that I have put you in a situation where people feel they have to make fun of – "

He interrupts me. "I love Fiona, mommy. I don't care that she is my mommy now. I want them to leave you alone. That's why I pushed him," he says.

I can't help but feel touched. He was actually standing up for Fiona and I.

"You are a good boy. You know that, right?" I ask him. "You have a good heart, baby."

"I'm sorry, mommy."

"It's okay, Kade. But we have to meet with the other kid's mommy tomorrow, okay? After school. To talk about everything. Fiona and I do. Not you. Okay?" I ask.

"Okay," he says, and we leave the ice cream shop and head home.

I know I need to call Trent before the school does, but I don't want to talk to him about the situation. He will only blame me and I can't handle any more blame right now. So, I drive home to talk to Fiona about it first.

"Alright, boys, go play in your room while mommy talks to Fiona real quick, OK?" I say as we walk in.

"Hey, Chloe. Where were you? I tried to call a bunch and I didn't know what to do about dinner so—"

"It's okay. I'm sorry," I say. "We just had ice cream, so they may not be hungry yet anyway."

"Ice cream?" she asks, confused.

"Kaden got in trouble today at school for pushing a boy over a chair who was making fun of him for having two mommies," I say abruptly.

"Sooo...he was rewarded with dessert first?" she asks, still really confused.

"He said he did it for us. That he didn't care that he has two mommies and that he just wanted them to leave us alone. I know that I shouldn't reward him for this violent behavior, but he is going through a lot and it just felt good to know he wasn't upset with me about it."

She interrupts. "And that he stood up for you. I get it, Chloe."

"Us. That he stood up for us. He said he loved you, Fiona."

"Wow. Poor little dude. Well, he's tougher than he looks, ay?" she says, and elbows me.

"Yeah, apparently so." We both laugh because that's all we can really do at this point. Fiona says she wants to come with me to the conference and there is no talking her out of it. I agree to let her come and decide to just let the school tell Trent. I avoid him until tomorrow. He doesn't call.

The following day, we barely make it to the school by five. We are literally running up to the door with the kids. I drop them off at the school daycare room before going in to meet with the teacher.

Trent is already there, of course, and I can see him sitting in her office, twiddling his thumbs. He looks up and sees us. He gives me a concerned look.

"Miss Fields. Fiona. Please sit down," says Kaden's teacher.

I look over and see the other child's parent. It is his father.

"This is Mr. Lewis. Curtis's father."

"Nice to meet you, man," Fiona says with her hand out. He doesn't accept the offer and sits still in his seat. "My son had to get three stitches," he says angrily.

"We will pay for any medical costs," Trent pipes up.

"I am more concerned with your son being a further nuisance at this school," he says.

"A nuisance?" I ask, heated.

"Yes, a nuisan – "

"We heard you," Fiona chimes in loudly. "Look, buddy, your precious son started the disagreement by being a bully to our little dude Kaden. Maybe you should talk to your son about respect for others and keeping his mouth shut unless he has something nice to say."

The teacher looks down at her desk before deciding not to say anything quite yet.

"He knows right from wrong," retorts Mr. Lewis, "And he knows that God doesn't approve of lesbian relationships. When he heard Kaden talk about having two mommies, he was just trying to relay a message that it was a sin."

I look over at Trent and he looks pretty angry now, too.

"Look. We don't want any more problems either, okay?" Trent says. "But let's leave God out of this one and stick to the point. Bullying isn't acceptable and neither was Kaden's violent outburst. So, both boys need to suffer the consequences of their actions."

Fiona is fuming. Maybe I should have left her at home, I think to myself.

The teacher agrees to separate them in class for now and make sure they are not in any of the same groups. We all start to walk out and Fiona walks right up to Mr. Lewis.

"Look. We know that you are the real problem. You are the one who doesn't approve of our lesbian relationship and your poor son knows no different. So my suggestion is that you keep your judgmental and homophobic opinions to yourself."

I walk out to Trent's car with him and Fiona goes to grab the boys from the daycare room.

"I'm sorry about all of this," I say.

"He's my kid, too," Trent says. "His genetics are half mine, I suppose."

"Yeah. Well, I'm the reason there was a confrontation at all. Because of my relationship with Fiona."

"Nah. You can't look at it like that, Chloe. There are always going to be obstacles now for you, but you are still the mother of my children and I won't let people make you feel bad for being who you are."

Wow. I am so impressed with Trent right now and how mature he is being.

"Thanks. You have no idea how good that feels, to hear you say that," I say, and give him a hug. The familiar touch of his tight jeans pressed against me brings back a comforting feeling.

"Well, how about I come grab the boys from Fiona's tomorrow night around six for the weekend? So you don't have to bring them to me this time."

"Yeah. That would be great, thanks. I'll see you then, Trent."

He smiles and heads to his car.

Fiona gets to the car with the boys a few minutes later. Her nasty expression conveys everything.

"Can you believe that guy?" she asks while buckling the boys in.

"Yeah, he was something else," I say.

"Get used to it, Chloe. Unfortunately, even though it is 2015, there are going to be people with the mindset of someone living in the 50s," she says, annoyed.

We don't say anything to Kaden about the situation on the way home and he doesn't ask.

Fiona: December 2015
Staying Clean

I wake up wearing the same clothes, I remember wearing yesterday. It is still dark outside and Trisha is curled up in her bed, snoring, with rollers in her hair.

I stand up and walk quickly to the bathroom to splash cool water on my face and change clothes.

As I step out into the halls, I realize it must be early. No one is awake but me, it appears. I walk down to the end of the hall where the Art Therapy room is and twist the door handle to see if it is unlocked yet. To my surprise it is open. I flip the lights on and begin to paint.

Hours later, I finally glance up at the clock and notice it is now mid-morning. I haven't had a bite to eat or drink, so I wander out of the Art room and toward the Barista. I grab a small coffee and a plain croissant and head to group.

Trying to focus only on myself and getting well and out of this place, I attempt to go in with a positive mind and outlook. I sit with my legs crossed in the usual group circle, Jade and Trisha at my sides.

"Good morning, ladies," Dr. Hall begins, in his usual cheery voice. "Today we will be playing another therapeutic game here in group," he explains.

I can only hope, it doesn't evoke lesbian thoughts for Jade this time.

"The game is called 'Fear in a Hat.' Has anyone heard of it?" he asks us.

No one answers.

"Okay, I will take that as a no. Well..." Dr. Hall begins to pass out miniature pencils and pieces of paper to each of us. "I want everyone to write down your biggest fear on the piece of paper, and after each of you is done, I want you to place your paper in this hat I have here. One at a time, each of you will open a piece of paper from the hat, not knowing whose fear is written on it, and read it aloud. I want you to then come up with a way to ease that fear. It is an anonymous game that I think will allow a fostering of interpersonal empathy for each other. Also, it might create solutions to your fears. So you may begin. And please take your time. There is no rush," he explains.

I stare at my small piece of paper and decide there is just not enough room to write all of my fears down. I go back and forth in my head about what I should write. I finally come up with something short and sweet. Something that fits on the paper we were provided.

I fold up my piece of paper and place it into the hat.

The first fear is read aloud.

"I fear that I will not be able to stay clean, once I get out of here."

The patient who has read the fear out loud suggests that to stay clean it may be useful to go to the twelve-step meetings and keep going to counseling once back home. She then adds that surrounding yourself with positive people is key to staying clean.

"Great advice," Dr. Clark announces.

Trisha draws a paper from the hat next. She reads it aloud. "I fear I will always self-destruct," Trisha reads. "Well, I think we all may fear that." She laughs, and then continues. "I think loving yourself and making sure to focus on that once you are out of here will help someone maybe not want to self-destruct anymore," Trisha suggests.

"I think that is a logical explanation, Trisha," Dr. Hall agrees. "Also, maybe jotting down things we love about ourselves would be another idea for a group exercise. What do you guys think?" he asks us. A few people nod their heads.

I draw a piece of paper out of the hat next. I read it to myself before reading it out loud. It barely fits on the paper. I clear my throat before beginning to read the novel which is now in front of me...

"My biggest fear is myself. I am afraid of myself in every way. I am afraid of my mind, my soul, my addiction, and my inner demons. I would rather be anyone else, besides me."

It sounds so terribly sad, to read this confession out loud. I look over and see Dr. Hall's face change as he feels pure empathy for this person, it seems.

"Well, I got a hard one," I say. "Hm...I am afraid of myself, too," I admit, hoping that this anonymous person may feel less alone this way. "I am definitely also afraid of my mind. But at the same time, I wouldn't want to be anyone but who I am. If you think for one second that any other person in this room is any more normal or secure than you, you are dead wrong. Everyone has their fears and their struggles, but that is what makes us alive. That is what makes us all human. Without it life would be...well, boring, maybe. My advice to you, Dear John, is this: embrace your fears, grab them by the neck and wrangle the shit out of them. They don't define you. You define them. Fear is not embedded in us: we aren't born fearful to walk, or fearful of monsters or scary faces; fear is learned. So, just as we learn to fear we can learn to not be afraid anymore. Those inner demons can be slain."

"Thank you, Fiona," Dr. Hall says, a bit stirred. "Very…insightful."

I feel a little embarrassed all of a sudden, having borne my soul in a room of strangers.

Jade goes next. She draws a card and looks right at me after reading it. I assume she believes it to be mine.

"My biggest fear is yet to come," she begins, reading, "But I will not let my fears of the unknown keep me weak. 'Ultimately we know deeply that the other side of every fear is freedom' – Mary Ferguson."

It is my paper. Of course, Jade got my paper.

Jade looks into my eyes and begins to offer me advice, because she knows this was my fear.

"Well, this person seems to already know the solution to their fears. To not let their fears break them down. To never let fear get in the way of being free. And I have to say I agree. Being scared is only an excuse. We all possess courage to do great things. To accomplish our dreams and live up to our potential, but it is only after we start living, and living our dreams and taking charge of our own lives and our own selves, that we can live up to our true capabilities. So my advice is to stay strong and power on, I guess."

Dr. Hall looks at Jade, then looks at me. I think he understand she knows it was my card, and so does he.

One by one, the rest of the group draws cards, offering their advice to ease the anonymous person's fears. As the end of the pile approaches and the hat is almost empty, Dr. Hall explains we have an uneven number of people and asks if someone would please draw again.

"Fiona," he suggests. "Will you be so gracious as to go a second time, and draw the last card?" he asks.

"I guess, sure," I say while opening up the final card from the hat.

I read it aloud without reading it in my head first. I am pretty over this game now.

"I fear for my safety. There are some crazy people in this ward. Fiona is fucking insane…Wait. What?" I say, confused as to what I have just read. Am I hallucinating, or did someone really write on their card – the card I was asked to draw from the hat – that I am insane and they are afraid of me?

"Fiona?" Dr. Hall says, acting as if I am psychotic now. "Would you like to re-read the card, dear?" he says.

I glance down at the piece of paper and open up my eyes wider, in order to read it correctly this time. I read it in my head. Yes. It is really there. I read it correctly the first time. I can't read this again.

"Um, I am not feeling so well, Dr. Hall," I decide to admit.

"Fiona, why don't you hand me the card and I will read it, sweetie."

I hand it to him and sit looking down at my lap, humiliated and confused.

He looks at the piece of paper, as I watch him out of the corner of my eye now.

"I fear for my safety," Dr. Hall begins. "There are some crazy people in this world – Not ward," he corrects me. "Fear is fucking insane," he finishes. "Aha. So, Fiona. Common mistake, sweetie," Dr. Hall announces to everyone, and I notice people are looking at each other as if I am actually insane and psychotic, as the paper suggests.

No, that is not what the paper said. I read it twice, and I am not insane. It said my name. I know it did. What the fuck is going on?

As people start to stand up and leave group, I remain seated in the circle. Dr. Hall smiles at me in a creepy way before grabbing his things and walking out with the rest of the patients. All except Jade leave, talking amongst themselves.

"Fiona?" Jade asks me while still sitting on the carpet beside me. "Are you okay? I mean, are you feeling okay today?"

"No. I'm not, Jade. I am really not. If I told you that Dr. Hall and Dr. Clark were evil people – I mean really demented – would you believe me?" I ask her desperately.

"What are you talking about? Is this about the stuff Dr. Clark stole from you?" Jade asks me, concerned. "Did you confront her?"

"Yes. I did confront her. And she stabbed me with a hypodermic needle full of a huge dose of Dilaudid," I blurt out suddenly.

"What?" Jade says with pure fear in her eyes.

I can't tell if she is scared that what I am saying is the truth or if she believes, like the rest of them, that I am insane.

"I know what I read on that card, Jade. I think Dr. Hall wrote that and that he chose me to read the card aloud so that I would appear crazy. So that when he and Dr. Clark try and convince the Court or whoever that I am to stay here he will have some proof. Please tell me you believe me, Jade. I need you to believe me," I beg.

"I don't know, Fiona. Those are some pretty serious accusations you are making."

"Do you think I am insane, Jade?"

"No. I absolutely don't."

"Then why would I make this up?"

"Okay. So they are evil; what now? How can you prove any of this? Beg for a drug test, to show that Dilaudid you weren't prescribed is in your system?"

I can tell she genuinely believes me now. It feels nice to have someone on my side.

"I don't know what to do. I have no ideas as of now," I confess, ashamed.

Dr. Hall walks back into the conference room, where Jade and I are still sitting alone on the carpet, cross-legged and awkward.

"Excuse me, Fiona. I hate to interrupt, but there is a matter I must talk to you about."

Of course, there is, I angrily think to myself. What now?

"May I speak to you?" he asks me, inferring that he would like either for Jade to leave us alone, or for me to get up instantly and follow him to some secret lair, I assume.

"Can't you just speak to me here, in front of Jade?" I say flippantly while giving him a wide-eyed stare. I don't care whether he knows how infuriated I am with him now. He needs to know that I am aware of what he and Dr. Clark are up to.

"I suppose, Fiona. But it may be something you would rather I speak to you in private about…for your sake."

"Nope. Go right ahead."

"Alright then. You had an early paint session this morning. Am I correct, Fiona?" he asks me.

"Yes," I respond, wondering what this is about and how he knows about me being in the Art Room early this morning.

"Well, your painting…it was…rather disturbing, sweetheart. I have it in my office and I would like to discuss it with you. We are just a bit concerned at this point, with your erratic behavior and lack of concern for your outbursts and all…"

"My outbursts? What outbursts? And my painting was not disturbing in the least…It is abstract, maybe, sure – but disturbing? I don't think so." I think back to what I painted this morning. I used pastel colors and painted my usual portrait-like art, this time of Chloe smelling a beautiful flower in my father's garden. Although it was abstract, I know she and I would know where the scene took place. I wanted to give it to her the next time I see her.

"Fiona, I would like to see you in my office, now."

"I didn't even initial my artwork. How do you even know I painted it?"

"We have cameras in all of the rooms here in the center, sweetie. Safety precaution, of course."

"Well I highly doubt you can find something 'disturbing' about my pastel portrait of my girlfriend, smelling a rose! But, yeah, sure…let me just follow you to your office." I am basically yelling now, confused as to what he could possibly find 'scary' in my painting.

"It's okay, Fiona," Jade says. "We can just catch up later."

"Fine." I try to shrug it off.

I follow Dr. Hall to his office and do not say a word the whole way there.

As I walk in, I see a dark painting lying on his desk. The color scheme is very dark: definitely no pastels. It is full of charcoal tones. The silhouette of a female figure sits in the bottom corner of the canvas, her face down in her lap; she is holding a knife and the only vibrant color in the painting is red. Red blood spattered about the bottom of the painting, as if this figure felt shame for having hurt someone, or herself. At least this is my interpretation of the dramatic painting.

I did not paint this.

Chloe: October 2015
The City That Never Sleeps

I can't help but tear up, playing with the boys, knowing that I won't be seeing them for a whole week. This will be the longest I have ever gone without being with them. It is going to be tough on all of us. I know they are in good hands, at least, and Trent promises to Skype me over the week and call often. I stay at Trent's until they go to sleep so that I can kiss them each goodnight one last time.

"I'll pray for Fiona's father, Chloe," Trent says as I am walking out to my car, "And for Fiona. That she can find peace."

"Thanks, Trent. It means a lot," I say, and get into my car to drive back to Fiona's house.

I hurry home to pack. Our flight leaves at ten tomorrow morning so we have to be out of the house by at least 8 AM. I walk in and find Fiona still pacing from room to room, gathering things she might need, then throwing them carelessly into her big suitcase.

"How did it go?" she asks me, still not focusing on anything besides the packing.

"Fine," I say, and grab my suitcase from the top of the closet.

I join in on the frantic packing.

"What about Marvin?" I ask as I look down at him panting nervously beside my leg. He can clearly tell we are going on a trip.

"I already talked to Viv and Winter and they agreed to keep him for as long as we need," Fiona reassures me. Man, she really has this all figured out. "Oh, and Chloe? Maggie says she has all of the days covered at Mugged. I called her to make sure, while you were at Trent's."

So, it is all worked out now. I am going to go to New York City with Fiona to comfort her while her dad takes a turn for the worse. I won't see my boys for a week and I will be in a completely new place in an inevitably sad environment. Why am I suddenly regretting the decision to go with her? She needs me, and I need her to know I am there for her, but I am terrified of what things will be like when we get to New York. I finish packing and force Fiona to call it quits, too. We relax for a while together before drifting off to sleep.

I wake up and think about what a terrifying dream I had last night. I dreamt our plane turned into a giant butterfly and we were trying to hold on to the wings, but inevitably lost our grip and fell into a huge body of water. I am still trying not to drown when I wake up gasping for air. I wake Fiona with my loud breathing.

"Chloe? You okay?" she asks.

"Yeah. Just a strange dream," I tell her.

We get dressed, have a cup of coffee and then roll our suitcases out to her car. Traffic isn't too bad, so we end up getting to the airport with time to spare. Fiona decides she wants to browse the gift shop, so we peruse the card selection and decide on the least mushy get-well card we can find.

On the plane Fiona is quiet. She sleeps for a while on my shoulder. She refuses any food anyone offers her. I don't want to push her to talk about anything so I let her rest as much as she can. We get into the City quickly and immediately take a cab to the hospital. I finally decide to bring up her father as we are pulling up.

"So, have you talked to your mom or dad to see what room he is in? Or if by any chance he has already been released from the hospital? Do they even know you are coming, or me?" I realize I just asked her about five questions all at once. I guess the no-talking thing was counterproductive after all.

"Um. No. They don't know we are here. And I am pretty sure he will still be in the hospital; I have a gut feeling. I will just ask at the nurses' station which room he is in when we get there, okay?"

She grabs my hand and gives me a half smile. She looks as if she is comforting me. I realize I am not very good at hiding my emotions from her. She probably senses I am nervous. We walk to the elevator, suitcases still in hand, and eventually locate Mr. Lennox's room. He is still in the hospital. I make eye contact with Veronica, who is sitting outside of his hospital room as we walk up.

"Oh my gosh!" she exclaims. "Fiona! Chloe! You didn't have to come here. What are you even doing here, darling?" she says, taking Fiona's hand and squeezing it tightly. Her rings dig into her flesh as she closes her fists and I think: Wow. That must hurt.

"I never heard back from you, mom, and I had to see him," Fiona explains.

"I know, sweetie. I meant to call. I have just been so preoccupied with your father. He has been sleeping a lot and he has no one to take care of him but me, you know, and then Junior has been having to handle everything with the coffee shop..."

"Mom." Fiona smiles. "I know. It's okay. That's why I am here. To help out. That's why we are both here, okay?" she says comfortingly.

"He looks pretty weak in that bed, Fiona. I don't want you to be alarmed, honey," Veronica warns.

"Can we see him now, mom?" Fiona asks.

"He is asleep, but there are a couple of chairs by his bed if you two want to check on him, yes."

Fiona and I walk into her father's hospital room. It is dark and all I can hear are the breathing machines. I watch as Fiona takes in the severity of how weak her father actually is. There is a wheelchair next to the bed, and it isn't one of those hospital wheelchairs: it looks like one he has purchased, very hi-tech. He is asleep and looks even frailer than before. He is barely recognizable to me. Fiona brings her hands to her face to cover her tears. All I can do is hold her as she takes everything in.

We sit in his room for two hours. He is still sleeping. We haven't spoken at all. Fiona just keeps looking at him in anticipation. Waiting for him to wake up. Veronica comes in periodically, asking if we want anything to eat or drink, but Fiona just shakes her head 'no' each time. Finally, Mr. Lennox begins to wake up.

"Daddy?" Fiona stands up and takes his hand in hers.

"Fiona," Mr. Lennox says in a surprised voice.

His eyes still look very much the same. Warm and inviting.

"How are you feeling?" she asks. "Can I get you anything?"

"What are you two girls doing here?" he asks.

"We wanted to be here for you," I say.

"What about Mugged, Chloe?"

Of course, that would be his second question.

"Mugged is just fine, sir," I say. "Maggie, the Assistant Manager, has everything under control for a whole week."

"Well, what a pleasant surprise waking up to you both," he says in a scratchy, weak voice.

He coughs loudly and Fiona immediately searches for a glass of water and hands it to him.

"Thank you," he says, and takes a small sip. "Well, they say I can leave here tomorrow as long as all of my tests come back okay," he informs us.

A nurse comes in and checks all of Mr. Lennox's vitals. She gives him some medication to take and warns him to not eat anything difficult to swallow from now on. She hands him a protein shake, but he shakes his head and says he has no appetite. He seems uncomfortable with us being in here and seeing him like this.

"Ladies, why don't you head to my house and get settled? Here is some cab money, or you can call Rick, my limo driver, and he can pick you up downstairs," he suggests.

"Are you sure, dad?" Fiona asks.

"Yes, dear. Veronica won't leave me alone, so I am sure, I will have plenty of help tonight," he insists.

Fiona gives him a big kiss and we head downstairs to flag a cab.

As we pull up to Mr. Lennox's home, I can feel how big my eyes are getting. Fiona pulls out a gate opener from her bag, which I didn't even know she had, and this huge cast-iron gate opens for us.

"Thanks," she says to the cab driver after we get out of the cab.

"Whoa," I say as I stand there and take in this immaculate stone mansion.

"Welcome to my father's gaudy home," Fiona jokes.

"It's beautiful," I say.

We are greeted by what I would call a butler as we walk in. A maid of some sort takes our bags and hugs Fiona. She seems really sweet. She brings us fresh towels in case we want to shower, and lets us know dinner is at six in the main dining room. I walk around Fiona's room and realize it doesn't look like anything she would decorate. There is floral wallpaper, which I absolutely love, but I know Fiona didn't pick it out. There are huge, ruffled throw pillows on her enormous bed, and a pink lamp on her bedside table. Clearly Fiona did not choose the color scheme for the room.

"So. It must have been pretty rough growing up a Lennox, huh?" I ask jokingly.

She glares at me with those jet-blue eyes. "Very funny, Chloe. As they say: Money can't buy you happiness," she explains.

"I know. I am just messing with you, baby," I say, and put my arms around her thin waist. "It's clear your father tried to suppress your tomboy side; that's for sure."

"Yeah, no shit," she agrees. "He basically was convinced that if he showered me in enough pink flowers it would rub off on me."

I look at Fiona, dressed in her whitewashed jeans and wife-beater, with a wide-brimmed hat covering her boyish haircut, and finally say, "Well, it didn't work."

We both laugh for a long time and then decide a bath in her huge, clawfoot tub would be nice before dinner.

There is a large mirror hanging in front of her bathtub and I can't help but keep looking at us the whole time we soak. We are an odd match, maybe, on the outside. Me with my long, blonde hair and hardly any artwork drawn on my skin; and her with her short, dark hair and androgynous appearance, marked with tattoos everywhere. Yet we are so picture-perfect in this moment. I wish someone else was here to snap a photo of us while in the tub. Lying peacefully together like we have done so many times now.

We eat dinner in our pajamas in the fancy, main dining room. Just us. And of course, the butler and the maid, standing awkwardly in the corners, seemingly guarding the huge table. I think Fiona can sense how ridiculous I feel in her Bert and Ernie tee shirt, which I never gave back to her after that first night I wore it. I am sitting there feeling that I stick out like a sore thumb. We both do, really. Fiona starts to laugh quietly and I can't help but join in. All of a sudden, we are both cracking up, awkwardly trying to hide the emotions we are actually feeling. That her father is dying. That we are here for what may be the last time with him.

Fiona: December 2015
Pitch-Black

As I sit confined in Dr. Hall's office – having to face the unpleasant task of explaining to him that I have not painted this morbid picture that lies on the desk in front of me – all I can think of is Chloe: of how desperately I need her in this moment. Or maybe I just want her. I long for her to defend me, the way she has so many times before to my family. But this – this is different. This is a prison sentence. One I don't deserve. This is entrapment. These two corrupt doctors are definitely out to get me. There is now no other logical explanation left. I decide that all I have on my side is the truth. I have to simply tell the truth and keep telling it until it – I hope – sets me free.

"I didn't paint that – the picture on your desk, if that is the one you are so concerned about. I didn't paint it. I painted a pretty, pastel picture of my fiancée Chloe. The girl in the navy polka-dotted dress, who came here on visitor day? Did you see her? Well, the painting I did this morning was of her smelling a yellow rose. In my father's garden. I wish I could help you more, tell you who did paint that darker painting sitting there," I tell him, pointing at the charcoal canvas, "But I don't know who did, sir. Sorry."

"Fiona, as I said, we have cameras in the rooms. It clearly shows you were the only one painting in the early morning. Although the video doesn't show a close-up of the painting, you are the only one in the room and this was the only painting in there when I cleaned up today."

My mind feels utterly blank, all of a sudden. I start to wonder whether I took my painting to my room with me, or whether I left it in the Art Therapy room. I can't seem to remember...

"Well, I don't know what to tell you." I am getting angry now. I can no longer hide my emotions, nor do I even try. What is the point? Apparently, they have some pretty great tricks up their sleeves anyway.

"Fiona. I am concerned about you, sweetie. You have been through a great deal the past year. I know you mentioned wanting to go home, but that is not in the cards for you right now."

"Fuck it. I'm out," I declare, and try to stand up to leave the room. Before I make it the two feet to the door, he blocks my path.

"Listen carefully. You are showing signs of schizophrenic tendencies. It may be in your best interest if we try you on new meds."

"Do I have a choice?"

"No."

I exit the office, leaving my dignity behind with Dr. Hall. It is evident to me that my freedom is gone. I have let it slip away.

I make it to my room, seeking refuge from the institutional monsters that threaten me, and I sit down on my bed. I start to think about the psychological thrillers I used to watch with my dad when I was growing up. We both loved a good horror film or a psychological thriller. Now I feel like a character in one of those movies. These places – these institutions – may be just as corrupt as they appear in the thrillers. Or maybe I am actually insane. It is hard for me to distinguish what is real anymore. My mind is so foggy. All the medications I am on and all the accusations that have been made confuse me. Maybe I did draw that picture. Did I? I don't remember doing it. How could I do something and not remember it?

Maybe the longer you stay in these places, the more insane you become. This is the longest I have spent in an institution without going home at all: without any freedom.

Marjorie has been in Living Waters for years. She is definitely a little eccentric upstairs, if not completely fried. Was the institution the cause of her insanity? The very thing supposed to fix the patient may be causing mental alteration. I mean, not everybody reacts to a certain type of drug or therapy in the same way. That's why some people have to try several medications – antidepressants, for example – before finding the right one for them. Maybe certain people don't function well when locked up, even though it is meant to be a path to recovery. I am not functioning in here anymore; that's for sure. I am basically just breathing. And barely breathing, at that.

I close my eyes as I lie back onto my pillow, and can only hope that when I wake up this reality will turn out to have been a nightmare. A horrifying nightmare – that's all. Before drifting off to sleep, I try to make out figures in the black inside of my eyelids with my eyes closed. I can almost see Chloe. I see her running around with the boys at the park in the hot Florida sunshine. I can almost feel the heat on my arms. I feel someone wrap me in a warm blanket as I fade out of my reality and into a real nightmare.

Come on, Chloe! You have to hurry!

I glance down the never-ending hallway before us. Having no shoes, we try to find traction on the slick tile floor of the institution. A warm – no, hot – sensation overtakes my body as I finally reach Chloe's delicate fingers and pull her down the hallway. A flame shows itself from one of the rooms.
It is Jade's room.
Jade walks out through the fire, unscathed by the flames. Her facial expression is that of a devilish spawn of Satan. Her pyrotechnics have caused the entire facility to go up in flames and Chloe and I can't seem to run fast enough to get away from the fire. Chloe trips and falls and there is a pool of blood beneath her.
"Go without me, Fiona," she calmly tells me as Jade reaches her.
"No; never." And I rush back towards her to scoop her up, determined to throw her over my shoulders and carry her all the way to the Exit.
Before I can get my arms underneath her to lift her, Jade lifts her first. Jade holds Chloe like a child. Chloe lifelessly gives in and curls up to her.

In an instant they are both gone. Vanished into thin air.
"Ahhh!" I wake up with a shrill shriek.
"Fiona! It's okay. You were just having a bad dream," Trisha says as she shakes me to try to bring me back to consciousness. "You are awake now, Fiona. It's okay," Trisha says in a soothing voice to me as she gently touches my arm.
"Trisha. This is worse than I thought. I can't – I can't do this anymore." I suddenly feel a panic attack starting. I put my head between my legs and take several deep breaths, realizing that Trisha has no idea about what is going on in my life, or with the doctors. Jade is the only one who knows. And quite frankly I am still a bit shaken up from having her be such a villain in my all-too-vivid nightmare just now.
"Do what, Fiona? Look, it is going to be okay. You haven't even been here very long, sweetie. It takes some getting used to. You know that, though, don't you? I mean, this isn't your first rodeo, am I right? You just need to relax and let them help you. You will be back home with your family in no time."
"I need to call Chloe," I announce, barely recovered from my minor panic attack. I rush out into the halls and sprint to the phones. "I need to make a phone call, please," I desperately ask the receptionist.
"Okay, but Dr. Hall has a special announcement in a few minutes so make it quick," she says.
I dial Chloe's number as quickly as my shaky fingers will allow. "Chloe, it's Fiona. It's me."

"Fiona! I was just thinking about you, baby," she says, and I immediately feel a sense of peace, hearing her soothing tone over the line.

"Listen. Chloe. This…situation with the doctors is worse than I thought. I mean, with Dr. Clark stealing my letters and all. It has gotten a lot worse since then. I tried to confront her about it. I tried to stand up for myself, like my normal, no-bullshit self. But it didn't go well. She stabbed me – "

"She what?" Chloe interrupts me, sounding shocked.

"I mean with a needle. She doped me up real good. Overdosed me on Dilaudid. It was terrible. I couldn't move…Anyway, I am scared, Chloe. I can admit that now. I am scared."

I look down and find both my hands are trembling just from talking about all of this to Chloe.

"Fiona. I am going to come see you. I will be there Sunday, okay? Can you just try to hang in there until then, sweetie?"

Sunday is a few days from now. I honestly don't know how to hang in there anymore. I am barely surviving.

"Sure," I answer, trying to sound as convincing as possible. I don't want to scare Chloe any more than I already have.

After I hang up the phone, a loud voice comes over the loudspeakers. It is Dr. Hall. He clears his throat and it sounds as if he doesn't realize he can be heard yet.

"Am I on?" he asks, still confused. "Oh! Hello, folks! I am sorry. Technical difficulties. So! Today we have a special treat for all of you. We are going to be taking a surprise field trip. Everybody needs to get to their rooms and put on some comfortable shoes, use the restroom or whatever else it is you ladies do, and meet me downstairs in the lobby in half an hour. Okay? See you soon! It is going to be a fun day, ladies!"

I don't want to go on a field trip. I don't have the mental capacity to enjoy anything right now. I just have to make it to Sunday so I can see Chloe. She will know what to do. I know she will.

I head back to my room to put on my Converse sneakers and, sure enough, I run right into Dr. Hall on the way.

"Fiona! I think you, especially, are going to love our outing today. I look forward to seeing you in the lobby in thirty."

He walks off and smiles back at me with piercing eyes that I am pretty sure he is able to shoot lasers out of. I can't help but make a baffled face. I scurry off to my room to get myself together before this outing he has planned. Trisha is already tying up her neon Nikes when I walk in to our room.

"Fiona. You look better. Did your fiancée calm you down?" she asks me with a smile.

"Yeah, she did."

"So, where do you think we are going?" Trisha asks excitedly. I can't seem to understand how anyone could be excited in this place. For all I know we are going to the meat factory to be slaughtered.

"I don't know. I hope it is relaxing, wherever it is." I try to sound optimistic.

Jade walks into our room suddenly. "Yeah, me too," Jade says. "Maybe we are all getting massages," she suggests sarcastically. It does make me smile a little. Her sarcasm has always been something I can relate to. She reminds me of myself sometimes. Her humor does, at least.

Everyone is present in the lobby, ready for our excursion, when Trisha and I arrive. I notice Jade over in the corner, waving at me. I try to act as if I don't see her. I still can't shake that dream where she set the whole place on fire. It was like a scene straight out of Carrie.

"Okay. Let's get to the buses!" Dr. Hall waves us all outside and we walk onto a few buses and take a seat. The sunshine is almost blinding to me, having not been outside very much in the past couple of months. I have to squint for the first few minutes until my eyes adjust. I take a seat in the very back of one of the buses, hoping for some solitude. Jade finds me.

"Fiona! Hey. Mind if I sit with you?"

At least she asked. "Nope. Go ahead," I say, and smile as sincerely as I can.

"Great. I have been wanting to know what happened with Dr. Hall earlier. About the painting and all. You seemed pretty shaken up about everything. I mean," she continues in a whisper, "You told me Dr. Clark stabbed you with a needle. That is pretty crazy. What did Dr. Hall do when he took you to his office, Fiona? You can tell me."

"Nothing." I am scared to tell Jade anything more right now. I realize I have said too much already. Not having Chloe by my side through all of this has left me no choice but to confide in someone here, but at this point confiding in Jade has maybe not been the best decision, after all. She seems too invested now. I don't want her to get dragged into all of this. It isn't safe.

"Nothing? Was it just a mistake, then? It wasn't your painting?"

"No. It wasn't mine."

It is the truth. At least, I am telling her the truth.

Chloe: October 2015
Spiraling

I have a hard time getting Fiona out of the car when we arrive at her house. She leans on me and drags her feet on the pavement the whole way inside. I plop her down as softly as I can onto the couch. She jerks awake suddenly.

"Huh?" she asks me, startled and confused.

"We are home," I mumble.

"I'm drunk," she exclaims, as if I hadn't noticed.

"Yes…you are," I agree.

"I'm sorry, Chloe." She slurs her words.

"I know. You have had a rough night. Why don't you slip off your pants and get some sleep?" I say as I try to unbutton her tight jeans.

"Chloe. Don't check me back into rehab." She looks at me, terrified.

"Rehab?"

I start to remember the conversation I had with Viv that night she brought Marvin home, and her saying she almost had to check Fiona into a center. Something about her spiraling out of control. But she said she almost did. Not that she had.

"Have you been to a rehab before?" I ask her, expecting an honest answer now that her inhibitions are extremely lowered by all the alcohol.

"I have been to lots," she admits.

"For what, Fiona?"

"For drinking too much, for drugs, for being GAY," she says mockingly.

Wow. How have I not known this? Do I even know her at all?

Fiona passes out soon afterward. I can't sleep. I lie awake next to her on the couch, wondering why she hasn't shared this with me before. It all makes sense to me, though; her struggling with addiction. She has had a bad relationship with her family. She doesn't drink often now – well, other than tonight – and she has made it clear her father did not accept her being gay. Also, Viv warned me she was depressed before she met me. I guess I just didn't realize how depressed she must have been. Viv's fear of her 'relapsing' might be valid at this point. Maybe Fiona and I are more alike than I thought. I have struggled with drugs and alcohol as well, in my past. But that is all it is now: my past. I don't want this to be our future. Her spiraling out of control, binge-drinking to cope with emotions, she has a hard time expressing. I am fearful of how her dad passing away will inevitably affect her. I love her so much, I think as I stroke her hair while she lies there sleeping next to me. Well, passed-out, really. She is still perfect to me, I think. Maybe perfection is not a flawless person who has no skeletons in her closet, or acts the 'right' way all of the time; maybe perfection is finding the person you believe is perfect for you despite all of their scars. I love Fiona's scars, and I feel a sense of peace knowing she is not as perfect as I once thought.

I wake up the next morning to find Fiona vomiting profusely into the toilet. I try to hold her hair, as she has done for me, and not vomit myself. She looks at me, horrified, when she is finally through.

"I'm so sorry, Chloe. I don't even remember last night," she admits.

"Yeah, I kind of figured that would be the case," I say as nicely as possible.

"Was I a total ass at dinner?" she asks.

"Pretty much," I assure her.

"Oh God. I will call Trent and Aubrey and apologize later," Fiona promises.

"I forgive you," I say. "But there is something I need to talk to you about."

She looks puzzled.

"When you were intoxicated last night, you admitted to having been to a few rehabs before, and that you may have an alcohol or drug problem?" I ask, concerned.

"Right. That." She starts to look as if she somewhat remembers saying it. "Yeah. I had a hard time in high school, fitting in, as you can maybe imagine. My mom made me hide a lot of feelings, but people clearly knew I was a lesbian at school. Well, I'm sure my dad knew I was gay well before the time I actually came out to him. So he sent me to a few rehabs after finding out I was drinking and using drugs. I will admit that I drank too much, and I have a hard time only drinking a little, but it felt a lot like he was trying to counsel the gay out of me, if you know what I mean. The therapy was geared more towards God this and God that. Anyway, I stopped drinking liquor heavily a couple of years ago. Actually, I stopped drinking all together for a while. You can see why."

I start to understand why her family warned me that she was prone to reckless behavior. It was because she is. I can't let things with her dad make her relapse.

"Fiona. I had no idea. I would have never let you order that Jack and Coke…or three of them."

"Yeah, I know. But I can take care of myself. It was just a minor slip-up. I wasn't expecting my dad to get this sick so quickly. And without me being there to comfort him."

"So do you think you will head back up to New York soon?" I ask apprehensively.

"I have to, Chloe. I have to say goodbye."

I still can't believe Mr. Lennox is as bad as Veronica has made it seem. The people I knew with A.L.S. lived months after they lost their voices and mobility. Their quality of life was poor, but they didn't pass away for a long time after losing those things.

"I want to go with you, Fiona. I want to be there for you this time…"

"I know, Chloe. I just don't know how we can make that possible, with the kids, and Mugged. Maybe you can just come for a few days again. You can say goodbye to my dad and then head back here to the boys."

"How long are you planning on staying?" I ask. I feel nervous waiting for her to respond. I am not sure I can handle another three weeks without her here. I feel so selfish even inquiring if she has a time frame. She should stay as long as she needs. I will still be here when she gets back; he won't. I suddenly feel an ache in my soul, thinking of that concept: the concept of her father passing away. I haven't known him long, but he has been a big part of my life, and my future. He has given me the opportunity to make a living for myself and my boys. Letting me have the chance to manage Mugged has been a huge blessing. I have to say thank you to Mr. Lennox one last time. To let him know how much I appreciate everything he has done for us.

Fiona finally responds. "I have no idea how long I will be there, Chloe. I don't want to jeopardize my job or my future here, but I need some closure, before he gets too sick to respond. Before he can't acknowledge that I am there, or that he can hear me…" Fiona starts to cry suddenly and puts her face in her hands, still sitting there on the bathroom floor, vulnerable and childlike. She looks so sad and helpless in the fetal position.

"I'm coming with you, even if I have to bring the boys this time," I say to her, there on the tile floor of the bathroom.

Has it come to this? I have to protect her from spiraling out of control. She needs me there this time; I know she does.

We stand up eventually, off the cold tile in the bathroom. I get Fiona a big glass of water and we plop down onto the couch for a few minutes before we have to rush to get ready to leave for work.

"Fiona," I say softly. "I want you to know that I love you just the same. I don't want you to be embarrassed now that I know the truth. I mean about the spiraling and the rehabs and the drinking and all. I have my demons, too. You know that. Perfection to me isn't the same as I thought it was before. Back when I was searching and searching for this perfect fairy tale of a life. What you and I have is perfect. Demons and all..."

She looks up at me and smiles as if she truly understands exactly the point I am trying to make. She doesn't need to say anything. She takes my hand and squeezes it tightly. That is enough conformation for me.

I try to keep busy through the day. I keep picturing Mr. Lennox and what he will be like when we get there. How helpless he must feel. I can imagine having been such a strong working man his entire life; this disease must make him feel completely altered. Completely diminished.

"We do the best we can with the hand we are dealt," I remember Trent saying to me that day. The day he listened to me sob my eyes out about Fiona and him and the battles I was fighting inside. I want to make the best possible life for me and my boys, and for Fiona and my future. At this point I assume her father may not tell her about the letters he discovered of hers. The love letters. Maybe he will just play dumb, as if they got left behind as she was packing that day. But he has already confessed to me that the last letter was a proposal and it is hard for me to forget that, even in all the chaos I have been through the past week. I want to marry Fiona. I want to take advantage of the freedom we now have to do so. I remember the feeling I had when I realized Trent might propose, years ago. I remember feeling anxious, but more in a logistical kind of way than I feel now. Now I feel more like I have this magnetic pull to complete Fiona. And she has to complete me. And that we won't be complete without professing our love for each other in some type of ceremony.

I still need to figure out the specifics of a gay wedding. As I start to think about the ceremony and picture Fiona and I there, both equal parts, I suddenly realize just that. We are both completely equal in this relationship. We are both female. This means that I don't necessarily have to wait for her to propose at all, this time, do I? I mean, Fiona and I definitely haven't succumbed to the gender roles at all in our relationship. She pays for meals sometimes, just as I do. She takes out the trash when she notices it is full, just like I do. And we both can master killing a spider or any bug now. She may look more like the male role on the outside, but she is just as much of a female as I am. Can't I propose to her? I realize that without any doubt I one-hundred-percent can. I have to talk to Trent about going with Fiona to New York for a few days. I have to give her something good to think about in order to stop the spiraling before it is too late.

I am running late after work today so Trent – or Aubrey, I assume – has picked up the boys, and I am driving to fetch them from Trent's apartment. I know I will have to talk to Trent about leaving for New York, yet again. I wonder if he will be upset or think I am a bad mother for leaving the kids with him again for a while. Or if I will end up having to take them with me. I discussed the situation at work today with the assistant manager. Luckily, she has no family and can cover my shifts again. Now all I have left to do is bare my heart to Trent about the predicament I am in.

Only Trent's car is in the parking lot when I arrive, so I hope he is alone: without Aubrey. I walk in and inform the boys I need to talk to daddy for a few minutes before we leave.

"What's up?" he asks. "How's Fiona? Has she recovered from last night?" He rolls his eyes.

"Yeah. About that, I am sorry," I say, and realize what a pain my relationship with Fiona might seem to him after this.

"It's okay. I know she is going through a lot with her dad. I am sure that's why she overdrank and acted a fool," he says, and laughs. I still don't find the situation very funny, but he doesn't know about the rehabs.

"Yes. I am sure that is the case. And Trent, about that. Her dad isn't doing well. Her mom has called Hospice now and it is just a waiting game at this point," I say.

"Oh wow, that soon, huh? I do remember it being a bad disease," he says, shaking his head.

"I need to go with her back up to New York. To say goodbye," I blurt out.

"Okay," he says. "And you want me to keep the boys for another, what, a week or so, Chloe?"

"Something like that, yeah. Maybe not a week. Probably just a few days. It is hard to get away from Mugged right now, with it being close to the holidays," I say.

"Right. Let me talk it over with the school and my mom, and Aubrey."

"I know I've had to lean on you a lot with them lately," I admit. "And I want you to know it won't always be this way and that I just really appreciate it."

"I know," he says, and helps me gather the boys' things before we head home.

Once we get home, I let Fiona know that I am able to go with her to New York. She seems relieved, but also a bit scared at the same time. I can't read her well enough to know whether she is more scared about her father's inevitable death, or whether she is scared that I will have some manic attack and run home scared shitless this time. Either way, I know the plan I have for her is genuine. That I want to propose while we are there. In front of her dad. So he can see how sincere my intentions are. It was something he confided in me about. Him being nervous that I would break her heart after he was no longer here to save her. He needs to know that won't happen. That I will protect her now. Forever.

After the boys fall asleep, I creep into their room and watch them, all snuggled tight in their blankets, dreaming. I kiss each of them on the cheek and say out loud, "Mommy loves you, angels." I stare at them for a long time, lying there so peacefully, the portrait Fiona painted of all of us at the beach in the background. They are blessed, I think to myself. To have so many people that love them and care about them. I'm not upset with Trent anymore about Aubrey. She is just one more person that loves our boys and wants the best for them, and for Trent. He deserves to feel the happiness I feel now with Fiona. He is worthy of that too. Fiona finds me watching the boys from their doorway.

"They were tuckered out, huh?" she asks, putting her arm around me.

"Yeah. They were," I agree.

We tiptoe to her bedroom and crawl under the covers. Fiona's skin feels so warm. So alive. I run my hands over all of her tattoos.

"What are you doing?" she asks, confused.

"Just admiring your skin," I say. Maybe that was a creepy way of putting it, I think to myself.

"It's pretty…colorful…and busy, huh?" she asks with a big smile.

"I love it," I say. "It completely defines you."

"I like that way of looking at it," she says. "That it defines me." She says it proudly.

"You are like a history book. Filled with pages of memories and important events," I add.

"What if you hadn't walked into the tattoo shop that day?" she asks me. "I mean, what if you didn't have that impulse to just get that caterpillar tattoo that day?"

She looks at me with her lips close to mine.

"I don't know," I say honestly. "I mean, I would like to believe that everything really does happen for a reason. That it was fate that led me to you that day. That maybe we just end up exactly where we are supposed to be. Like right now. This is exactly where I am supposed to be. Here with you, in this bed, feeling your heart beat close to mine."

"I can't picture my life anymore without you in it," she says. "It's as if I forgot what it was like before I met you. I promise I won't drink like that again, Chloe. I promise. As long as you are there with me to say goodbye to my dad. I need you," she admits, and buries her head in my chest.

"I know, Fiona. I'll be there."

Fiona: December 2015
Daylight

The bus ride seems to take forever. Jade talks the whole time: she talks about her brother and her family, and they sound a lot like mine. Although I can relate to a lot of what she is saying, I wish she would just shut up. I miss silence.

Dr. Hall announces that we have arrived and I can't help but notice how familiar everything looks, outside the window. All of the medications, I have been taking, seem to make my memory terrible so I can't quite pinpoint how I know this place…yet. As I step down off the bus and walk towards the huge building I suddenly realize exactly where Dr. Hall is taking us.

It is The Butterfly Sanctuary. The last time I was here was with my father, Chloe and her boys. Before he died. Once again, I feel as if this has all been set up to strike a chord with me. To send me back into a depression and make me miss my father. These doctors just keep getting cleverer. Digging deeper and deeper. I fear that at some point they may dig a hole so deep that I will not be able to get out. I may suffocate to death underground.

I try to act unaffected by the location. I don't want to let on that I have even been here. Maybe they will think they got it wrong. Hopefully they will feel they failed.

"Ladies, welcome to the Butterfly Sanctuary. Have any of you been here before?" Dr. Hall looks right at me.

I shake my head. I feel I am pretty convincing so far.

"No one? I thought for sure that at least one of you would have. Well, you are all in for a treat. We are going to walk through and I want you to just enjoy the beauty. After we leave, when we get back to your rooms, I want you all to write a one-page entry on how you felt. I want to know what feelings the beauty invoked in you. Okay. Let's go."

I try to contain my emotions, as we enter one of my favorite places of those I can remember being at with my father. And Chloe. I hold my hand out, knowing it is unlikely for the butterflies to land right on your skin. Immediately a blue and black butterfly – like the one I painted with Chloe and her boys in their room in my house back in Florida – lands directly on my fingertip. It sits there for a while, suckling on my finger. It seems to be cleaning itself, or maybe just taking a time-out for a moment before it takes flight again. Back into the wild. I raise my finger just a little bit, closer to my face, hoping not to startle it away, and examine it. I can see all of its coloring so clearly now. It is exquisite. Jade marches right up to me…

"Fiona! There you are!" She startles the butterfly away with her loudness.

"Aw, rats. I wanted to take a picture of you with that butterfly!"

Really? That was her plan of action?

"Oh well," I say unenthusiastically. And walk away.

"This place is great, isn't it?" She follows me like she always does. I just can't seem to shake her. It is as if she is always there.

I can hear Trisha talking in the background. This is not like the other times, I have been to these places. Usually it feels so serene and calming. But today, all I hear is noise. I feel so distracted by the voices that I can barely focus enough to take in any of the normally beautiful surroundings. I see Dr. Hall in the distance, snapping photos and laughing with some of the patients. He disgusts me. He is so fake.

I take out a journal I brought with me and sit on a bench by myself. I start to sketch. I finally feel a bit of peace and quiet, and then Trisha walks up to me.

"Hey, you doing alright, sweetie?" she sweetly asks me as I am still looking down at my drawing, barely acknowledging that she is even there.

"I am fine. Thanks. I am just drawing my emotions. I can express my experience better that way. For the journal, I mean. The entry we have to turn in," I explain.

"Fiona?" Dr. Clark walks up to me. I didn't even know she was coming.

"What are you doing here?" I ask her, a bit startled.

"Fiona, I am here for the same reason as you, sweetie. To enjoy the beautiful butterflies for just a little while." She smiles, and for the first time in quite a while, I feel she looks sincere. I feel I can see who she really is underneath all of the mystery and evil she is laced with.

"Oh. I just didn't know you were coming."

"I know, sweetie, I know," she says.

I try to sit by myself until it is time to go. I catch Dr. Clark looking at me several times from a distance while I talk to my friends, who don't seem to get the picture that I just want to be left alone. Eventually we all get back onto the buses and head back to The Meadows. All in all, it was a beautiful day. Maybe being in a familiar place full of good memories was just what I needed to snap back into reality. To get myself well, so I can go home unscathed by the attempts of the doctors to break me. I can do this. I can see the light now at the end of the tunnel. It is still there – it has to be. I know it is.

As I walk back into my room after an eventful yet liberating day outdoors, I am greeted by the smell of pills and cheap laundry soap. No more brisk smells of flowers and earth outside. I am back to the reality of my world right now.

I am back in Hell.

I am alone in my room, so I decide to take advantage of it for a minute. I walk into the bathroom and don't even bother to shut the door. I look in the mirror. My hair looks a bit disheveled, longer than I would normally wear it. I am wearing one of my favorite shirts. It is a rainbow tie-dye shirt Chloe and I made with the boys one day we were bored, back in Florida. It reminds me of being free, and of being happy with my family. There is a knock at the door so I quickly step out of the bathroom to see who it might be.

"Fiona?" asks Dr. Clark, but already standing inside my room.

"Oh, hi. What's up?" I say, trying to act unaffected by her presence.

"I was wondering if you would be up for a counseling session with me today. Just me and you. Like old times. Would that be okay?" she asks sincerely, and I am caught off guard, remembering how close we used to be. Before I found out she was a thief and a homewrecker. Oh, and before she stabbed me with a needle and sent me into a temporary coma: that sure hasn't helped our relationship.

"Is there a reason for it?" I ask. "I have counseling with Dr. Hall tomorrow morning."

"I know, sweetie, but I feel you are in a good place today. Maybe we could really get some good things in today if we talked?"

She seems very persistent. She is right: I am in a good place today. I feel like my old self. The butterfly gardens helped bring me back to reality. They reminded me of how important it is for me to get the hell out of here, no matter what it takes. But will talking to her ruin my mood? I am hesitant to commit.

"Yeah, I guess that's fine. Can I grab a Coke first?"

"How about I make us some hot tea?" She grabs my hand and squeezes it warmly. I give her a puzzled look and wonder if she has some master plan to trap me in her office and lock the door.

"Okay. That sounds nice." I guess I am feeling rather brave today.

We head towards her office together. She immediately microwaves some water and serves me hot Chai Tea after a few minutes.

"Fiona. I would like to talk to you about some things, sweetie. Now, I don't want you to take them too literally, okay?"

"Um…okay."

"Fiona. Do you know where you are?" she asks me while taking out a yellow notepad that reminds me of my father's office when I was a kid. He had stacks of those old yellow notepads everywhere and I would draw him pictures on the first pages of all of them for him to eventually find. It was a little, amusing game we would play.

"Of course. I am at a mental institution."

"Yes. Can you tell me the name of it?" She turns on the tape recorder on her desk. It sounds fuzzy and I start to feel a bit of anxiety, wondering why she is recording me. Dr. Hall never records our conversations. I feel uneasy.

"Why are you recording?"

"Oh, just protocol." She smiles.

"I am at The Meadows."

She looks up from writing and gives me a strange look.

"Uh-huh. And have you been here before? At The Meadows."

"Yes, my father brought me here as a teenager. I remember now," I say.

"What did he bring you here for? I mean, what did he think was wrong with you?"

"I was just rebelling, like a normal teenager. Well, I think, in all truth, he wanted to change me. I think he thought if he could medicate me or get me the right doctor, I would suddenly become straight or something."

"And did he get what he wanted? Did it help you?"

"No."

"Tell me about your friends, Fiona. You seem to have a few close ones. Can you tell me about each of them? Maybe tell me what it is you like about them individually."

"I wouldn't say I have 'friends' here. They are more like annoyances."

"Annoyances. How so?"

"Well, Jade – for one – talks too much. And Trisha is always there in my room when I am just trying to be alone. My mom and I thought originally that I wasn't going to have a roommate. And didn't you guys say I would get my own room soon?"

"Tell me more about Jade, to start with. What is it that you do like about Jade, Fiona?"

"Oh, I don't know; she is an artist like me."

"She is? Well, that's wonderful. Anything else she brings to the table?"

"She does yoga and she is always in a good mood even though it seems she has had a hard life lately."

"She has? What do you mean a hard life? What is she here for again?"

"I don't know if I am supposed to tell you all of this, but she tried to kill herself and fell from a building or something. She was almost paralyzed. She is lucky to be alive, really."

"Wow. That sounds terrible. I feel sad for her, don't you?" Dr. Clark asks me.

Of course, I do. I just said that, I think to myself. She is acting weird.

"Oh, Fiona, how do you like your new medication, the one I put you on, honey?" she asks all of a sudden. "I have been meaning to ask you if you feel more…well, lucid, maybe. Are you able to concentrate or think any clearer?"

"Sure," I say. I guess I do feel a little better lately. A little less confused.

"Great. I hope you feel even better in the next couple of weeks. Sometimes it is hard for me to know the right medicine for you. I hope this helps."

"Yeah, okay."

"Well, Fiona. Do you spend a lot of time with your friends here? I mean, how often are they with you?" she asks me.

Man, she is really more into my friends than into me right now.

"Yeah. They are around a lot. Jade especially. She seems to never go away."

"Why do you think that is?"

"I don't know. She is needy, I guess. Maybe lonely."

"I bet she is lonely. She is in here, away from her family. Anyone would be lonely. Don't you agree, Fiona?"

"Yes."

"Are you lonely?" she asks.

"With all of these needy women around me, and Dr. Hall – " I begin to respond.

"Who?" She interrupts me suddenly. "Dr. who?"

She looks shocked. I must have struck a nerve having mentioned her "Boyfriend."

I decide to repeat it, just to rub salt in the wound.

"Dr. Hall, I said."

Chloe: November 2015
Departure

The sky is filled with dark clouds as we arrive at her father's mansion in New York. Fiona has deep lines on her face from sleeping on my shoulder the whole plane ride here. I watch as she looks up at the house before starting to put one foot in front of the other and walk down the long driveway, towards the front door. She breathes heavily and doesn't say a word to me the whole trek. I take her hand in mine before she opens the door.

"Listen, it is going to be okay. You are a strong woman," I say. Something she has said to me many times before. Now I need her to know she is strong and courageous too. She has to be strong for her father.

She doesn't respond and Louise, her maid, opens the door and greets us welcomingly. I see Veronica in the kitchen on the phone. She notices our arrival and quickly hangs up the phone and walks towards us.

"Girls. Oh, I am so glad you are here," she says with forced cheerfulness.

"Is he in his room?" Fiona immediately asks.

"Yes. He is resting. You may want to give him some time to wake up before you go up there. He has been rather agitated when he wakes up, the past week or so."

Fiona begins to walk up the spiral staircase, disregarding everything her mother has just warned her about, and I am not sure whether I should follow her or not. I decide to trail slowly behind. I head to Fiona's room first to drop off my suitcase. Louise has already taken Fiona's upstairs. Fiona is already out of sight – in her father's room, I assume – as I reach the top of the stairs. I walk into her pink, feminine bedroom and set down my suitcase, out of breath. I walk around the room, trying to picture Fiona as a teenager living in this space. How out of place she must have felt. It doesn't resemble her at all.

I walk over to the dresser and see a stack of pictures. I start to flip through them. Most of them are of her and her father. Her mom probably pulled them out for Fiona. There is one of Fiona sitting on his lap as a little girl. She has a bowl-cut hairstyle and is wearing chucks on her feet. He is in his usual suit and tie. Neither one is smiling at all in the photo. Fiona is barely smiling in any of the pictures I flip through, actually. I decide I should try to go find her to make sure she is holding up okay.

I find her just where I thought I would: in her father's room, in the dark, watching him as he lies there sleeping. There is a home-health nurse who has a whole station set up in the corner of his large bedroom, trying to act like she isn't there while Fiona sobs quietly to herself in the dark room. I put my arm around Fiona and try to think of the right words to say, but nothing comes out of my lips. I just hold her as much as she lets me while she stands there in tears.

About an hour later, Mr. Lennox wakes up. He shouts something that doesn't make sense to us and I can tell how slurred his speech is now. He coughs loudly and the home-health nurse runs over to him and adjusts his breathing machine while trying to calm him down. Fiona just stands there staring at him with a fearful look in her eyes, and it appears to me as if she has no idea what to make of the situation. He looks at her angrily and keeps yelling and yelling, but she doesn't move. She just stands there with a blank stare spread across her face.

"Daddy?" she finally, desperately says. "It's me, Fiona."

"Maybe you should give him a few minutes," the nurse explains. "He has had a hard time waking up the past few days," she reassures us.

I have to pull Fiona out of the room to get her to move.

Veronica comes up the stairs just as we are exiting his bedroom.

"Oh, I tried to warn you to give him some time, girls!" She angrily raises her voice at us.

Fiona is still in some kind of trance, just standing there staring, motionless.

"Fiona?" I try to break her trance.

"I think I am going to step outside for a minute," she eventually responds.

"Okay. Do you want me to come with you?" I ask her.

"No…no." She starts to walk away.

Here I am, feeling helpless in New York yet again. I know it is good that I am here, but Fiona doesn't seem to want me to take care of her. I can't go into Mr. Lennox's room with him like this and Fiona doesn't want me to follow her. I decide to walk downstairs and sit on the couch in the living room alone. I start to think about how maybe I am completely insane for thinking this would be a good time to propose to Fiona. With her dad dying. For some reason before the trip, I thought it would be something that might give her some hope. Maybe take her mind off of things and give her something positive to think about. But I am realizing now the depth of the situation and how entirely sad it all is. I can't propose to her in the midst of all of this. How could anyone be happy for us at a time like this? Was I expecting them to jump up and down and throw us a party while Fiona's dad lay in bed like a vegetable? I can't help but feel overwhelmingly ill, all of the sudden. I put my hand on my stomach and contemplate throwing up a few times before deciding to get up and walk to the kitchen to get a glass of water. I look out the window of the kitchen to the backyard and see Fiona outside, in her father's gardens: the gardens where I had planned to propose to her sometime during this trip. She has a cigarette between her lips and her eyebrows are frowning, as if she is deep in thought. I consider walking out to her, but decide to stand there instead and watch her from the kitchen for a few minutes. She looks much thinner and taller from this distance. She looks different. She seems to be talking to herself and hasn't sat down at all since I have been watching her. She is just pacing back and forth, puffing away on her cigarette. I feel more alienated from her now than I have ever felt before. Why won't she let me in? Why won't she let me comfort her? She promised me she wouldn't relapse – that she wouldn't drink like she did at dinner that night with Trent and Aubrey – but I have smelt alcohol and cigarettes on her every day since. I start to worry about her relapsing. How can I be so in love with this person that I suddenly feel so disconnected from? As if I don't know her at all anymore. She seems like a completely different person from the one I met in the tattoo shop that day. "Who is Fiona?" I wonder.

After watching her have a conversation with herself for about ten minutes, I finally decide I should walk out and check on her.

"Hey!" I shout to warn her I am approaching. I don't want to startle her and whoever she may be talking to.

"Oh. Hey," she responds right away.

"I just wanted to check on you," I say. "That was pretty rough in there."

"Yeah. It was," she agrees.

"Well, maybe we should head back in and see if he is more awake now? More lucid?" I ask her.

"Okay. Probably a good idea," she confirms. "You see this bench?" she asks me after I turn to walk back inside. I look back and see a stone bench in the garden next to a huge and beautiful Azalea bush. "I used to raid my dad's liquor cabinet as a teenager. I'd come out here with a pack of cigarettes in the dark, completely annihilated, and sit on this bench and smoke a whole pack of cigarettes staring up at the sky, asking God why He made me this way? Why He made me be born into this family where I didn't fit in. I would sit out here all night sometimes, and think of ways I could make my dad happier. Ways I could change myself to fit in. You know, this one time in high school a kid threw their entire tray of food at me. But I didn't cry. I didn't let him know I was even affected by it. I stayed in those clothes the rest of the day. The teachers asked me if I wanted to call my dad and go home, or have him bring me a change of clothes, but I didn't want him to know. I was scared of how embarrassed he would be by me. For not fitting in. For being a loser. I didn't want to let him down."

"Fiona, that's terrible," I say, and try to grab her hand.

She pulls it away.

"I bet you can't relate to that, can you?" she asks me.

"What do you mean?" I feel so far away from her; she seems as though she is suddenly turning on me, like some kind of wild animal. Like we aren't a team at all...Like I am her prey.

"I mean, you were this pretty cheerleader who probably dated the hot jock and nobody knew you were a lesbian and you just fit right in," she says mockingly.

"Fiona, that's not fair. I had – "

She interrupts me. "I mean, you don't get it, Chloe. You don't understand what I have had to overcome to be this strong-looking lesbian who isn't afraid of what anyone thinks, because you never had to go through what I have!"

She keeps yelling at me but I stop hearing her. I feel incredibly dizzy all of the sudden, and hot. I feel like I am in a nightmare.

"I have been through things too, Fiona!" I yell back at her, and immediately feel guilty for screaming at her when she is clearly not herself. I can tell she is really hurting, but it is not fair for her to attack me like I am some bitchy high schooler who doesn't care about her at all. I love her. I just want her to be happy again, like she was in the beginning of our relationship. Before all of this stuff with her dad, and before I knew about all of the rehabs and her extremely addictive personality traits. Where has that person gone? I want her back.

"I'm sorry," she says. "I'm sorry, Chloe. You're right. I am sure, you have been through plenty of rough times, too. I mean, I know you have been. I was there."

I immediately forgive her for her violent outburst. She is so fragile and vulnerable that I am afraid she may break if I upset her more, or stay angry with her.

"It's okay. Now, let's go and see your dad. In a better mood than he was before. Okay?"

We walk inside and upstairs to her father's room. He is calmer now. He is awake and watching the news on his television. The nurse and Veronica motion for us to come in and sit down beside him. He looks at Fiona right away and smiles. I know he recognizes her and is happy to see her this time. His eyes have the warmth they usually do. She smiles and takes his hand in hers. Neither of them speaks: they just hold hands. She leans her head on his chest and he can barely move his hands to stroke her hair. He doesn't try to speak. I think it is clear what is felt.

"I love you, daddy," Fiona finally says with her head still resting on his chest.

"His speech is poor," the nurse reminds us. "So it's best he doesn't waste the energy trying to respond." She looks at him, almost advising him not to. Fiona doesn't sit up for a long while. She just rests on him in his dark room. I feel a little out of place, but he eventually smiles at me and I know he is glad to see me too.

"Thank you, Mr. Lennox," I say quietly. "For giving me the opportunity to take care of my family and be a part of yours," I say graciously to him. His smile gets bigger and he tries to nod, but his breathing is poor and even that seems hard for him. This disease is hard to witness. I know he is completely aware of who we are and that we are here with him. But he is trapped there in his body unable to move a muscle; paralyzed and helpless in his bed. The act of simply doing nothing at all is what is killing him, I think to myself. Even though, I know that isn't the culprit. Fiona still hasn't come up for air. She is lying against him, looking just as helpless as he does. My mind starts to fear how bad her erratic behavior is getting. Her violent and reckless outbursts are becoming more frequent. I still can't believe how she attacked me down in the gardens. I definitely can't propose to her there now, knowing what darker memories are also tied to that spot. All I can think about now are her drinking and her belligerent outbursts. There are no happy memories tied to the gardens anymore, of her and her dad painting. Now I know the truth.

Eventually, I decide to leave the room. It looks as though Fiona might actually be asleep now. I wander around the hallways and notice there aren't many photos hanging. There are a couple awkward school pictures of Fiona where she is barely recognizable to me. But most of the walls are bare. I see Mikey Junior's room, full of sports paraphernalia: awards and trophies that he must have won over the years. I keep walking and come across Mr. Lennox's office. It is unlocked, so I convince myself it is okay to walk in. He has more awards hanging on his walls than anyone I have ever seen. He has his diploma from Julliard. I didn't even know he had gone to Julliard. He also has several business awards for Mugged. Some sort of art trophy sits on his desk next to a stack of papers. I notice he has a rather large filing cabinet beside his desk. My boredom allows me to convince myself that it is okay to open it and take a peek into his life. It is a very organized filing cabinet labeled with names. I see Veronica Lennox first, followed by Mikey Junior. Then, last, Fiona Lennox.

I flip through some of the papers in Fiona's file. First, I notice her birth certificate and some sort of art class completion form. Then there are lots of receipts. The amount on the first one is ten thousand dollars! "Holy cow!" I think. What kind of gifts has he gotten her over the years? When I look closer, I realize it isn't a gift receipt at all. It is from one of her rehabs. At the top is the name of the center and then, following, is a description of why she was there: why she was admitted. "The patient was abusing prescription medications and attempted suicide," it reads. Suicide? I can't even begin to imagine Fiona in such low place that she would try to kill herself. That doesn't seem like the Fiona I know. Until her father got sick, she was this positive, uplifting person in my life: a strong and confident woman who would never take her own life. How is it that I am just now finding out she has such demons hidden away? She has a much darker past than I ever imagined.

I continue to flip through some of the slips from Fiona's past rehab centers and find most of the reasons for admittance are the same. There seems to have been a pattern: she would get addicted to something, then either abuse the medication or try to commit suicide, according to the files. Apparently, Fiona has seen many, many therapists over her lifetime as well. I start to feel guilty – sick in the pit of my stomach – so I decide to dart out of his office. As I am shutting the door, I turn around and bump right into Mikey Junior.

"Ah. You startled me," I say, frightened.

"Were you…looking for anything specific?" he asks me, clearly questioning my motives and knowing I was snooping.

"Um. No, I was just lost," I say, shaking. "This is a big house," I add.

"Yes, it is," Mikey says, still looking at me like he knows I found something startling in there. "Look, I saw you looking through the filing cabinet," he says finally. "So, you might as well tell me what you saw." His blue eyes give me a menacing glare.

Great. I really don't feel like getting into all this with him right now. I haven't even processed the magnitude of the situation yet. "Oh. I'm sorry, it's just…I…I don't know," I say, not having any words that can justify my actions at this point. "You want the truth?" I ask.

He nods and waits for my response.

"Fiona has been really distant with me ever since your dad took a turn for the worse. I guess I just wanted some insight into why she would be that way, or whether I should be worried about her or not, with her drinking and violent outbursts."

"Well, did you find what you needed?" he asks me calmly.

"No. I mean, yes. I mean, I don't know," I say, flustered, wondering if he is going to tell everyone in the family that I was rifling through his father's office.

"Do you want to talk about it?" he asks me, and re-opens the door to the office, like he is some kind of therapist. I wonder how many shrinks he has seen in his lifetime. Although, he appears so professional and put together, he does belong to the same family.

I follow him back into the office. He sits behind his father's desk and I sit across from him as if I were his patient.

"Alright, Chloe. What did you see?" he asks. His voice is always so steady and calm. It impresses me. And right now, it intimidates me too.

I pause before admitting the truth. "I looked through her file. I saw all the rehabs and the reasons she was admitted. Is that really true? Has she really tried to kill herself that many times?"

"Fiona has...had a harder life than you might assume. People think that because we were raised in a wealthy family, we have it all. But you must know, with your own identity struggles, that people can be cruel. Even parents. My dad wasn't as accepting back then. He put her on a lot of medication. I think he legitimately thought she was sick. As though if he put her on some specific blend of prescription drugs her brain would think the right way: that she would no longer be gay. I mean, he knows now that isn't the case, but it took him a long, long time to accept Fiona the way she is. When she turned eighteen and could make up her own mind about what she wanted to put into her body she stopped taking the medication altogether. Cold turkey. Well, you can imagine how that went. She went borderline psychotic. They admitted her based on the assumption that she had tried to kill herself because she was depressed and didn't want to live anymore. But what actually caused it was her trying to get the medication out of her system too quickly. Stopping the prescriptions so abruptly gave her suicidal thoughts. That was the first time. The second time she was Baker-Acted – Do you know what the Baker Act is? It means she was committed against her will. By my father. He claimed she had stolen money from him for drugs. Whatever is written on that slip is a warped version of the truth. He told whatever lies he had to tell to save her from going to jail. If he hadn't, the stealing she did would have resulted in jail time. She still wasn't happy, though. She was back in rehab. She has had court-ordered therapists and routine drug tests, among other things, for years. I am surprised you went this long without seeing this side of her, honestly."

I sit in silence, trying to understand how I have fallen in love with such a mentally ill individual. Someone so fragile she has tried to take her life multiple times and has been addicted to God knows what for God knows how long. How am I going to confront Fiona about this? How am I going to deal with all of this? I don't know what to say to Mikey Jr. at this point. I sit for a long time and he seems to understand I need the time to process it all.

I finally blurt out, "But I love her."

"I know you do," he agrees.

"But what do I do now?" I feel so helpless. It is clear she isn't going to have the mental capacity to handle her father's death. I'm not sure what triggered all of the relapses before, but I can see her starting to spiral out of control now. And I suddenly think about my children. What if they saw this side of Fiona? I can't let them ever see her like this...

"That's up to you, Chloe," Mikey says, and looks me right in the eye. "I understand if you want to run out of this house screaming and never look back. Plenty of her ex-girlfriends have before. And I didn't blame them. Fiona is so easy to love, yet so hard to love, all at the same time," he says to me. "She is so nurturing when she is happy and healthy. But when she is sick or in a low place, she can be almost impossible to console."

I know what he means now.

"I love her too, Chloe. She is my only sister. But she is my family. We are blood." I can read the sincerity in his eyes.

I interrupt him. "She is my family, too. I have a ring. I wanted to propose to her...I mean, I want to propose to her."

His eyes widen as he stares deep into my soul. "Are you sure, Chloe? I mean, that you can take care of her when she is low like this?"

Suddenly it makes so much sense: why her dad was so hesitant to let her propose to me. Why he stole those love letters. He was trying to protect Fiona. But he was also trying to protect me. He knew I would inevitably find out who she really is and that I might break her heart, just like all of the girlfriends before me. But I love her. How could I leave someone I love so much, and in such a vulnerable state? This does change a lot and I need to talk to her about it, but I still want to marry Fiona. That I know.

Mikey promises not to mention any of this to Fiona or Veronica until I am ready to confront Fiona myself. He also promises not to ruin any proposal I have planned. He agrees the timing is bad, with Mr. Lennox this close to dying. I decide I will just hold on to the ring for now. Especially, until I talk to Fiona about all this. She needs to know that I know about her past, and that I love her despite all of it.

I eventually wander back into Mr. Lennox's room and find Fiona still resting against him. He too is asleep now. Veronica is no longer in the room: just the home-health nurse, still stationed in the corner, dispensing all of his medications into little cups. I tap Fiona's shoulder to see if she is okay.

"Chloe. I must have fallen asleep. What time is it?"

"You have been asleep almost an hour," I say.

"I'm sorry. Are you okay? What have you been doing?" she asks.

"Oh, I was just talking to Mikey a little bit and looking through some pictures your mom pulled out, of you with your dad."

"Oh, Mikey is here? Let's get out of here for a little while. I'll let him sleep," she says, and looks fondly at her father before we walk out of the dark bedroom.

Fiona and I walk into her bedroom and she lies down on her back, exhaling loudly.

"Chloe, I am really sorry for the whole garden thing earlier – " she starts to apologize, for the second time since the incident.

"I know you are, Fiona. It's okay. Let's just pretend it never happened," I say, wishing I could erase it completely from my memory.

"I just don't know what is going on with me lately," she tells me. "One minute, I am so mad at my dad for ruining our chance at a normal relationship and the next minute, I completely forgive him and can't stand the thought of being without him."

"I am sure that is pretty standard, Fiona. I mean, for someone going through what you are and with someone whom you have had a rocky relationship with your whole life."

Really rocky, apparently. It is hard for me to look at her the same way. I know my feelings for her haven't changed, but I suddenly feel like I have to shield her from any trauma due to the fact that she may relapse at any moment.

She seems so much more fragile now than she has ever seemed to me before. I have to tell her I know.

"Hey, Fiona, I need to talk to you about something," I say.

"Okay, what's up?" she asks.

"I know about the rehabs and I know about why you were there."

"Yeah, I told you about them, I know," she says, puzzled.

"No, I mean the real reasons you were admitted. I read the reports," I confess.

"What reports? What do you mean you read the reports?"

"While you were napping, I snuck into your dad's office and looked through your file and there were these receipts and reports or something…Well, they said how you overdosed on prescription pills and tried to…" I can't seem to get the words out of my mouth. I can't seem to say it out loud, that she tried to take her own life.

"Tried to what, Chloe? What did I try to do? What did you read?" she asks, waiting for me to say it out loud to her.

"Why would you do that, Fiona? I just need to understand how you could…get to that point…where you would…"

"I didn't!" she says loudly. "All of those rehabs you read about are bullshit! They were a prison! My dad fucking made me stay in there locked up against my will. It was sadistic. It was cruel!"

"I'm sure it was, but, I mean, you weren't stable…you took all those pills, and you stole from him?"

"I would never steal from him, Chloe! Don't you know me at all? Do I look like someone who would steal from someone; especially their father?"

She doesn't. I mean, before reading all of that I would never even think she was capable of such a thing.

"No, I guess not," I say quietly.

I feel so confused. Here she is telling me the things I read weren't true and that her dad was just keeping her in there. But Mikey Jr. told me the story. He told me the truth.

"But I talked to Mikey…" I blurt out.

"Ha! Mikey…and you don't think my dad brainwashed him?"

"But I just don't understand why your dad…how your dad could do that to you? How could you do that to your child? I would never do that to my boys."

"That's because you are a good mother, Chloe. But my dad wasn't a good dad."

"If everything you are saying is true, Fiona…then why are you even here now? I mean, I know he is dying, but why would you even come back here? Why did you paint that big mural on the Mugged wall, like you two were fine?" I ask.

"For you, Chloe. I reconnected with him for you. Remember? You needed a job. I hadn't talked to him in over a year. But I knew how much it meant to you. And then I guess I just sort of got sucked back in. And, I mean, he is still my dad. He always does this, though. He pulls me back in right when I have got away from it all."

I suddenly feel partly responsible for Fiona's recent behavior. I was the reason she called him in the first place. Would she even be here now if it weren't for me? She would inevitably have found out he was sick, probably from Veronica, but who knows if she would be here, this invested in him again?

"I'm sorry, Fiona. I had no idea. I would have never had you reach out to him, had I known he kept you in some type of rehabilitation prison."

"He would pay off the therapists to keep me sick," she says.

I feel sick. I run to the bathroom and start to dry heave over her bathroom sink.

"Chloe?" she calls. "Are you okay?"

I'm not sure that I am okay.

"Be right out!" I yell, and close the door to the bathroom.

I look at myself in the mirror. I hardly recognize the person staring back at me. When I started dating Fiona, I felt so liberated. I finally felt free. I love her. I want to marry her. But at the same time, I am not sure I even know how to be around her right now. She has so many inner demons. More inner demons than even I do. We are more alike than I thought we were and I am not sure if that is a good thing or not.

I finally get myself together and decide to walk back out of the bathroom and put on a strong face for Fiona. She isn't in the bedroom, though, when I walk out. I walk down the hallway and find her in her father's room again. This time she is completely alone with him. Veronica and Mikey are nowhere to be found and even the Hospice nurse has stepped out. She starts to talk to her dad, but he is completely unresponsive this time. He looks like he is barely hanging on. I watch her from the doorway without her knowing.

"Daddy?" she starts. "It's me, your daughter Fiona, again." He doesn't move at all. "I know that I wasn't the little girl that you pictured having. I know I let you down. I know you were scared what the world would do to me. But I could have taken care of myself, daddy. I mean, I could have made up my own mind. You never let me have a voice, growing up. You always masked my true self with all of the pills and the therapy and the bribing and convincing. I just wanted to be heard, you know? I wanted to be able to be myself. Especially with you. But you wouldn't let me!" Her voice starts to sound a little angrier now, and louder. "Why would you leave me in those centers? With all of those strangers? I was so young and afraid and you just abandoned me there and let someone else deal with me. What a cop out! I spent half of my life trying to make you happy and then one day I just snapped. But we are more alike than you think. You are a true artist, like me. Mom suppressed that side of you. She cared more about money than about you being happy. She wanted you to make a name for yourself so you guys could have nice things, but I know you missed your art. All of my tattoos…the ones you hate so much…they are my voice. I know they aren't 'pretty' to you. But art isn't supposed to just be some pretty picture; it is supposed to invoke a feeling in someone. And I know it did that in you. I wanted to make my inner voice heard so I drew all of those emotions on the outside for everyone to see. And that proves I am stronger than you. That I do have a voice. I eventually stood up for myself and didn't let you get to me. But you let the world change you. You let them win. You are not strong. You are a coward."

I watch as Fiona pours her heart out to her father while he lies there so helpless. He can't defend himself against her. He can't move; he can't speak. Part of me feels proud of her in this moment – for standing up for herself – but the rest of me is horrified. She is being abusive to a helpless invalid. And she is so wrapped up in her own pain that she doesn't even realize it. How could she call him a coward?

"Daddy. I love you. I will always love you. And despite all of the hurt you have caused me, I forgive you. I want you to know that. But I also want you to know that you didn't break me. I broke free."

I can tell she suddenly feels my presence and knows someone is watching her. She turns around quickly and sees me in the doorway. A look of terror sweeps across her face, but I smile at her reassuringly. She needs to feel that I believe what she has said is the truth. That he hasn't broken her. That she is still strong, despite all of the hardships she has had to overcome.

She runs to me and I immediately hold her close, as tightly as I can. She starts to sob loudly and we leave the room. All of a sudden, a loud, incessant beep begins in Mr. Lennox's bedroom. It's coming from his machines.

"What is that noise, Chloe?" She looks at me with complete fear in her beautiful blue eyes.

I know what that noise is and so does she.

"Nurse!" Fiona screams at the top of her lungs. "Nurse, there is something wrong!"

I hear people scatter downstairs and the nurse, along with Veronica and Mikey Jr., come running up the stairs. Louise follows, leading what appears to be a priest up the spiral staircase. Veronica abruptly stops in the doorway. Mr. Lennox opens his eyes one last time and takes a big breath, as if he is grasping, one more time, for life. His eyes look frightened, not warm and inviting like before. Just frightened. Fiona falls to her knees and sobs.

He is gone.

Fiona sobs and sobs, unable to stop. I think she feels like she just killed him with that desperate and resentful speech she could not control.

An hour later the priest has arrived. He says a prayer over Mr. Lennox's lifeless body as we all gather around the sickbed. Fiona, Mikey and their mother – one after the other – touch him one last time. Fiona seems to be holding it together pretty well now, considering, but we all knew the end was close. Veronica seems the most devastated to me. She can't stop crying violently and keeps staring at his lifeless body lying there in his bed, rigid. Eventually, Fiona grabs her hand and tries to lead her out to be with the rest of us, but she convinces us she needs more time with him. We leave Veronica alone with him and we all walk out into the hallway together.

Mikey and Fiona hug for a long time while I just stand there, helpless.

"I can't believe he is really gone," Mikey says to Fiona finally. His voice remains just as calm as it always is and I can't believe it. He seemed to love his dad. Then I think, maybe that's what Mr. Lennox taught Mikey: to stay calm no matter what. Maybe this is Mikey's way of showing his love.

"I can't believe it either," agrees Fiona. "He was ready," she says, trying to reassure Mikey that he was. "You know dad probably couldn't stand not being able to work and dictate what everyone was doing around him."

They both manage a laugh and I join in awkwardly.

Mikey looks right at me. "I am glad you are here with us," he says to me.

"Me too," I say, and take both Mikey's and Fiona's hands at the same time. "I am just so sorry for your loss," I say. It sounds so cliché. But it is all that I can think of to say.

Veronica eventually wanders out of the bedroom with her eyes red and swollen from all the tears. I let Fiona and Mikey hug her first; then I embrace her too. She walks to his office and shuts the door behind her, clearly wanting to be alone.

Fiona, Mikey and I all sit together downstairs and drink hot tea while watching the news. We barely speak. We just sit there, planted on the couch where Fiona's father usually sat, and let the coroner pass us without acknowledging what is actually happening. Eventually, the Hospice nurse comes in to inform us we are free to go through his things and that afterwards she will destroy all the leftover medication and clear the medical supplies from the room. Veronica says she needs to notify his attorneys so they can prepare to examine his Will and start the process of settling his estate.

I hadn't even thought about all of his assets. He was extremely wealthy. I am sure Fiona has some kind of trust fund set up in her name. Veronica leaves, and eventually Fiona asks me if I want to go upstairs with her and look through some of his things. I agree to accompany her up the long spiral staircase and help her start to deal with the death of her father.

Chloe: November 2015
Truth

The next couple of days are a bit of a blur. The phone has been ringing off the hook ever since Mr. Lennox's passing. There are countless families close to him that give their condolences and drop by with food for the Lennox family. The kitchen counter is beginning to look like they've opened some sort of deli, with all of the baked goods spread across the countertop. Apparently, the Lennoxes have been members of a pretty large church here in New York for a long time, so the funeral service will be held there in a couple of days. Veronica has written an obituary for Mr. Lennox that shows what an 'honorable' and devoted father he was for so many years and mentions all the prestigious awards he has hanging in his office. Fiona finally looks through the daunting stack of family photos her mother pulled out for her, to pick a couple to display at the funeral service. Compared to her mother Fiona has been holding up quite well, considering. She informs me we have to gather a few items for Veronica from Mr. Lennox's bedroom, after choosing what pictures to display from the pile. Veronica is apparently still too shaken to enter Mr. Lennox's room.

We walk into the dark bedroom and I notice the hospital bed is still there, along with the nurse station and all of the machines. It looks as though, after the Hospice nurse removed the supplies, no one has been back in at all. Except the men from the funeral home to take away the body.

"I'll be just a second," Fiona informs me before venturing into his large walk-in closet.

I walk around the room and things start to pop out at me more, now that he is gone: a framed picture of him with Veronica, for example. It looks like they might have been on their honeymoon. They look many years younger. Both wear swimsuits, and are laughing and drinking margaritas on a boat with a beautiful view of the ocean in the background. I wonder why he would still choose to have this photo displayed in his bedroom. They look genuinely happy, though. I also notice the plethora of books stacked beside Mr. Lennox's bed. He has a couple of Thoreau classics, and a novel by Kerouac, but what sticks out to me the most are a daily devotional and a book titled "Connecting with my Daughter." I flip it open and see he has a picture of Fiona from when she was a little girl that he has been using as a bookmark. The book seems to be a how-to on steps to have a better relationship with your daughter that he was in the middle of reading. He seems like such an anomaly to me. Here he was, reading this inspirational how-to book to get closer to Fiona, but he had her locked in institutions for years when he could have been connecting with her then. Maybe Fiona is right: he really had repented and was trying to make up for the years of pain he caused her. I sure hope so. I would like to think God really gave him that pass and that he is at peace. I realize Fiona has been in the closet for a long time, so I decide I should check on her to make sure she hasn't been eaten by some kind of bear that has been living amongst all of Mr. Lennox's suits.

"Fiona?"

I find her sitting on the floor of the closet looking through a big stack of papers.

"My letters," she says, and looks up at me while shaking her head in disbelief. "He took them," she says to me.

I want to tell her right then that I have known all along he had the letters. The love letters Fiona wrote to me during a time we weren't speaking. I never did get to read them. I am caught off-guard by her finding them this way, after he has passed. He can't explain himself to her, though, which is hard for me to witness. He told me he hid them to protect her. That he stole them because he was scared, with the last letter to me being a proposal; scared that I might say no and break his daughter's heart.

"Why would he do this? I told him I had forgiven him for everything. And I had. But this is just one more thing he has crushed," she says to me.

I consider telling her the truth, but she looks so fragile that I don't dare. She can't have her sense of what is real and true disturbed now. What if she can't accept it? Maybe in a few months, when this is all over and we are back at home. When I am sure she is stronger, then I will tell her. I think Mr. Lennox deserves that much.

"Oh, it's okay, Fiona. We can't dwell on the past anymore. And, hey. At least you found them, right? Now I get to finally read these infamous love letters," I say, trying to sound encouraging.

"Right," Fiona says, and gathers up the letters. "Maybe later, okay?" She puts them back into a folder Mr. Lennox must have been hiding them in, and walks out of the closet.

"Did you get the things for Veronica?" I ask her, noticing she only has the letters in her hand.

"No, I'll just…get them later," she says evasively, and storms off, out of sight.

I want to follow her, but I have been doing a lot of following her around for the past couple of days. I decide to let her have a minute by herself and I call Trent from Mr. Lennox's office with the door shut.

"Hey, Trent," I say as he picks up the phone.

"Chloe. I heard about Mr. Lennox, I was just going to call, I'm sorry I didn't call earlier," he informs me. I meant to call him last night, but we have all been so preoccupied with everything at the house that I didn't even remember to call the boys to say goodnight.

"It's okay. How did you hear?" I ask. It was only yesterday that he passed away, I think to myself. News travels fast when you are wealthy.

"It was on the local news. Since he just opened that Mugged and all; just that the owner had…passed away," Trent explains.

"Right," I say. "Well, how are the boys?" I ask.

"They are good. My mom watched them yesterday while I worked. They seemed to have a good day."

I miss them so much suddenly. I miss the normalcy of having them with me and doing childish and happy things with them. I wish I could give each of them a big kiss.

"Well, tell them I miss them."

"You can tell them yourself. They are right here."

"No, I am afraid I will lose it," I say.

"Okay. I get it. I'll tell them," he assures me.

"Look, the funeral is in a couple of days so I will be back by Friday, okay?"

"How's Fiona?" he finally asks me. How do I explain to him how Fiona is? I don't know myself, from one minute to the next, how she is. One day, she is screaming violent and irrational things at me and the next, she is apologizing and holding it together perfectly well.

"She is doing okay," I tell him. "A little in shock, still," I say.

"That's understandable," Trent says.

"Well, just let the boys know I love them and miss them and will see them in a few days, okay?"

"Of course, Chloe. Will do. You take care of yourself, okay?"

I wander downstairs and look at all of the beautiful flowers people have sent. It looks a lot like the garden out back has now moved inside. I hear someone coming down the stairs and turn and look up at the spiral staircase to see Fiona. She is standing towards the top of the stairs, wearing a fitted black dress. I almost take her for someone else, at first. I have never – nor ever thought I would – see her in a dress.

"You look stunning," I say.

"Thanks. It was my mom's. You think it is appropriate for the funeral?" she asks me.

"It is absolutely appropriate," I say, and can't help but stare at how exquisitely beautiful Fiona looks, all dressed up in her mother's tight black dress.

"She has others," she informs me. "If you want you can come up and look through them for one to wear?"

We spend the next hour or so trying on Veronica's fancy and expensive array of black dresses. We model them for Veronica and Mikey Junior. It seems to take everyone's mind off of the sad truth of what has happened. It is a good hour.

I lie in bed next to Fiona. It is the night before the funeral. Everything is in order. The gigantic flower arrangements we have picked out, have been shipped to the church. The out of town guests are at their hotels. The music has been selected. The priest is ready and the readings are assigned and the food has been ordered for the reception, which will be held here at Mr. Lennox's home. Veronica has been displaying some interesting behavior ever since Mr. Lennox's death. She has suddenly taken up sewing, which is something she apparently has always wanted to learn to do. She also has decided she wants to sing a song at the funeral. Fiona assures me she used to sing, but it has been a long time since she has performed in front of anyone. I guess death brings out a passion in people that otherwise may be lacking. I toss and turn almost all night, and right before I enter a deep sleep I wake to a loud thunderstorm.

"What time is it, Chloe?" Fiona asks me in a hushed voice.

I glance at the clock next to me on the bed side table. "It's six o'clock."

The thunder roars louder now outside the window. I stand up and look out at the raging storm. The rain is blowing onto the windows and the trees are swaying aggressively in the yard. Mr. Lennox is even causing uproar from the sky, I think.

"At least everything is inside, except the burial," I say while still watching the storm from Fiona's bedroom window.

Fiona and I decide to get up and get ourselves ready for the day now that we can no longer focus on going back to sleep with our anxieties over the day brewing. I eventually put on the black dress I have borrowed from Veronica and head downstairs, leaving Fiona upstairs, still getting dressed. I make my way to the kitchen and pour two large cups of coffee for us. Mikey walks in shortly after and does the same.

"Good morning," I say as he grabs a croissant from the plethora of food still draped across the countertops.

"I guess the storm woke you too?" he asks while taking a big bite of his bread.

"Yes. It's a loud one." I see a flash of lightning through the kitchen window and wait for the big boom of thunder to follow. As it roars the walls seem to shake a bit around us. I feel like I am back in Florida, with the weather this way.

"Are you going to speak at the service?" I ask Mikey, not knowing whether he has decided to say anything or not.

"Yes. I plan to say something. I have it written down. What about Fiona? Will she read what she wrote?"

Fiona wrote a letter to her father after he died that day, and mentioned she might want to read it aloud at the funeral, but she hasn't told anyone for sure.

"I'm not sure what she has decided."

"Well, she should. She needs some closure," Mikey says, and Fiona walks into the kitchen as he says it.

"What do I need?" she asks with a smirk.

"We were just saying you should read your letter to dad, at the funeral," Mikey says to her, caught off-guard.

"I will," Fiona agrees.

I'm glad she has decided to speak. She does need closure.

"You know, I was thinking," Fiona says. "You are lucky you knew dad so well, Mikey. I mean, looking back, I feel like I didn't know him at all."

"That's not true, Fiona. We just knew him differently. You know things about him I probably don't, and I know things you may not know about him. But you knew him."

"I don't know. He still seems so…mysterious to me."

He seems mysterious to me, too, I think.

Eventually, Veronica makes her way downstairs wearing a beautiful black dress, with lots of her gaudy gold jewelry on and huge high heels.

"Shall we head to the church?" she asks us as I stare at how unaffected she seems by the situation suddenly.

Rick, Mr. Lennox's limo driver, is waiting for us out front as we exit the front door, all in our black attire, to attend the funeral. Veronica carries a large, black umbrella so we don't end up soaked by the storm. No one speaks on the ride to the church. I stare out of the window, anticipating the tortuous service that awaits us. The storm doesn't let up at all once we arrive. We end up wet by the time we reach the doors to the church.

There are loads of out of town guests and relatives, awaiting the Lennoxes' arrival when we walk in. I get hugged by family members and end up explaining I am not a cousin to almost every single one of the other guests. I also have to explain I am from Florida, when they comment on how tan and blonde I am. I am pretty convinced most of Fiona's relatives hide the fact that she is a lesbian and I am her girlfriend, and just inform others I am a distant cousin. I can hear them chatting from afar. The church is decorated very elegantly with gigantic floral arrangements adorning the pews and altar. Everyone in Fiona's family is so glamorous. It is a big turnout, but I am not surprised at all by how well-known Mr. Lennox is in the City. We eventually find a seat on the front row and the service begins.

"Dearly beloved," the priest says. "We are gathered here today not to mourn, but rather to celebrate the well-lived life of Mr. Michael Stephen Lennox."

I can see a handful of people begin to tear up as I look around at the crowd. Fiona, Mikey and Veronica seem very cavalier so far. None have shed even one tear since we arrived. We sing a traditional hymn before the priest calls on Mikey to speak first.

"Hello," he greets the crowd as he takes the microphone. His voice doesn't quiver. "I'm Mikey, for those of you who may not know me, or who haven't seen me in quite a while. Michael was my father. I was named after him, being his only son." He looks at Fiona and smiles. She smiles back. "When I found out my dad was sick, he didn't want me to tell anyone. Not even my mother. Which was harder than you think. She has always been very…intuitive," he finally says, and the congregation laughs, agreeing that Veronica must be intuitive, as Mikey has explained. "But I kept my word. As I always did with dad. I didn't tell anyone. Not my sister and not my mom. He didn't want the pity he knew he would justly receive, had they known he was sick. Eventually, though, the disease started to show on him. He wasn't his usual fit and healthy self. And the family noticed. You see, he was always the strong protector in our family. But taking on that role had its difficulties, too. There were holidays we didn't see everyone…or anyone. At least one of us – he or I – was at the office every single holiday. With great power comes great responsibility."

That was said by Peter Parker – I know this because Kaden loves Spider Man.

Mikey continues speaking.

"And he had that: great responsibility. He may have let some people down, in the family, along the way." He looks right at Fiona. "But he had a lot on his plate. At all times. So I would like to take a minute and recognize what an honorable and hardworking man my father was for so many years. He had a hard time showing it sometimes, but he loved each and every one of you out there. He talked daily about how important his family was to him. Dad, I promise not to let you down. You have trained me well over the years and I will take on this role for our family now. I will protect and honor the family name and business and keep everything in line for you. I love you, dad."

Mikey looks at a big, blown-up photo of Mr. Lennox displayed on the altar before walking back to his seat beside Fiona. Other than wiping one single tear from his eye, he remains as serene as always.

Fiona is next. She hasn't shared with me at all what she is going to say. I just know it is laid out like a letter to her father.

"Dear Daddy," she begins. "I remember that as a little girl, you used to lift me up onto your shoulders and tell me, 'Here kid, you can see things more clearly from up here', as if my vision was skewed by my lack of height at that age. And I believed you. Because when we are little that's what we do. We believe everything our parents tell us. Whether they tell us Santa Claus is real, what to wear or who to vote for, we believe them because they are the higher authority. But as I got older, I realized you weren't always right. You didn't always have my best interest at heart, nor did you have the best plan laid out for my life. You see, I wanted to make you proud, like Mikey did."

She looks at Mikey and he forces a smile, probably wondering where this is going, just like I am. I stare at the crowd and they all have puzzled looks on their faces, especially Veronica.

"But I was never Mikey, dad, and I know that was hard for you to accept. I…" Fiona takes a deep breath, as if she is trying not to fall apart now. "I loved you. I love you, daddy. But you hurt me. The scars run deep. I just…I just…want you to know that I will remember the good things. The butterflies…the flowers in the garden…the landscapes we painted together…the elaborate vacations we took…the way you looked at mom, up until the day you died." She looks at Veronica, who is now sobbing. "I want to forget the things that leave a bad portrait of you in my mind. You see, 'they' say you wouldn't have the good without the bad, right? You wouldn't be able to tell what a good day is, without having some bad days, too, right? So I am going to try to forget the bad and only focus on the fact that I am grateful for each happy day we had together, and for the last few months I spent getting to really know you as much as I possibly could. Thank you for doing the best you could.

Fiona."

There is a pause before people begin to clap. Fiona sits back down next to me and Mikey Junior and I notice her entire family is crying now. She has hit a nerve in them, being so brutally honest up there. I think that's good.

Veronica sings an old love song to Mr. Lennox and it is clear to me there was still love between them, even at the very end. Everyone stands as she finishes her ballad and cheers loudly for Veronica. I think what an artistic and talented family Fiona has come from. She must have good artistic genes.

The congregation follows us out to the graveyard after the service, to the plot of land where Mr. Lennox will stay. The rain is still coming down hard and the wind is fierce. As we stand outside watching Mr. Lennox be lowered into the ground, I feel a strange sense of relief. As though, all of this misery we have been through in the past few months is coming to a close. Maybe we can be at peace now: Fiona and I. Maybe the spiraling will stop and things will go back to normal. I can only hope.

I listen too many of the same stories over and over again, back at the house after the burial. Stories about how Mr. Lennox was raised a poor man and achieved this big and extravagant life all by himself, with the great drive that he always possessed. I remember him telling me, that day at the coffee shop, how he saw that same drive in me. I think about what he would say to all of the guests complimenting him if he were here. I picture him shaking hands with each of them, greeting them and telling them thanks for coming to my funeral. He was always so professional and businesslike, even with us. I can't find Fiona. It takes me nearly half an hour to make it past all of the guests, up to the stairs and away from the crowd in search of her. I finally reach the top of the stairs and peek into her bedroom first. No Fiona. I look in the office. No Fiona. The guest bathroom. No Fiona. "Hey, Fiona!" I finally decide to call down the hall.

"In here," I hear her rough voice call back to me.

She is in Mr. Lennox's bedroom at the end of the hall.

"What are you doing in here, baby?" I ask her from the doorway.

She is over by the nurse's station, which is still there, just as it was when he was alive.

"Just needed a minute," she says to me quietly.

The black circles under her eyes are hard to hide in the bright light of the lamp next to her. She looks frail, and I start to wonder when she last ate.

"Well, I'm sure everyone can understand that," I finally say. I walk to her and hold her close to me. She feels smaller in my arms than she has ever felt to me before. Her skin is cold and her arms and waist feel bony. I realize how long it has been since we have truly been intimate with each other.

"I don't like this…distance between us," I say to her. I feel bad for making her feel bad about how she is dealing with this, but it just sort of comes out.

"I know. I hate it too, Chloe," she says, and she sounds so sincere and warm again all of the sudden. She squeezes me tighter, looks up at me and kisses me passionately. She tastes of cigarettes and alcohol, but I don't care. I just need to feel close to her again. I have to.

"I miss you. This is all going to be okay, baby. When we get back to Florida and have the boys…and we can just snuggle up and watch Netflix again…" I say, and she starts to cry.

She breathes heavily through her tears. "Yeah. You're right, Chloe. It will all be okay now. I'll be down in a little while, okay?" she reassures me.

"Yeah, okay," I say, and start to leave her. Clearly, she needs a little more time.

"Hey, Chloe," she says as I am about to turn the corner. "I love you so much. Forever. I'm sorry."

"I love you too, baby."

I walk back downstairs to listen to more flattering stories about Mr. Lennox.

Relapse

The guests disperse, little by little, as the day wears on. Soon, I can actually see through the crowd again. I look around the living room, trying to locate Fiona. She isn't there. I walk to the kitchen and am held up for a while by Mr. Lennox's best friend Ted, who tells me all about how Mugged came to be, a story I have heard about four times before, but I stand and nod in order to not be rude while I keep an eye out for Fiona. I still can't seem to find her in the crowd. After all the guests have left the house I wander around downstairs, still looking for Fiona, to make sure she is doing okay. She is nowhere to be found. The last place I saw her was upstairs in Mr. Lennox's room, so I decide to walk back upstairs to see if for some reason she never made it back downstairs. I see Veronica standing in Fiona's bedroom alone, crying. I walk over to her.

"It's going to be okay," I say, and touch her gently on her back.

"It was just a hard day," she assures me.

"I know. I can't imagine how hard it was for you. Your song was fabulous," I say, acknowledging how brave she was to perform it.

"Oh, thank you, dear. It was nice to sing in front of someone again. It has been years since I have done that, and it felt so…liberating, actually." She smiles.

"Well, you have a very talented family," I inform her.

"Thank you. You are a blessing to us, Chloe. You have truly made Fiona a happy soul again."

"Wow. Thanks," I say. "Have you seen her, by the way?" I ask Veronica, thinking she may know where Fiona is.

"No. I haven't really seen her at all since we came back to the house," she says with a puzzled expression.

"I'm going to go check in Mr. Lennox's room," I tell her. "That's where I left her about an hour ago, alone, so she could have a minute."

"Okay, I will accompany you," Veronica says. We head down the hall towards Mr. Lennox's bedroom together.

As we walk into the bedroom, I see a body in the fetal position, lying on the ground next to the nurse's station. It doesn't turn to us as we move closer. It just lies motionless in a ball on the ground.

"Fiona!" I shriek as I realize it is in fact her lying helpless on the floor.

I immediately decide to turn her over and notice her eyes are not focusing and her mouth is foaming a bit, saliva drooling out of the corner of her lips.

"Call an ambulance!" screams Veronica to Mikey Junior, who is now outside the bedroom looking in on us in a state of panic.

I shake Fiona, trying to get her to wake up enough to realize it is me. "Fiona! Can you hear me? It's me, Chloe. Wake up. Focus, Fiona. Look at me!" I yell, terrified.

"What did you take, Fiona?" her mother asks her. "What did you take, sweetie? Tell mommy what you swallowed."

I guess at first, I thought *Fiona was just having some sort of seizure*. It is only now that I am beginning to realize she may have done this to herself, like all of those times before: another attempt at suicide, here, on the very day of her father's funeral.

Veronica suddenly sees something under the nurse's station and reaches frantically for it, shoving her arm under the rolling metal cabinet. She scoops out a handful of prescription pill bottles. No pills, just the bottles.

"His pills. His...medications..." she says, realizing Fiona has swallowed them all. "But the Hospice nurse said she destroyed everything!" She is reading the labels while she talks. She pauses, looking confused. "These are older, prescribed by his doctors. They don't have Hospice labels."

It is then that I realize what Fiona was doing in her father's closet for so long that day. Not looking for her love letters, the ones he hid from her. Finding those was an accident. She was looking for her father's pills: whatever stash Mr. Lennox had left. She planned this!

"I think she found them in his closet," I say to Veronica. "I think she knew they were there."

She is still lying helpless and motionless with her head back on my arms now, unable to hold it up. Mikey runs over to her.

"The medic will be here in just a moment, Fiona. Hang on, sis. Hang on," he says to her. He starts to cry. "Why did you do this again? Why?" It is the first time I have seen his emotions get the best of him.

I say nothing. I have no words for this moment. I left her up here. Alone with her memories and all the equipment that reminds her of her father's illness, not even knowing this would be a possible outcome. Why has she done this? What was she thinking?

It takes what seems like hours for the paramedics to come running up the stairs.

"Ma'am. I'm going to need you to back away," says one of them as I sit there holding Fiona's head, trying to look into her beautiful, jet-blue eyes to figure out why she has done this. "Ma'am!" the paramedic says, louder, and I finally hand her to him. He begins speaking to Fiona. "Miss. We are going to have to pump your stomach so I need you to swallow this tube here. Okay…" he says as he puts a large basin in front of Fiona. She tries to push it away, but her strength is gone and her attempts are weak. She turns her head away from the tube, but inevitably they force it down her throat and she begins to heave up whatever is left in her hollow stomach.

I stand, stunned. I watch as Fiona vomits profusely for thirty minutes. She eventually lies there with her head on the side of the basin and our eyes meet. She has a blank stare with a hint of embarrassment. A second paramedic wheels in a stretcher and places her fragile body on it.

"Can I go with her?" I ask as they start to wheel her out.

"Go, Chloe," says Veronica. "You can go with her in the ambulance. Mikey and I will meet you at the hospital."

I ride next to Fiona in the ambulance, watching her as she flows in and out of consciousness. I attempt to hold her hand the whole way, but her grasp is weak. I can't help but be mad at her inside. What a selfish act she has committed! Why today? Why ever? Why would she pull such a stunt? But I thought *I was making her happy. She is supposed to be my soulmate who has saved me from my mundane life.* All of a sudden that mundane life I once had is looking pretty good to me. It is looking pretty desirable. I miss my simple life back in Florida with my boys. I miss being a housewife and a mother. Is this what being a butterfly really feels like?

I sit in the hospital room next to Fiona, waiting for the rest of her family to arrive. They have intubated her so that her breathing is regulated. As she begins to wake up, I explain to her that she has a tube down her throat and should not try to talk because the tube won't let her. I look at her and ask her, "Why did you do this, Fiona? Why did you do this to me, and your family? After everything we have all been through today…the last couple of months…the last year! Did you really try to…kill yourself…again?" I sit and look at her and she is trying to shake her head and I can tell she wishes she could talk, but she can't. I think about her father and how this is how he felt at the end. He wanted so badly to talk and probably defend himself, but he couldn't. "Well," I finally say. "I'm glad you failed yet again."

She is still trying to communicate something to me while shaking her head, but I look down at my lap. There is a bulge in the pocket of my black dress. I remember that I placed the ring for Fiona in there, just in case I decided to propose today. As morbid as it may seem, something about her being all dressed up in her beautiful black dress made me suddenly want to marry her again. I place my hand over the bulge to cover it.

Veronica and Mikey hurry into the room and ask me how she is doing.

"She's fine. They intubated her, though, because her breathing was still weak," I inform them.

Mrs. Lennox strokes Fiona's sweaty hair and kisses her softly on her cheek.

She is handling this way better than I am, I think. But she has had more practice with this sort of thing.

An hour later, a nurse comes in to remove the tube from Fiona's throat so she can attempt to breathe on her own. I turn away, not able to watch.

The nurse advices Fiona to take it slowly when drinking anything, and tells her that her throat may feel sore and her voice will be hoarse for a while. She also lets us know the doctor will be in shortly to speak with us.

Fiona clears her throat loudly and I can tell she is feeling sore, like the nurse mentioned. She makes a sour face and swallows hard a few times before trying to speak.

"I wasn't trying to kill myself," she finally says sternly to all of us. "I just…I just wanted to numb the pain. I wanted to feel better, not to die," she explains.

"Fiona – " Veronica begins to say.

"Wait! I'm not done." Fiona cuts her off. "I know I have a…history of this sort of behavior, and I know that I have been drinking too much lately and I was rude to you a few times, Chloe, but that does not mean I would try to kill myself!"

I want to believe her. I want to believe this was some kind of accident and that she was really just trying to feel better, but her past shows differently.

"Chloe, you were right." She starts to cry. "I think when we get back to Florida and get the boys back, and we can just relax again, away from all of this…things will go right back to normal. Right?" she asks us.

Veronica looks down, avoiding making eye contact with Fiona. Mikey hasn't said a word since he entered the room.

A male doctor and a blond woman dressed in a blue suit walk in.

"Fiona," the woman in the suit says to her. "How are you feeling, honey?"

"Dr. Clark?" Fiona asks, "What are you doing here? Mom?" Fiona looks right at Veronica, who is still looking down at the tile floor. "Mom, did you call her?"

The medical doctor walks over to Fiona and takes her hand.

"I called her, Fiona. Your records show that you have a long history of suicide attempts and drug addiction, theft, and alcohol – "

Fiona interrupts him. "What is going on here?" she asks. "Just tell me what is going on?"

She starts to cry again and pushes the doctor's hand away.

"Miss, we need to get you some help. We want you to get better. Your family knows you have been through a lot lately," he says.

"Am I being…committed against my will, again?" Fiona asks in a hushed voice now.

Can they do this to her, with her being twenty-eight years old? I think to myself. I don't know the protocol for these sorts of situations. And the doctor is right. She does have a long history of failed suicide attempts and addiction. But she swears she didn't do this on purpose.

"It was an accident!" I exclaim all of a sudden.

Fiona looks at me with horror, aware of what is coming.

"No!" she screams. "No! No! No!"

"Nurse!" yells the doctor as Fiona tries to stand up, but she's too weak and falls back onto the bed.

The nurse gives her a shot of something in the arm that calms her down immediately and she falls asleep after blinking her eyes several times at me.

While Fiona is sleeping her psychiatrist, Dr. Clark, explains to us they can legally keep her at a state center for seventy-two hours before she has to decide whether she wants to move to a private institution or be released. She has to give her consent after the legal stent. She explains to us that this is not supposed to be some cruel sentence she has given Fiona, but a chance to get healthy and happy again, and that she has faith that Fiona can do that with a short stay at the center. We are not allowed to see her for the few days she is there, but we may speak to her once a day on the phone.

I can only imagine what Fiona will say when she wakes up and hears they are forcing her back into a psych ward again.

It's only seventy-two hours, I think to myself. She can handle that, right? How bad can a few days really be?

When Fiona eventually wakes up, her face is panic-stricken. She looks confused and the wear she has caused to her body is apparent now on her face. I take her hand.

"Hey, how are you feeling?" I ask her.

"Where did the doctor go? I need to speak with him and my psychiatrist. I need to explain to them that it was an accident."

I can tell Fiona is so fragile that she might break if I tell her there is no talking them out of it, and that she is inevitably going to end back up in a center for at least three days.

"Okay. Well, when they come back in here you can talk to them, Fiona," I assure her.

She takes a deep breath and lies her head back down against the pillow on her hospital bed. "Did Mikey and my mom leave?"

"They just went to get a bite to eat in the cafeteria."

"I miss the boys," she says.

"I miss them too."

"We just need to go back to Florida. Right when I get out of here, we need to just get our things and leave, Chloe. It will all be fine."

I want to tell her that I am not sure it is going to be fine anymore. That I don't think there is a chance in hell she can convince the doctors to let her go…but all I do is nod my head and try to stay positive for her.

Eventually, the psychiatrist and doctor walk back in. They inform Fiona that she is being released from the hospital, but will have to stay at the State Center for three days. Fiona absolutely loses her mind. They end up having to put her in restraints and give her another shot of something to calm her down, or rather, put her to sleep for the second time.

"We are going to take her there sedated," Dr. Clark informs me.

"But I need to say goodbye. I need her to know I do not agree with you. That I don't believe putting her back in there is the solution!" I yell.

"Chloe, I know her pretty well, sweetheart," Dr. Clark says to me. "I have been her therapist since she was eleven years old. I know her habits, and I know the warning signs. I went to school for a long time to help people like Fiona. And I know what is best for her."

I start to remember what Fiona told me. That her dad paid off her therapist to keep her. Is Dr. Clark that same therapist? She is the only one…

"I know that you took money from Mr. Lennox to keep her locked away!" I blurt out loudly.

"Chloe, that is absurd. That is a ridiculous allegation," she says, looking extremely angry at this point.

"I won't let you keep her in there more than three days," I say sternly.

The doctor comes back and they start to wheel Fiona out of the hospital room.

"Wait!" I shout. "What about her family? I am sure they would like to say goodbye!"

I haven't even had a chance to say goodbye. She is going to think I am in agreement with this. And I am most definitely not.

"She gets a phone call a day," Dr. Clark says coldly to me.

As Fiona is being wheeled down the hall, I watch her open her eyes.

"Wait!" I run down the hospital hallway, right up to Fiona's stretcher. "I love you, Fiona. I won't let them keep you there. I promise. I am so sorry," I say, and I suddenly feel my impulsive character taking control of me. I grab the engagement ring that I still have in my dress pocket and hand it to Fiona. I let her hold onto it tightly, so no one sees me give it to her. I don't know what she is allowed to keep with her in the center.

"Marry me, Fiona."

I see Fiona read the inside of the band that I had engraved for her: "I choose you, my other half."

"Yes," she says in a hushed voice. "Yes."

I keep watching her as they wheel her farther and farther away from me down the hall.

"Chloe!" she shouts. "Chloe!"

I explain to Mikey Jr. and Veronica that they have taken Fiona to the state center, somewhat sedated because she was so uncooperative. They are upset they didn't get to say goodbye. I assure them she will call one of them, using her phone call this evening. Veronica informs me she is going back to Mr. Lennox's house to get Fiona's things and drop them off at the institution. They probably won't let her see Fiona, but she will at least have some of her own clothes and toiletry items.

I decide it is best that I catch a quick flight home this evening, if at all possible. I feel lost here in this city, knowing Fiona is locked away somewhere and I am without her. Veronica and I ride back to Mr. Lennox's together in the limo. Few words are spoken on the ride home. I can't manage to come up with anything uplifting to say. Everything has been such a whirlwind since we have been here.

After arriving back at the mansion, I quickly get on the computer in Mr. Lennox's office and book a flight home for this evening. I gather my things, kiss Veronica and Mikey goodbye on the cheek and take a cab to the airport. I am anxious to get home to my boys and to get away from the emptiness I am feeling in this house.

During the entire ride to the airport, I think about Fiona. I wonder how we got to this point. I reflect on the last couple of months and try to focus on the many good days we had, just as Fiona said she was trying to do with her father. There have been a lot of good days, I tell myself. I think about the fact that I have now proposed to someone who I love so much, but who is institutionalized for allegedly trying to kill herself, and this isn't the first time this has happened in her life. What will I tell Trent? And the boys? They are going to inevitably ask questions and I have no idea how to defend Fiona's actions to them. I have an unsettling feeling all the way home, until I get to Florida.

I finally walk into Fiona's house. It is nine o'clock at night. I haven't talked to Trent or the boys at all today, with things having transpired the way they did. I decide I need to give him a heads-up that I am home a day earlier than I had planned.

"Hey, Chloe," he says as he answers his cell phone.

"Hi," I say timidly. "I...I am back in Florida."

"Oh? Already? Okay, well, the boys are asleep, but you guys can grab them first thing tomorrow morning if you want...I know you really miss them..."

"It's just me," I confess.

"Oh, Did Fiona have more family stuff to take care of?" he asks, confused.

"Sort of, yeah," I lie.

"Okay...You guys are okay, though, right?" he asks me.

"Yes." I mean, we are okay...I proposed. We are engaged. But I can't tell Trent all of that now. Not with her in the mental state she is in and while she is locked away.

"Good." He sounds relieved, actually. "How was the service?"

"It was fine. It was...beautiful."

"I'm sure it was. They have the means to go all out and I am sure they did," Trent assumes.

"Right...okay...well, I will call you in the morning and come pick up the boys, okay?"

"Yep. Talk to you then, Chloe."

My heart starts to beat faster as I hang up the phone. Here I am in Fiona's house, without her. I wait and selfishly hope that she will use her one phone call this evening on me. That she will reassure me everything is okay and that her calming voice will reappear and I will sleep soundly, knowing things are all going work themselves out. Just like we both convinced ourselves that they would.

The phone doesn't ring all night. I sit alone in Fiona's house and don't sleep at all. I stay up the entire night, questioning every decision I have ever made in being with Fiona.

At six o'clock, I decide the boys are probably going to be waking up soon, so I put on some cut-off shorts and my Bert and Ernie shirt and drive over to pick them up. I get to Trent's apartment by 6:30 a.m. and knock quietly on the front door.

"Chloe?" Trent says, squinting in the sunlight. "What are you doing here so early? The boys aren't even awake yet...I – I'm not even awake yet." He looks a little upset that I woke him. He's wearing an old pair of shorts and not even a shirt yet, and I notice right away that he has lost more weight. I'm sorry to see him so stressed out.

"I'm sorry. I just...I need to see them," I say, and walk past him to the boys' bedroom.

I peek in and see they are cuddled up together on their bottom bunk. They look so sweet. So completely innocent.

"Chloe? Have you slept?" Trent asks me, concerned.

"No...I mean, a little," I lie to him.

"You look like hell, Chloe. Why don't you go lie down on the couch until they wake up?" he suggests.

I go plop down on his living room couch and immediately my cell phone starts to buzz.

"I'll be right back," I say to Trent as I walk back outside the front door to take the call.

"Hello?" I answer, not recognizing the number.

"Chloe. You have to help me. They are going to try to keep me here, Chloe," Fiona says in a panicked voice. "They aren't going to let me leave. I can't stay here..." Her speech sounds slurred and I can tell she is on a lot of medication by how muffled she sounds.

"Calm down, Fiona. They can only keep you two more days, baby," I remind her.

"No, you don't get it, Chloe. They can keep me as long as they want. My dad turned my trust fund over to Dr. Clark. You have to help me, Chloe...Listen carefully to everything I am about to say..."

I can hear a doctor in the background – who sounds like Fiona's therapist Dr. Clark – walking up to Fiona.

"No! I am allowed one phone call a day!" Fiona screams. "No! Give me the phone back! Chloe!"

Fiona's voice fades away and all I can picture is her being caged like a wild animal.

"I'm sorry. It is time for Fiona to take her meds," Dr. Clark says in an eerily routine voice over the line.

Click.

Fiona: December 2015
Insanity

I sit in my room alone after being interrogated yet again by Dr. Clark. Why does she have to ask me so many questions? I just want to be left alone. Actually, I just want to go home and be with my family. I think about Marjorie and wonder how she is doing over at Living Waters without me. It has been almost two weeks that I have been in a new place.

I hope she is happy.

I reach under my mattress and pull out all of the pills I have been hiding. All of the ones I haven't been taking for quite a few days. I can't decide if the brain zaps I have been having from not taking them are worth the sudden clarity or not.

At least I feel alive again. At least I feel human.

I realize I haven't seen Trisha in a while. Or Jade. My room seems awfully quiet.

I decide I want to change clothes; maybe put on a little makeup while I am alone. Something I haven't had the energy to really do in a while. Having been taken off the Lithium, I have felt a burst of energy in the past few days. It is very refreshing.

I open up my closet and browse through the clothes.

All of a sudden, I notice that none of Trisha's clothes are hanging in their usual place.

Has she moved out, and they didn't tell me?

I feel anxious and decide to go hunt down Dr. Clark again to confront her about Trisha.

I see her talking to someone in the halls, but I interrupt her, not caring in the least how rude I am being.

"Um, excuse me, Dr. Clark! Did Trisha move out? Why are none of her things in our room anymore?"

"Fiona. Well, hello again, sweetie. Why don't we talk in your room, sweetie?"

"Why can't you just answer me? It isn't that hard. I mean, I know she must have moved out. Is that why you kept me in your office so long today, talking to me? So she could just sneak away without saying goodbye? That is pretty messed up, Doc."

"Fiona. Please. Let's head to your room."

I trail behind her, trying to stomp my feet as annoyingly as possible on the hard floor to prove how upset I am about this fucked-up situation. I mean, these doctors sure are ruthless!

"Fiona. Please sit down on your bed, sweetie."

As I sit on my bed, I glance over and notice Trisha no longer has a bed in our room either.

It is perfectly clear that she is gone.

"Fiona. Before I say what I am about to say, I want you to know that I have dealt with people like you before. People that have...well, I just want you to know you are not the only one who has experienced this sort of thing before. Can you say you understand this before I explain something to you, sweetie?"

"What on earth are you talking about? Please don't try and change the subject like you tend to do – "

She interrupts me in a tone of voice, I am not familiar with from her. She sounds aggressive, almost. "Fiona! This is serious. I need you to just listen. Until I am done. Do you understand?"

"Yes, sure," I say, and feel very anxious.

"Fiona. Sometimes people handle trauma in very unusual ways. Sometimes when people have had a rough or dark past, they develop some...bizarre tendencies. Coping mechanisms, really, to deal with the pain or grief they might be experiencing. Now, I am sorry to say it did take me some time to figure out what was going on with you, but I am pretty sure you have been experiencing some very serious delusions – very detailed hallucinations. You have been in a schizophrenic state for some time now, honey. It was just recently that I figured this out. I had no idea you had completely made-up characters in your world. To cope with the pain you were feeling. I would like to try to get you off the medications, to see if some of the delusions subside. It is rare, but sometimes certain mixtures of the drugs you have been taking can cause hallucinations. They can be very real, even – "

I interrupt her frantically. "I stopped taking all of my medication a few days ago," I admit.

"Aha. Then that could explain your sudden realization of Trisha being...gone. Do you understand what I am saying, Fiona?"

I sit in complete shock. I try to respond. I try to wrap my head around what she is insinuating, but I feel so faint. Nothing comes out of my lips. My mouth just stays open for what feels like an eternity.

"Fiona? Are you okay, sweetie? It is going to be okay now. Now that we know what is going on."

"So…so…what you are saying is that I am completely insane? Trisha is not a real person? She is just some imaginary friend my crazy mind created. Like I am a four-year-old child?"

"No. No, Fiona. Like I said, these things have happened before…"

"But they don't happen often, do they? I mean, has this happened to any of your patients, before me?"

"Fiona, you know I am not allowed to answer that."

"Right. So no. It hasn't. Just me." I suddenly don't know what is real or fake anymore. "And is there anything else? I mean, what else isn't real?" I ask, praying there is nothing else.

"Jade. She isn't real, Fiona. And do you know where you are, sweetie? Try to really think about it…Where are you, Fiona?"

I sit and feel as if I can actually think straight for the first time in a month. I look around and things look much duller than they have the past couple of weeks. My room looks so desolate and stale. It even smells different. I peek out of the door and see a familiar face – one with a soft, innocent smile – looking back at me.

"Do you want to play monopoly, Fiona?" Marjorie asks me.

Dr. Clark smiles at me and knows I have come to grips with where I really am.

I am still at Living Waters. Marjorie is smiling at me from the hallway. Her hair is in its usual messy bun on top of her head.

At least, I know Marjorie is real.

Clarity

It is as if some switch has flipped in my head now. Trisha, Jade, Dr. Hall: none of them are real. They are all made up. As if I have written some psychological thriller inside my head. Just like the movies I watched with my dad, growing up. Except this time, I am the psychopath.

I ask Dr. Clark lots of questions, trying to understand my own mind. And why I would make up such elaborate tales, with such vivid characters?

"Why would I do this? What kind of person does this? As an adult," I ask her in tears. "Does Chloe know? Does my mom know?"

"I don't think so, Fiona. I have not shared this with anyone since I realized what was going on."

"But I just don't understand. I don't know what is real. What has really happened? And what did I make up?"

"Why don't we play a little game? Something that could give you some much-needed clarity at this point. How about you ask me some questions? Ask me whether something really happened or not, when you remember it, and I will tell you – to the best of my knowledge – whether it is a real memory or an imaginary one. Is that okay, Fiona?"

"Okay. Did I never go to The Meadows? I mean, I vividly remember my mother coming and the both of you driving me there, to The Meadows. And I had a roommate: Trisha. And my mom was upset that I wasn't alone in a single room. Was that a dream of some sort? All of it?"

"You never left Living Waters, sweetheart. It could have been a dream; it could have been an elaborate hallucination or delusion that let you escape the isolation you have felt here. But no. You have been here the entire time."

"And how did I never notice Marjorie anymore? She was my best friend. Did I just abandon her? Have I pretended the whole last couple of weeks that she didn't exist? She must really hate me now. Deep down…"

"No. I have seen you play Monopoly with her a couple of times. It is possible you might have imagined you were playing with someone else."

I think back to when I must have imagined playing monopoly with Jade. I guess I was actually still playing with Marjorie.

"And Dr. Hall. How could I imagine all of those memories with him? He led group. He set up all those therapy games – "

She interrupts me. "I led group, Fiona. It was all me, sweetheart."

"And the butterfly sanctuary. He was never there?"

"He isn't real, sweetie. So no. Just me."

She looks sad for me. She looks compassionate again. Like the therapist, I remember from my childhood. The one that cared deeply about me. And getting me well.

"And the needle? Did you stab me with a needle? In your office?"

"I did. But it was not to be cruel or frighten you. You were in a strong delusion, Fiona; one that was turning you against me. I had to protect myself. And you. You left me no option. That is when I figured out what was going on: that you were not living in reality anymore. That you were delusional."

"I see. Well, I am sorry…"

"I know. It is not your fault. You know that, right? None of this is your fault."

"So you took my letters to help me?"

"Yes. I was hoping they would give me more insight into your mind and what you were imagining."

"It all makes sense now. I can't believe I am so…insane."

"You have been through a lot in your life. You father, his death, your sexuality…"

"Can I ask you one more thing? And you may not even know the answer to this one…"

"Of course. Go ahead…"

"Was my father…I mean, was he really…gay?"

"I am not allowed to reveal that to – "

I interrupt her suddenly. "Please. So you did really counsel him as well?"

"I did. Yes."

"Well then, please. Please, Dr. Clark, just tell me the truth. You know you will not get in trouble. I will never – "

"Yes, Fiona. Yes. He was gay."

"Wow. So that is what was real. Out of all these memories. That one was real."

Dr. Clark looks down at her lap. I feel bad for making her break the rules and tell me something so confidential. Even if my father is gone, I can tell she really takes her job seriously. It is going to eat her up.

"Thank you, Dr. Clark. Thank you for caring. Thank you for caring about me enough to give me some closure. To bring me back to reality. I really owe so much to you."

"You don't owe me anything, sweetie. I have known you since you were just a child. I have seen who you really are. You are one of the most generous and loving people, I have ever had the privilege to know. Even after everything you have been through. After all that your father put you through, and how cruel the world was to you at times. You were able to forgive. I think that proves your true character. You deserve all of the happiness in the world, sweetie. I want you to know that you are completely deserving of that happiness."

I am sobbing like a little girl now. I can feel for the first time in over a month. Being completely off the medication and hearing how sincere a person Dr. Clark truly is has struck a chord with me. She is right. Everyone deserves to be happy. I deserve to be happy.

"If it is okay with you, I would like to make a phone call now."

"Of course, honey. One more thing, Fiona. It is my mission now to get you well. I strongly believe you will be healthy again. With time."

I simply nod my head and smile at her before walking out of her office into the halls.

Closure

"I would like to make a phone call, please."

I dial Chloe's number with a shaky hand.

"Hello?" She answers on the very first ring.

"Chloe. It's me."

"Fiona! Oh, I am so glad you called. I have been meaning to call you all day. Actually, I have been meaning to call you every day the past few days. I am so sorry, sweetie. I miss you."

"I miss you too, Chloe. Listen. I need to talk to you about something, okay?"

"Is everything alright, Fiona?"

"Yes. Everything is great. Listen. I need a little time to think. I need some time…Can you give me some time, Chloe?"

"Of course. Can you tell me what this is about, Fiona? I mean, any idea when you are getting out yet? I have been meaning to come see you, but it is just that things with Trent's job and Mugged – "

"No. Please. Don't come see me right now, Chloe. I think it would be better if you didn't. At least for a while. Can you just kiss the boys for me? And try to enjoy every day with them. I love you, Chloe Fields. Until the day I die."

"I love you, too Fiona Lennox." She pauses for a long moment, but I can tell she has something more to say. She takes a deep breath and finally says, "Listen, I know that you have been somewhere 'else' lately. I spoke with Doctor Clark a while ago, when I noticed how confused you were…about where you were living. Also, there were certain names you mentioned to me that no one had ever heard of…Fiona, I hope I'm doing the right thing here. Trisha and Jade aren't real. Please say you know that. Please say you figured it out."

"I figured it out," I say quietly.

"I think now you can get the help you need. It's going to be okay, Fiona. It isn't your fault. I want you to know that. I love you. I will see you on the other side. Okay, Fiona?"

It is hard for me to hold back the tears now. The tears I am shedding for the loss I know I have just suffered, and created. Chloe has known all along what a delusional basket-case I really am. I have to let her go. For now. Until I am well enough to give her all of me. To give her what she deserves. I can't love her now. Not until I love myself again.

"Fiona?"

I finally pull myself together enough to respond one last time. "Okay. I will see you on the other side. Goodbye, Chloe."

"Goodbye, Fiona."

After hanging up the phone, I feel a sense of relief. I have finally, selflessly, done something I am proud of. Something I know was the right thing to do. Chloe doesn't need to be burdened by all of the details of how sick, I have actually been the past month and half. She needs to just let me go. I want to believe that I do possess the ability to get myself well again. That one day I really will be sitting in Mugged with Chloe and the boys, and Mikey and Marjorie. And my mother...

I want to believe I will be on the other side of these walls again.

The world can be a cruel place. So unaccepting of what it doesn't understand. I don't want to admit that it has broken me down to such a weak person: a person who has to create alternate realities in order to avoid coping with the truth. I want to believe I can still break free. Someday I know I will find peace again. I will visit the butterfly sanctuary. I will go to my father's old house and paint in his garden. For now, I need to simply focus on...me. Someone once said to someone they loved very much...

"How does one become a butterfly? You must want to fly so much that you are willing to give up being a caterpillar."

When I am healthy enough to fly again, and I know I will be, she will still be there.

This love will never die. Only transform.